Millionth Method

Tabitha Hudson

Under the Table Publications

Under the Table Publications

ISBN: 978-1-4787-9762-3

PRINTED IN THE UNITED STATES OF AMERICA

I began to struggle heavily in the year 2010. I had to make a decision about what was best for my four daughters and my partner of eleven years, Rainen, and myself. I mulled over the decisions I had to make for several weeks. I had gone looking for a pen to make a grocery list and instead found a rather rude surprise. There were email addresses and phone numbers for three different women in Rainen's college backpack.

When confronted, he swore they weren't females he would ever meet in person. I found the betrayal too bold to ignore. I had noticed him drifting away since I had helped him to get back into his education. I didn't figure he needed yet MORE time with hooches. I thought he needed to begin to work with his brain instead of his back which had been severely compromised by his Juvenile Scoliosis. He used this diagnosis to get away with many things during our relationship (which now spans fifteen years and the lifetimes of my daughters). His family had made excuses and more excuses and enabled him to live a small life rather than expect anything more of him. I knew—JUST KNEW he was destined for greatness with his bright mind and wild inventiveness. If only he would push himself a little more.

When Rainen and I got together in 2001, we made certain agreements to keep either of us from being trapped in a loveless relationship. I felt I had been for the year and a month I spent married to a man who obviously was in love with someone else. At the least, I knew he didn't love ME. I found I was pregnant by him a second time and I didn't want there to be any weirdness for our children so I guess I did ruin myself with demands for marriage. Once we got married it was too late to discuss if he was already in love with someone. I assumed if he had been, he would have told me. He did not say that.

I was married to a man who didn't want me. He chose

instead to drink each night to the point of passing out. I made shy advances and later in the marriage, bossy demands for sex but he didn't seem to find me attractive any more. No doubt he was missing her. I chose to give the marriage a year to see if he would straighten up for his daughters. No such luck. I decided to let him go and be with her if he wanted. He didn't like my company and he didn't like sex. We had nothing in common. He didn't seem to like his kids much either. I figured some other woman probably had a decent shot at it since I had obviously failed to do whatever it took to be wifey. Though I did spend a weird amount of time cleaning and cooking and caring for his darling daughters. I even took better care of myself hoping I could manage to at least interest him. No real reason to stay in it, right. I suggested a separation.

I was very depressed and lonely during this time. I hadn't even begun to heal. I wished and waited, I talked and argued and I begged and pleaded with him to talk with me or a clergyman or a therapist. Anything to save my daughters the same awful fate of growing up with no father. Or worse a father who resented them because of their mother. When I started the affair, he seemed relieved. He didn't want to touch me. Now he didn't have to. The affair wasn't with the man he wanted to villainize--Rainen. He still to this day wishes it was Rainen. He wants to be angry at the man for some reason. Despite my work and his lack of same, the separation started.

I began to close the doors and not answer the phone for anyone. My mom lived in the same town as me and my kids. I wished for her. We saw her rarely. If I was in the mood to drink, she was there! I knew my family couldn't be counted on to care what happened to me since they all "warned" me about Carl. Like I didn't know. But I never saw that side of my so-called family unless someone needed something specific from me. No long phone calls or drop-bys just to hang out.

I still taught my daughters and ran my household while I tried in vain to figure out what to do with myself and my girls next. It is a scary world when you don't have any skills or education to rely on. (You would think I learned this lesson and started to deal with my own shit.) I received bare minimum support for the children because Carl didn't think I was worth giving spousal support to—once again--the beauty of me is that it was so very easy to damage me back then. I started to realize I was alone. I began to think it might be better if I didn't try to put the marriage back together, if he felt that I deserved to be homeless and without, while caring for his kids.

My father Paul, and his new wife, Mae, were trying to get me out of my four walls, so I expanded my relationship with them as best I knew how. I went to family dinners and spoke with my sisters from his side. I stayed busy with as many things as I could to avoid the real issue I was dealing with.

I felt I had no one. Mae knew her older brother, Kaylen and I were going through the same thing at that point in our lives. His ex, Rona, was way bolder and lied at every opportunity she had. He ended up in jail with no real cause for it. He took care of his children and made sure his ex had spousal support. Seemed like the least any man who has been married for years and had children with a female could do. I found him refreshing. He was intelligent and seemed ready to change his life for the better. I began to speak to him regularly and it became a very positive thing to get a letter from him or to sit and write him a letter. I was as honest as I could be with him. I told Kaylen I was in a very bad place and needed a friend and he said he would be that friend. Obviously, he was not being as honest with me. He wanted to jump into a brand-new marriage as fast as possible to keep the ex off balance. I guess I was the newer model he sought to upgrade to. I felt saddened by this since I was amid the same shit and I began to wonder how long till I was too old and he needed to trade me in? I found out quickly he wasn't quite the man I thought he was. This was disappointing but not unexpected. I barely knew the man, after all. I was honest and he didn't see the value in being honest.

I can remember being so surprised when after writing for a while, I received a letter with a very shocking portrait of Kaylen's... man parts. Laughs a little at how completely unlike him that seemed. I am sure I blushed awhile and didn't read the rest of the written parts due to embarrassment. He was not shy. What a bold move. I had to answer that one, didn't I? I know it was in poor taste but it was so unexpected! Had to give you a look at the always thinking and never routine Kaylen. The things that were most unusual about him were the contradictions of being a minister and being in jail. He had been married to a woman who asked for odd things and trying to accommodate her to keep her happy. He had children and a decent job and seemed well-adjusted. I couldn't see a down side. I kept asking questions and trying to learn about the hidden aspects of Kaylen. He was so genuine and nice to me, that I began to fall for his games. He began to say disturbing things about jail. My brother and just about all his friends and mine and most of my family had been in at some point in their lives. So, when he started to spout off about how most of the people in jail were stupid, I naturally took offense. I had grown up with these people and knew their kids and felt a simple loyalty to where I came from. He started to exclaim how anyone could make it in jail, and all they had to do was act like a badass. I laughed and wondered who he had tried this with that made him so sure. I spoke to a few guys I knew and asked if they could make sure he didn't get his ass kicked too badly when it came time and he popped off to the honchos. He was a good guy and did have kids, after all. No one I knew understood why I would talk to this poser and certainly couldn't understand why I would align myself with someone so obviously full of shit, as they put it. I just grinned and said they had some questionable ties as well, and we all got a laugh out of it.

I didn't have many vices, but pot has always been a stabilizer for me. My pot dealer attempted to befriend this man while they were both in jail, thinking he would need to know my new friend. We found out exactly what the agenda was. Kaylen told the older gentleman that he wouldn't be paying for marijuana or for me to sit on my ass and smoke it while he worked for that money. He told him a myriad of bold things with no holds barred and made himself the enemy of most of the friends I had in jail. They knew where I came from and didn't ever think less of me. I worked for my reputation from that clique because I paid cash for my weed, when so many females who hung around used their charm to get what they wanted. I only dated who I chose and only if I deemed them smart enough to keep me interested. I hadn't dated anyone from that clique in my life and I didn't see who could change my mind. After all—my brother knew them all and he was a raging idiot, about to get out of prison for the eighteenth time, so what good could come from it? I would befriend any one of them and if they needed me, I was there as much as I could be.

Kaylen made comments about how he would "make me" quit smoking pot if I knew what was "good for me". I determined he must not think much of me with such an attitude. It saddened me to no end to understand he was just like Carl. I quit writing him and started staying home in the house so full of hateful memories. I answered the phone for my brother once and a very old friend Jerry. They both tried to get me back to my hometown where I would miraculously remember what fun was so I could get over that jackass ex-husband of mine. I sighed heavily and told them no. They were trying to interest me in getting with Jerry. He had several kids and thought my kids were being raised right. He also talked to his mom about me and they decided I was the perfect new mom for them. Everyone knew while I was fighting with Carl, I had given him my piece of shit car to make sure he left. Jerry used this information to his advantage and began to try to set himself up with a house and a car, since stability was so important to me. I never led the man on. I was friends with him and did love his kids to death, but I could not see myself with Jerry at all relationship-wise. He simply was not the man for me. He and my brother were playing matchmaker in any way they could though. If Jerry wasn't getting anywhere with me, they would find someone else. Anyone else to make sure I was not with Carl anymore. The sentiment was beautiful and their big giant hearts were surely in the right place. They just had no clue how to appeal to me in my sadness. I had withdrawn far into myself and my own little world. Sometimes, I just need to be alone and figure it out for myself.

Turned out my good friend of a few years, Rainen was living in that same town at the time. My brother and friend took it upon themselves to enlist his help in operation "get Tabitha out of her slump". They asked him to call and get me interested in coming to the little town south of my small city. I didn't have a car and I used that excuse if possible. I could at least be silent and alone with my failure at my house.

Well, they were persistent and didn't take no for an answer. I'm sure my brother offered to pay for the party at Rainen's if he could only get me to come down. My brother was not above anything and he had just been released from prison--again. Unbeknownst to me then--with a serious health diagnosis! I knew I wanted to see him but I didn't want to socialize or be around men hitting on me in my sad state. I told them I would have my kids with me so there was no crazy partying and I wasn't in the mood for idiocy so anyone pissed me off and I was out of there. I was rather unreasonable when it came down it. I always had this theory that if my brother wanted to be around me, he could damn well do it on my terms. Thugs. Whatya gonna do?

Chuckles...they of course agreed to whatever I wanted. I didn't think of going there to get with anyone. I didn't want to be around any men really or any of the people I knew there in my old hometown. They had effectively ditched me when they all got married and then when I did, I didn't think anyone knew or cared. I was having a very hard time through those years. My friends appeared if they had something they wanted to say about themselves. I knew this and so stayed away from them all as a rule. With friends like that. Ha-ha.

The little get together at Jerry's house was a huge failure. We ended up at Rainen's house. I did make sure my little girls had food and toys and fun while we were there. I didn't even care how cute Rainen was, still mostly aloof to my shy flirting of the past. I planned to go home the following morning regardless of any plans the boys had made.

We spent the day in jovial chats and talking about whatever came to mind. We smoked and drank and ate. Damian enjoyed the time he got to see his spoiled nieces, and I felt reconnected to some friends I hadn't seen or hung around in a very long time. My girls were delighted to have Uncle Dummy back. He was excited and threw little Alyc around in the air and caught her with ease. She was always the center of attention with my brother. I could often find her asking him, "What did you bring me?" and he would promptly start emptying pockets to find her random bills and coins and other simple things like super-balls, small candies, cool pens, and her favorite and mine, blue smoke bombs. He was very in love with all children (though especially enamored of my own...) and was adamant he would have his own someday. He was the most responsible person when it came to his ideals about having them when he chose and was ready. So, he was forever passing out condoms in his crowd and making snide comments to me and any other female who had babies too early for his taste about how everyone "knew what caused babies, right?" Can't help but laugh over his genuine worry about the state of the world and how kids were treated wrong...we would know, with our trying childhood. His sometimes more trying than mine...

As I tried to lay down on Rainen's couch after a nice day

of hanging out and eating and drinking a little, I fidgeted and fussed with the little space. My Alyc finally kicked me off. I sat in the floor for several hours. I was so sad. I went over and over what had transpired between Carl and I at our last meeting. It didn't calm or soothe me in the least.

I looked over at the bedroom door and saw Rainen's light on. I intended to try to talk and perhaps gain some clarity on the situation. It was difficult for me to admit to needing someone during that time.

I went to the door and asked him if I could just lay down next to him. It was a bad idea. I could see that he was one of the crowd who had sex first and asked questions later. I didn't even think as I saw the look cross his face, as he looked at me in my conservative green silky pajamas. I had no wish to seduce anyone.

For once in my life I went with the wild me. I crawled into his arms and we ended up staying that way for the rest of the night.

I got up early and showered and dressed me and my girls, while not knowing what I should do or say. He kept smiling at me and making any excuse to touch me as he passed by me, whisper how he liked the way my shorts fit, or smell my hair. I had no idea how to act with him. I never spent much time flirting and the situation left me at a loss. When my brother got there, he laughed and said he knew that I would end up with Rainen. Darius congratulated him on being the first from the entire clique to be able to get to me. I felt like I wasn't on a healthy track with this and I began to stay quiet and thoughtful.

I was mortified because I knew I couldn't go right back to the way things were at my house. I had to change what was happening to me.

I had just started talking about a divorce instead of separation.

I really had no idea what came next. The boys asked if they

could come along to drop me and the girls off in Roswell. I agreed because my brother had suddenly started spouting advice like a damn guru. I needed to have people around me and the wisdom of anyone. I didn't know but found out later, Darius had already been talking to the people he knew in jail, and they decided Kaylen was bad news. I agreed, though for much different reasons. I was still sad I had opened up and trusted someone who thought so little of me. Rainen and Darius took it upon themselves to make sure no one would be taking advantage of me. Carl seemed like the first thing that needed to be resolved. My brother was angry at him because I got married and I told no one. Darius had expected to give me away. You know-- see me in the dress and the whole nine yards. My view: why revel in a marriage that didn't mean anything to the groom? Carl didn't want to advertise he was getting married- why should I?

But it made Darius angry to see him destroy and manipulate me so easily. He started watching my house to make sure Carl didn't try to come back. He ran him off well. Carl always thought I called Darius to come by and be rude, but that was all my big obnoxious brother, knowing with the cancer, that he wouldn't be around to care for me and his nieces much longer. Darius sat outside my house down the block and waited for Carl to come try to reconcile. He then proceeded to get in his face and be rude. Carl never seemed to understand how protective Darius was after learning he was dying.

Rainen didn't want to let go of my hand or leave at all. I could not even begin to send him away. He wrapped me in all his fiery, glorious love and made sure I didn't feel sad. Even though it had only been a few months, I felt close to him. I had known him for two years prior to this. I didn't think I could feel love again, so to find I could feel anything again, was a huge relief and joy to me.

I woke in the morning and he would curl around me. It made me feel like I was right where I needed to be when I was in his arms. He became riled at Kaylen's pursuit of me. Kaylen going so far as to propose to me in front of my father, who did not at the time, like Rainen. I tried to remain friends with Kaylen but he would have none of it. He ran off and got married to the first twenty-three-year-old he could find that would have him. I wished him well even though he hated me openly and spoke poorly of me to anyone who would listen.

Rainen didn't want to have to stand up for me with regards to the men who stayed around. I didn't want him to have to. But when Carl became rude and attempted to withhold my children's support time and time again, Rainen felt it his duty to tell him where to go. Rainen made Carl respect me, which I found sweet and endearing. No one could make me feel like I was beautiful or smart or funny like Rainen. He sidled up to me in the strangest moments to put an arm around me or drop a kiss on my head. Right when I was holding back tears or almost falling apart.

He even listened to what I wanted from a relationship. He seemed committed to making me see him as a mate. He was amazing to my girls, always being what they needed. Making Ionthe giggle outrageously as a chubby little baby who wasn't used to male attention, and drawing Alyc into long conversations making her think her responses out. She responded with intelligence he was often amazed at in one so young. He drew me out too. He thought Carl shouldn't be allowed to come back to us—Rainen wanted to be a part of me and my little family even if Carl was too stupid to see what he let go.

Rainen and I struggled in the beginning. I didn't care and neither did he. We would make it and we had our little house of joy, so what did it matter?

We ended up moving in with my father when the rent could not be paid due to Carl and his withholding of the important support. I was working at Denny's waitressing but it didn't pay for much besides feeding the babies. After Rainen got his job with a retail store to hold us over, we moved quickly again while I was pregnant with my third daughter. The pregnancy was hard on all of us. My brother finally told me he was dying of cancer after I found out I was pregnant with this daughter. I was supposedly unable to have any more children, according to doctors.

It shook me. My brother told me repeatedly to not let Rainen go because we were going to take care of each other and become a great family. And I don't know if he made Rainen feel obligated to stay somehow. Rainen said he hadn't. While I was in the hospital I heard Rainen was cheating with several girls. He thought I was fragile and he was taking on so much in responsibility, I knew he would have to break somewhere along the way. When these accused girls arrived later at my house to show off in front of me, I began to wonder if I would ever have the love I looked for so long.

It really brought me to a new level of depressed.

I did everything I could to keep him interested and I think he was. To be fair, when he considered my eyes and said he loved me, I believed because he seemed to be truthful. I kept trying. Despite the idiots trying to break us up. My family and his. Hateful and unhappy about us being together, I assumed they were trying to share their misery.

It didn't seem to help. When I went down the list of things I could give him in the bedroom to revamp his passion, we crossed them all off and then went back for the one thing I had hoped he never would. But it did bring him back.

He just couldn't have enough when it came to sex. I was into anything that would keep him. I stayed at home just like with Carl. I begged this man I worried didn't want me for attention just like with Carl. I spent time and effort on making everything perfect for him. I just wanted his life to become something he would love and enjoy. He seemed to want the same life I did.

When I noticed Rainen didn't seem to want me, I told him to go look for others he could find attraction for, since I knew he wouldn't with me. I just could not put up with another failed relationship. I had put on serious weight and it was affecting my perceptions of myself. I didn't do well when Darius died before my third girl was born. I withdrew and became deeply and darkly depressed.

Rainen proved what he wanted by going out all night one night and hunting for himself a girl. He didn't come back till nine thirty in the morning while the agreement was for him to return before sunrise for my little girls. But instead we all woke wondering where he was and why he wasn't back yet. You know—where's daddy?

That was where he lost me.

I tried to be as open for him as I could possibly be. It just wasn't enough.

So back to me finding the email addresses and phone numbers of college girls... I sat alone in the house. The older three girls were at school and the baby- my fourth daughter- was sleeping in her bassinet.

I piled a huge stack of his belongings, clothes and Cd's and tools and anything else I found. I sat with lighter fluid in hand and wondered if I should just set his shit on fire and leave. I could take the baby and go get the girls and we could leave. Go anywhere. Any fucking where but here. I could let him come back and find his shit burning while I drove away to a new life as he looked for us. Believe me when I say, I sat there for two and a half hours thinking about what to do.

I had pushed him forward to his dreams. He had pushed me to the back burner while he found stolen joy for himself and forgot me. I knew then that I could continue to change slowly, or I could do something very drastic and wild. As I would have when I was young and still myself. I could keep this man. He loved me after all. I was already painting and writing even way back then. I knew I could dream myself a new and bright future if I wanted it.

I asked him to please talk with me about taking us to

Oregon. It was his favorite place to be and he wanted very much to go back. What could it hurt?

No one would miss me here. I had asked my mom and sister repeatedly over the years to be a part of my life again, but they were so busy being drunk and creating problems for themselves, that I couldn't even get through to them how bad it was for me. My father and step mom were divorced and the step mom was going through her own life changes and could not be there for me. To be fair, I could have tried to be there for her more as well. She did have to leave the state and I understood. I could barely stand to be in the same town as my ex. Poor her. My father was incorrigable.

I had no friends to speak of and when I tried to create deeper more meaningful relationships with Rainen's friends (the only ones I ever saw) they seemed to shy away like I was trying to be a skeevy girl rather than that I was desperately lonely and needed a friend—any friend.

My ex...well he didn't see the value in me being such a good mom. I offered him the world and he treated it like liver. I gave him privileges that everyone agreed was a waste of time since he didn't utilize them. He didn't think it necessary to be a part of his girl's lives. I figured he could move on and be happier without us there to remind him of his failure. And he did.

I never begrudged him his happiness. I didn't want anyone to be unhappy.

I started packing. It seemed like a far-fetched plan but I was all in. We could be right there for Rainen when his back needed to be worked on. The top surgeons in the world were based at an Oregon teaching hospital that is quite popular for the top docs. The construction work he did ruined his back and that was the main reason for me pushing him to work with his mind instead of his back. He was so smart I thought he would easily be able to do anything he wanted.

He received his diploma with honors which made me so proud. I demanded he walk and do the ceremony thing. We shouted and took pictures and were so damn proud of him. He began school and immediately made presidents list for his high grades. He sought his masters in engineering. I knew he could do anything. While he recovered from his surgery, there I would be, I promised, to care for him until he could do it for himself.

When we arrived in Oregon in 2010, I had no idea the promise I made would come to be called on so quickly. His back began to curve instantly upon arrival. Me-stay at home mom for thirteen years-had to find a job in a dwindling job market with all the college educated masses out of work and applying for the more menial work—MY jobs. McDonald's called me to thumb their nose over having a four-year college graduate in business restaurant management apply for the same job of front counter help. They stayed on the phone for five full minutes telling me why I wasn't a good fit. I found them to be presumptuous dicks and told them so.

I filled out endless job apps. Three thousand forty some-thing of them before I got called for more than a first interview. I decided I had to get some college under my belt. I began to work, go to school full time, play insurance advocate for Rainen and his many doctors, take care of my four daughters online schooling and still take care of Rainen all the time as well. I didn't know anyone in Oregon and though a few were kind, many made me feel like I should never have come. Only a few of Rainen's friends wanted to be friends with me and I didn't even care most of the time. I was still so depressed.

Then the online bullying started. My YouTube, email, school sites for me and my girls, and my phone was hacked. I didn't do anything cool so I wondered who would find so much joy in causing me pain. I was suicidal and the bullies all made sure that was exploited. I guess we are all lucky I had been dealing with suicidal thoughts since I was four years old or it might have ended very differently.

Rainen was dealing with an ungodly amount of pain

during this time. I saw and tried to help whatever way I could. He constantly blamed me for there not being enough food or there not being enough money, or me not being enough anything. He told me some time before our twelve-year anniversary he didn't love me and he hadn't in ten years.

I lost it and couldn't deal with anything. My very first childhood boyfriend ever, Cain, had contacted me and he said he wanted to help. I suspected he didn't really want to help so much as be in the middle of my business. Which was true any way you look at it. Very funny. I knew what he was about and I tried to be gracious but he kept on laughing at me while I was already going through quite a lot at home. It wasn't very funny to me to be going through so much and having everyone I ever knew bail on me at the same time. I see now looking back at this experience, that I could have been a better friend but I couldn't get my emails out or letters sent until it was too late. I needed someone and I felt like I would die without some peace for my soul. I felt that Cain's name was the only vital part of him that I needed to write and stay upbeat. I assumed he would never become the friend I sought but at the same time, I needed someone in the worst way. It would never mean to him what it did to me anyway. I knew he felt I was stupid. And I also knew what he was saying behind my back. I heard a lot more than anyone knew. What I didn't know I dreamed. And that just added more pain and stupidity to every day. I withdrew and grew profoundly distressed. I asked Carl for what little help he might be able to do, and he repeatedly said he couldn't. Cain began to talk to me. He found I was without and thought it might irritate Carl to help me. I imagined that was why he did. I knew better but had little option.

My bad choice. I slept with Cain after he lent me the money. I knew better. I never apologized except that it hurt Rainen. Maybe I just needed to know someone was out there and didn't find me all bad. I could have said no, and afterwards, I felt stupid plenty. I had to sleep with Rainen before the trip, even when he had just said he hadn't loved me in ten years. He was sure to use me roughly so I didn't forget where I belonged? He stamped me with his body so I would never feel pleasure while I was with Cain. Cain was apparently of the same mindset and used me twice as roughly. When I got home I spent two weeks trying to heal my body from the rude treatment from the both. Still walking to find jobs or applications with that major pain inside fresh was extremely hard for me, but I made the choice, so I didn't feel I needed to bitch. I didn't want to hurt Rainen.

I didn't want to be with the ex either. He was newly married and having kids and just loving his life. He knew what he was doing. Trying to make it appear I was selling myself to him for the help that he just KNEW I didn't really need. His wife never knew because he of course is a great husband. Treats her quite gently... seemed stupid for him to keep gunning for me because I was having five seconds of what he thought might be joy with someone other than him. Over it you say? I think the gentleman protests too much!

Shakes head. So now you have the history that will help you understand these letters and the meaning behind the letters to no one. I was never so stupid to think I would get anything in the way of real friendship from Cain but I was so grateful for his help. He really did have to be kind to do it. Even if he wanted to do it ultimately to hurt me. Both mentally and physically.

I disliked the lies I had to tell to keep the fighting down while I dealt with the behavior from Rainen. He knew I was talking to Cain, which was only happening because I figured Cain had something to prove, Rainen's treatment became rough and he started to get violent. The one day, before I ever took the trip to Texas, I had been talking to someone on the phone and as I got finished, Rainen asked who it was. I think it was my cousin, but I couldn't be sure, now. Only I was sure it wasn't Cain. Rainen asked if it was Cain. I was in such a bad mood from his behavior after he told me to go ahead and talk to Cain on Facebook, that I just stood there for a while and fumed. I finally threw the phone at Rainen and it grazed his cheek. I stood there holding little tiny Lily on my hip and waited for the screaming. But instead, I found him barreling towards me and he slapped me as hard as he could. I stumbled and almost fell. I turned and took Lily out of the room while he stood there smirking at the older girls like he had finally solved that issue and weren't they impressed with him.

That moment changed my mind about so many things. I had never seen Rainen hit anyone. I never knew he would get so violent so fast and I even wondered if it was my fault. I put the girls to bed, and I gathered my phone and my jacket and took off walking. I walked for three hours in the rain and I was so glad no one could see the welt or small bruise on my face in the dark. Very Beatrice of me. And after all I did to get away from how she had mothered me. I didn't know what I was going to do. If I had been smart I would have seen that he wanted me to leave and he only did the best thing he could imagine that would make me leave. I was sure he came back for a woman but I was so in love or in illusion-whatever. I went along with most of what he wanted to make sure this would work. I was devastated with this turn of events. He spent the entire time he was at the house with the girls trying to convince them he was a good guy who just lost his temper. I didn't say anything to them about the incident. I figured they knew by that, there WAS no excuse for the bullshit. I stopped right then even caring if I did anything for him. He revealed secrets of his own to me, and those didn't make me sympathetic. He looked and looked for anything to re-bond me to him. I was lost to him.

I smiled when expected to, I cooked as usual, I filled out applications while Rainen went online and hunted girls. When I was there I talked to what friends I had online but they seemed to sense me holding back and they started ignoring me collectively before long. I sent a goodbye out so I could begin to take care of Rainen full time and not worry him with my online escapades. After all, that promise is why I came. So, I had to make it matter. Even if he didn't want me or care what he did to me or said to me anymore. He tried to show me the beauty of Oregon. I saw it. He didn't realize I was not enraptured with him anymore. I didn't care if he was the most beautiful man I knew, I didn't care if he was kind long ago. I didn't care if he thought I was awful. Since I wasn't beautiful, I couldn't be worth a shit to him. All the cute Oregon girls thought he was amazing. And he was. And is. All I could do was to start to wall myself off so I could take on what would surely be the hardest thing I would ever go through. And I knew I would have to do it myself. No one was here for me. No one would try to be my friend and I couldn't see why. I had to let them all go to it would appear. I didn't mind really. It seemed simple to let it all go.

I knew the girls would be the only reasons I did anything I promised and they would also be the reason I made it. When I did. I knew the online bullying was going on. I didn't care too much about it. I am not big into all things tech. I thought maybe my oldest was even in league with her dad and they were helping each other make me miserable. Seemed silly but I guess I knew a little something I didn't KNOW I knew. I wished I had someone who cared to just talk to...

I didn't need to worry about it, though. Just get through it.

2011 (no identifying date but the year on this writing)

Someone somewhere lives for me. They might love only me, if they knew me. There just IS no balance to this reality. I don't seek a fairy tale of an honest lover any longer. I don't even look for beauty within people anymore. There is no realness to this balance. I shouldn't have to shout to the universe. I wait for a presence without anger. Who is bound by deep feelings. Who still cares. I sigh and pull myself up for one more round. Why anyone should fear me, I could never say.

--I don't know when I wrote this only that it was written on the back of an envelope. Probably while sitting in the huge three building learning hospital where Rainen was constantly receiving checkups and CAT scans. If I had to be honest, the lack of belief in love must have come when I first began to speak to Cain and Rainen got angry. It was the first time he hit me and I was devastated. I began to know that this was not going to be some ordinary promise I was keeping here. I couldn't keep pretending nothing was wrong, at the same time I knew I must. Who would be able to see it and believe it. Rainen never had behaved like this before and remember I had no friends to speak of. I had spoken so highly of Rainen, even when he was horrible to me. I felt my loyalty was all that preserved his friendships and familial ties. I had to force him to talk to his family and make him be nice to others. I couldn't get him to be even passably civil to my friends. Funniest was that the friends all disliked him and never asked how I was doing. Like they knew he was violent and they instead chose to close their eyes to me because I was heavy? I am sure some of them thought I deserved it, not knowing what I had already had to go through in my youngest years. I don't know what motivates evil. I only know I won't extend my hand in friendship to them again. Any of them, Cain.

2011 (no identifying date but the year on this writing)

Simulating peace is still OK with me. I really needed it right now. This is way too much shouting and packing and homework and unpacking. Thanks universe. The eviction was my fault- I see that. I prefer to be happy while I get high but alas! No shyness about my situation. I know I am the only one who can do it. Therefore, I will put on my cape and go out into this wild new place and get myself some work. But for this five minutes, I am just the girl Tabitha. This is where I find the quiet I am looking for while I am surrounded by noise of all kinds...

--Rainen was telling me each day that I was the reason we

were failing and if I couldn't do more, then what good was it for us to even be together, since I would have broken my word to him. I chose then to make my word matter and that is why I chose to keep smoking pot. I needed to retain some coping mechanism that could help me keep it together. I knew I would have no friend or help since some shit you deal with yourself. I tried to keep everything away from my girls and make sure I just smiled more. I tried to make sure the crying was well away from them.

021811

I pull myself up from the lowest I have ever been. I unfurl my black wings and make myself quiet. This is the four o'clock in the morning world where it must stay silent... leave me again and again. See if I care. I am the beast you run from in nightmares. You will know it wasn't right.

I am accustomed to walking alone. I am invisible but that makes me dangerous. The rain soaks right through me... it fills me with a clean I can't describe. The cold touches me like freezing steel on burning skin. I turn back to the night.

--This was when I was doing multiple interviews in a day and walking all over town to generate more applications and help. Rainen told me not to bother him with my bitching since it was my fault. I accommodated him by starting to write again. I was already tired of Facebook and didn't even care if anyone ever talked to me again. I had been dealing with an uncle's poor health and trying to keep the hospital from killing his life support. He was a strong man and recovered with the help of another cousin (I knew she was a powerhouse. What a great girl to take so much time and work so hard!!) She had the capacity to deal with it since I couldn't. I couldn't even explain to the family WHY I couldn't visit him and talk to doctors on top of what all I had to do in a day. I was so exhausted and helpless feeling that I would slide onto the tub floor in my shower and just lean against the wall and cry. I was trying to make my own little family work and no one else even cared. My kids were in the front of my mind each time I stood up from the floor and angrily wiped the tears away. I would not quit. It didn't matter who liked what I was doing or not doing. I was doing the right thing.

021811 0510a

I don't want to share shit with the world. It's chilling. I didn't want this world to bear any more pain. I'm sure there are worse things than what I have endured. I still can't take the nightmares and put them away so easily. The slimy hands and the smell of the whiskey is too much. I wish someone else could see the nightmare through my eyes.

--After the violence and fighting started in earnest, I found myself having nightmares about my awful pseudo-childhood with the step father who had abused my mother and I for so many years. No surprise when I was dealing with some of the same arguments and many of the same behaviors. I had never seen these emerge in Rainen in even a slight way. It tore me up to have the dreams replace the monster stepdad with Rainen's face. His smile had always brought me so much joy and now it was just a small trip to childhood trauma. I tried to remember pain changes behavior. I tried to remember that we don't all deal well with physical pain. I had been dealing with physical pain from a very young age and mental pain for the entirety of my life. I couldn't see why he couldn't internalize at least a portion of it. Perhaps it made me expect unreasonable things from him.

When I started to dream again prolifically, I began to stay up again. This time, no liquor- with only good habits. Painting and writing, sewing, making simple jewelry and putting together scrapbooks of my life and pictures. I wrote every single day and sometimes for hours in the early mornings, when I knew nightmares were inevitable. I used to drink whiskey to help combat them. It stopped working so I decided to stop using it. I smoked sometimes—when there was money for it. Or when Rainen would "front" weed. He spent so much rent money on it that I began to fight with him over it. I smoke, too, but I would never get us all kicked out for it. He would, though. Laughs but it isn't funny. It was sad. I had to talk to the dealer's wife and set a limit and have the dealer not answer the phone for Rainen when he was at so much debt. The dealer and his woman thought me stupid, but I knew what they were doing. Trying to get us out on the streets. I had no stomach for the games everyone seemed to be playing. One honest soul?? Seemed far away into a future I couldn't see.

I have met some great people back here in NM. I had to leave my bubble to do it and that is why I wasn't widely known or liked before. Plus, when you're fat it seems like people can't bring themselves to look you in the eye. It's fine. So many had disparaged my name, I didn't care if they did. I was never worried since I was related to so many awful people—I always had shit talked. Even though I tried to clear their damn debt and get them set up with whatever I could do. At least the little sis and mom. It never mattered. I was reliable but no one saw past my stupid last name.

022811

I know what's next...this guy won't be hateful or lie. He is the man of my heart. Blame is easy to misplace. Convince yourself it's all my fault. You need your space. I just lock up my soul. I won't keep living like this.

Keep your apology and your fucking kiss. You say it because it's what you imagine I want. But did you try asking what I want? Remember, I want a relationship-not a train wreck. The day is coming when it won't hurt anymore. I realize this isn't love.

--I had a hard time reconciling when Rainen blamed me for the evictions and bills piling up. I worked on my credit and tried to keep it good enough to keep getting the loans from my bank. It was sometimes all that kept us afloat. And the second part of this is all Cain. He said many things I could tell were false and meant to dig at my situation. I didn't even get hurt. I knew he had some revenge issues. I told him to go ahead and get through it. I just ignored the slights to my strength and my honesty. I had to lie every time I talked to him because of the fight it started each time I was honest and told Rainen who I was texting. Then Cain would miraculously find another thing to do so he didn't have to talk to me, once the fight was full-blown. I don't care about it. I go see him because I feel for him. I know he doesn't return them. It is fine. I didn't want his little pink houses life. I am pleased he is doing so well. I took the only inspiration from Cain that I could... that he was happy and guess what? I could be too. I can still use that to soothe myself even though I know who he is and that he damn sure can't be anyone else at this late date. Sometimes he is a good person. I can't always tell and don't want to waste any more time trying. Fake friends are NOT better than enemies. Ha-ha-ha-ha!!! They are about the same.

022811

You manage to hurt me. Fuck me over. I'm just a woman. "A bitch." You sleep with me. Would it kill you to be kind to me? I smile for one moment and shake my head. I stumbled onto this. You love me, you hate me, you can't be real to save your life. Smile, look pretty, but don't make a sound. Or have an opinion...

Mean words, slaps, punches to the wall by my head, all fine. What happens when I go elsewhere for peace? I must make some kind of refuge for myself. He caught the pain and looked away. You didn't care.

--Everything I wrote incorporated both Cain and Rainen for so long. The two tormentors. I was so hurt over it. I finally gave up though I can't say when. Cain decided to walk away from his lie of friendship and I didn't stop him. I'm the one that got away and he was so sure I would want the life he had. I could not ever resign myself to a life of wifey. It took him a year to get ahold of me and try to weasel back in. I let him believe whatever he wanted. I nodded and smiled and kept on doing what he did. Putting visits off and making sure to ignore as much as possible. I don't care if he loves me or hates me. I am bored of fighting for love and friends who won't do the same for me. I agree he should fear Rainen. Rainen mistakenly blames him for the breakup. And Rainen offered to tell Cain's wife if he didn't leave me alone. That seemed to finally make a difference. Years later, Cain lied and said Rainen did try to get ahold of his wife. Rainen didn't but it's funny Cain lies so much while spouting good morals. I don't usually lie. I have but it makes me uncomfortable as fuck to do it.

030511

If it's all over just be real and honest about it. No one I know chooses to trust me. Only lie. I am wearied of living like this. Why can't people be who they are instead of faking so much. I gave my life to you. Bad idea, I guess.

--Rainen didn't seem to care. When I bared my heart each day to him and tried to have an honest moment he would shoot me down and continue to tell me some real or perceived wrongness with me. I heard it so long I began to turn off his voice in my head.

032811

I let myself be hidden behind what could be. Try to block out all the many discordant voices that know nothing. They seem hostile for no apparent reason. I was so thoroughly ignored. It seemed they should be grateful for me removing myself. I feel tired and low; my mind is troubled today.

I can be tired but I can never quit. Live life—when can I be spared. No one cared and no one dared.

--The cyber bullying went on and on. I have so many names its tacky. I know who is and isn't my friend. I never cared who had money. After all—I didn't. Who cares. But friends who will kill your soul are not friends, I think. Rainen and his friends are on my shit list and so are many others. You think I fucked you up? Obviously, I was horrible the whole time and you had nothing to do with it. Laughs. I am being judgy. They are all good people and if they stay the fuck away from me, well I am fine with them being any old way they like. How's that for generous spirit. Laughs at my simple revolution. If irony was Swedish meatballs... ha-ha. I would like irony a lot more. Laughs.

041211

No one sees my wings of fire and thorns. My eyes used to be full of doubt. You let me go long ago. I don't care anymore. I never changed. I modified my behavior while I spent time again in Rome...what else do we do. I slam a lot of doors. I don't care about that either. I can't seem to get away from my dreams and there are people in those dreams I know I am supposed to talk to.

I know they're liars, I don't get the choice on this one. I fight demons in dreams you will never need to know about. If I don't sleep the night in your arms then why would you need to know. I will find a respite from the dreams in someone's arms someday. Not yours for sure. I won't weep for a knight that reluctant. No one had to save me—I just needed the bravery of one friend. You are not sure of me and I am sure of myself. I can say goodbye when I need to now.

--I wrote this for Cain. I kept seeing him in dreams

randomly. I knew I was supposed to help him with something but I couldn't decide what. I knew he was OK but something was prompting the shittyness. It needed some help from something. His wife didn't cool his attitude or teach him to be kind. At least unjudgy. Laughs... I find the whole marriage-mess a failure if someone doesn't help you to see the best you and then help you achieve it. Of course, he wouldn't dare to let his wife know THIS Mr. Hyde existed! She might not think the same of him. Or maybe she would cheer him on. In such a case, they would have to be made for each other in heaven. Laughs. I hope they are not so morally bankrupt they would both approve hurting someone like he did me. It is a distinct possibility. Though, I am a bit jaded when it comes to him, I will admit.

060811

One female against legions. The world is loyalist. I don't think it knows about pain. I don't want to feel today. It's too real for my simple soul. Simple questions about sleeping with no dreams. The stars disappear but the creeks and groves sit the same under the peaceful rains. I am restless from dream trysts with bad things. I'm tired and sleepless from my old weights. It catches up at strange moments. I don't care if I am the smart one. It must feel better than being the dumb pretty one.

I don't know why I am trying so hard to make him see I am real when he isn't. I could use a hopeful patch right now.

--Rainen was hateful to some of the people I met while in Portland, purely because they were lesbian. He thought many untrue things of me, then. I told him I would not deal with that and to keep his fucking mouth shut since he couldn't or wouldn't say anything nice while they saved my life so many days and nights... talking me down from the ledge, as it were. I couldn't ever fault the friends I made on my own. Randi you know who you are. And how many times I talked to you about all the stupid decisions I made and how I tried to be better. You made me feel like I could still be real. I saw the love you and your Julee had and I was so heartened by it. Rita, even though you laughed about my struggle, you still sat and listened. You are such a hippie and a great soul. Joyful and a gardener like me. You made me feel like I was never alone. Beth, you were so beautiful and sweet. You made a huge difference by just seeing me as a person. Instead of wife, mom, worker, student. It was nice to be in the company of others who could draw me out of my head. It was so hard to get out, those days. My art professors and indeed all my teachers were kind and open and caring. I learned so much and fought for something more. Anything can be misconstrued, but I felt they went out of their way to show me that I had a way out if I wanted it. The promise was all there was. I couldn't see the end of the longest night in my life. But I could make life happen while I waited. And because of Una, and Michele, and Elizabeth, and the others, I made it through it. Thank you for making me shine under all the rust and tarnish. You amazing and remarkable people. In a place where I had no one, the good people I met were the one joy I could see in the day. I saw my girls and took all the joy and beauty I saw in my heart each day. What mother wants to think of herself in only those terms. You stepped out of the forests and right into my heart. You may not know it yet but I am eternally grateful and I sure wish I could let you know. Maybe you will read this book someday and see...

062211

I have to sit very still in the darkness and keep my silence. DON'T YOU DARE CRY OVER HIM. The echoes of the hateful, hurtful screams swirl around in my head like smoking pitch. It gets to me. I don't sing anymore. I knew this place was going to challenge me, but I had no idea it would take so much out of me. If I keep telling him what he can do to help me and he doesn't listen, then I can't do anything more to create understanding.

Where am I supposed to fucking go? Back in time? To when you loved me? Just take the soul right out of me. I don't fucking need one. Can you tell the truth for one revolutionary minute?

--There was a low day when I sang to Lily and tried to soothe her while she was sick and Rainen told me he was "fucking sick of hearing" my voice and my song. He screamed until I shut up. I chose to not sing again while I was there. I only received a few gifts from my mother. Singing was my favorite. I remember singing once more at my friend Brooke's party. We had fun I guess. The comment about truth was my nod to his lying when he left the house. I smelled perfume, cigarettes and all kinds of other neat shit when he came in. I stopped asking where he went and he wouldn't answer me anyway. "None of my business." That's what he said. So, I made myself blind and quit giving a fuck.

062211

The words beg me to stay and love you more. Your actions show me all the numbers and pictures. I see her when I leave each day. You sure have a dream of being the big player on the block. Let's do this then. Can't you leave if you are well enough to care for yourself and be such a stud? Do I really need to watch? I look and see when you laugh quietly outside and say goodbye to her. (And me. Though my goodbye will last much longer than till bedtime.)

What happens if I look for something new and exciting? Something JUST for me. I don't ever do that. Maybe for once, I can be brave and let you walk away since you want to so badly.

I will keep being myself, no matter how badly you dislike it.

--He started being low with the neighbor women and I even heard a lovely story. She let me know where I got the little infection I found I had with no provocation. Technically, he could have gotten it sharing a cigarette with her, which is likely. Nonetheless, I began to say no to sex with Rainen because I couldn't trust his answers. How did I get it if not from him? He had to make physical contact to get it to me. Even if it was just on his hands. I was ashamed. And I spent some time clearing it up. But I looked for answers to questions I didn't need to ask. How disheartening it was to me.

062311

You are from the past, jealous boy. Lie all you want. I don't want you, anymore. Can't tell the truth with a kindness? Bad raising. This new man I once loved sets me free and then finds he is too in love to let go. When he smiles the sun rises and I know I love him. He is somewhere else with some stupid girl. He has no idea what my intrinsic value is. I don't advertise it. Thank goodness.

--First about Cain. I know he was raised better, and I thought the words might remind him. His mother was disgusted by me, true, but she wouldn't want him to try to hurt me on purpose. Would she? I don't know. Maybe she would laugh with him. Who knows anyone's mind or heart these days? She was amazing to me in the far past. His mom, I mean. I learned so much about how to mom properly from her example. I don't think she ever knew and I don't think she would care if she did. I am so cynical these days. She thought since I was from my mom's family, I was just like her. She was so chagrined when she asked if my oldest baby was Cain's...I think I would have told her not even had she been his. I am an honest woman. I don't lie about parentage. That hurt me. Sort of like she never wanted me to be with him. How could I have not seen her just going through the motions of liking me?

062411

I am holding onto my dream of peace despite the words being shouted. Breathe Tabitha. The reality of the lie is obvious. I am trying to forget it all. You took my years like they meant nothing. You go ahead and forget me. You don't get to take that back now.

--Rainen in his terrifying ogre phase was something evil to behold. I spent many nights shaking in the dark and trying to recover equilibrium enough to sleep. His shouting encompassed a myriad of my faults for the day... the main one that I would not agree to be back with him. He would scream that he loved me and I would be with him or no one. I worried some of these nights and stayed awake for no real reason except unease. Failed to sleep, mostly. I couldn't imagine how I was passing college classes and working and taking care of kids and Rainen at the same time. He was surely destroying me. My hair was falling out in clumps and my ulcer pained me every day. If I could have eaten, I would have. There was food thanks to crazy mom couponing and making the stuff stretch like mad. I would shake so hard I would sometimes throw up before my morning run to the bus. And sometimes I would fall asleep in class. I had no way to know how to cope. I should have stood up for myself and left. But where would I go. No home and no time to make a new one. I was devastated.

062311

It was a crazy whim that gave you the thought to speak to me. (Whatever stupid mystery I represented.) Couldn't you just let me be? You saw me happy in the rain and decided I couldn't be with someone else and be that happy. What did I do to you?

I have to wake each day all over again waiting to fight today. Have to always kill my dreams, do you?

I don't care anymore. I will keep walking in the cold rain.

Enjoying the only good things I can see—that rain. These babies... I grew and so I have to leave?

If you traded your dreams, then go for it. I can't. I know what I am doing.

--Cain's. He only spoke to me when he thought he could stir shit up for me. I knew. I would exhaustedly sigh when I saw his name. I used to get excited like I was going to get interaction with someone who knew me and might even care about me. After many times, I stopped caring when he texted. I would answer whatever I thought he wanted to hear and get off the phone as fast as possible. I knew some of the bullying felt like him. I flipped cards on it all the time. Many people being involved made it tiring to whittle it down to exacts. I did see him in the cards and I got it loud and clear he was in the know even if not doing it. Which made me feel he was fake. I fought for him and over him so much and I knew while I was doing it he was going to fuck me over. He didn't disappoint. He came back trying to get me to trust with stories of loving me and being there for me. I listened with half an ear, knowing all along... each time he changed his picture on Facebook, he seemed in some fierce competition with me. Pictures geared to let me know he was so thrilled and look! Didn't I see? I loved Rainen truly. I wasn't competing. I just wanted my own love. That was all I ever wanted. He was sure to make it a laugh. He belittled my time in the horrible hospital while I wrung my hands and prayed Rainen wouldn't die on the table. He sent sex texts and tried to make it a joke. I sent him texts geared towards getting off the phone as fast as I could. Mostly I could say, "I have had a helluva day", and then he would not text again for weeks. No one would see what I was going through without thinking I deserved it for some fucked up reason. I knew I would get no real honesty from him. Nor did I expect it from minute one. I was hopeful, not naive.

062411

We don't always remember where we were when our love fell apart. Life lessons are love and trust. I live it even when I don't want to. I was the one who believed. You didn't think I was anything. My heart retreated from you and let it be. I just need to get away from this place and these same old hates that can't seem to work themselves out.

If you don't hear a word I say then it doesn't even matter. Giving yourself to me wasn't as easy as you imagined, but if you think it's easy for me—DON'T.

Of course, for Rainen.

072411

Now I am just sitting here waiting for the day to end. Held my breath all morning. And now it seems to be at a screeching halt. Something went wrong. Something I said made the peace end again. I see you smile in your sleep when I check on you. Must have been a lovely dream. I wish I could be there with you instead of here pacing, worrying over waking you for more meds. Can't wait too much longer. And those same nightmares wait for me when I go back to sleep. I will just stay awake and fight the sleep. To stay away from all of it.

Rainen again.

081611

Can you dream out loud? I am limited, I confess. These dreams aren't for sharing in the light. When I wake, I am upset. Nightmare cities and houses made of glass. I walk corridors endlessly. I don't usually speak and can't go anywhere. It is obviously my fault, since I go climb in bed like a special kind of idiot. I spoke with quiet dead who had their mouths neatly sewn shut. I woke and had a hard time believing in this world.

I turned in the dream to go back. The second time he rose,

I died with him. Brother of mine, I loved you through the hardships we both went through. I didn't mean to hurt you so badly. I hate letting you go, but if I don't, you won't get the rewards you earned with your own experience.

Be at peace, Darius Michael.

--I dreamed about my older brother and it had very creepy shit in it. I thought maybe I should quit calling on him. My sign to let him go be at peace. I loved him and he would have been there if he could have. He always was. I miss you Darius. So fucking much!!

090611

What if I got up right when you spat the hateful words out? What if I ran so far and so fast you got lost looking? Where would you turn? I bet there wouldn't be a problem. I hope the new one is someone who can stroke your ego forever. I fell so hard for you that I couldn't see past what you were showing me. Love is dangerous for sure.

090611

I have always felt this from when I was a child--all the words the bad people would attribute to me. I thought I must be bad in some way. I watch every move I make as though I am a bird of prey waiting to strike myself for being evil. Waiting to see what I do. How I will live up to my potential or fail. Waiting for the sunrise so I can go do all the billions of jobs that require my presence. I can prove I am worthy. I know I don't have to prove it to myself but every day finds me making my list way too long to even finish the entire thing. Why do I expect myself to be perfect? I don't need to be thought of as Miss Wonderful, but I would like to see myself as a finisher and a productive and good creature. I want my girls to see fierceness. They know what it takes. I have fought so hard and I know, now. I never had to fight. Just stay alert and focused.

And never quit. Something I don't think I had a chance to learn in my mother's house. My mother didn't finish much she started. I saw and learned inconsistency. I am unteaching myself every day. It is something I have to teach myself. I know I am good. I know I am going to make it.

--I spent much time trying to figure out my faults and work on them. I couldn't imagine I was going through this just to cry. So, I found each spot that hurt when I touched it, and I opened it up and looked inside. I found a lot out about myself. The big thing—I AM NOT MY MOM.

102111 1126p

My day today has been full of letting go. Letting go of fights I can't win, letting go of people I already knew weren't for me, letting go of my conceptions of what I am. My night tonight is full of beautiful silence and my own dear company. What a relief it will be to see the clouds come back and pour down the rain. The moon is only barely visible and she seems to be shining only for me. I feel like the only person left on the planet.

--I think it was graduation in Forest Grove that night. The entire apartment complex left. The town was silent and I was there out on the balcony with no sounds. It was easily one of my favorite moments.

110211

The world is full of fire if you look. My soul hides under the mushrooms and clouds and trees and it grows. Cooling shadows of this lake make my heart swell. The wind blows my hair back and I pull the rain to me. It's sort of a shelter for me. I belong in the rain where I can feel my fire. It needs the rain... laughing.

--I was so much within myself that I found it hard to enjoy outside things. I learned to draw myself to the things and places I could get peaceful.

111711

Dare me to live and I am. Say I can't do more but I did.
I am loving without failing. I am jumping with no looking
down. Too much, too soon; too little, too late. Here we still sit
blessings between us...

--Rainen and the girls obviously. He had threatened to
take them away if I even thought of moving away without
him. Then he began to up his game as a dad because he knew
he was a superior one most of the time and he knew I would
come back to him if he proved what he could be like again. He
was always a great dad. Not good for me though.

111711

Complicate my life totally. Turn away from who you were.
These times try even me. I can't tell you how it is or how we
will get through this. Walk with me in the rain soaked streets
full of trees. I leave the walls behind for this.

Only for myself.

112511

Watch the sorrow melt into the lament of a lifetime. To the
woods and waters wild... hold my hand tight.

"Float Away"-KMK

122111

Can you reach one extra inch? Can you teach someone
hard of learning? Within, without, but only for me. You aren't
the shadow.

For Cain.

2011 (No dates beyond placement in notebook)

There is always darkness. It doesn't always require fear.
Or light. I sit through many reminders. One more time today

even. I am lost in my own resurrection. I gave myself to the wonder and magic and it took me. If the words you all said were true then none of you would want me anyway. Little wonders. Thank gods...

--I didn't want to be wanted by hateful asses. Lying about me was a quick way to make sure no one wanted to talk to me or be friends even when I was trying so hard to understand the druggies and the con men and the hurtful, fake friends. I made every excuse for them all. I am NOT Jesus and I hope I can love you guys when it's finally over and I am finally free.

All the cyber bullies and the fakers...

2011 (No dates beyond placement in notebook)

There's a dance inside... I sing new songs that loose joy from my secret side. I am doing what I said I would do. It brings me peace to know my word is real. It doesn't matter what he says while he hates me for his pain... I loved him then even if he didn't think I was perfect. I love him now and he doesn't know because I can't tell him anymore. I'm not sure anyone can shake me, now. I don't even care anymore.

--He made promises and broke them. Rainen knew how I hated it so he did it every day for a year. I wrote them down and started checking them off myself so my girls would see promises kept mean something. Even though I was discouraged I began to keep them one at a time. Funny but he never even worried one second over anyone thinking HE was a liar.

2011 (no other identifying date-just placement in the note-books tells me where this letter belongs.)

Tabitha,
I don't know why you think that you have robbed me of anything. You never held me hostage or kept me down in any way. I am a grown damn man and it was me who made the choices I did. I made several choices in our eleven years together that

did more damage to you and those beautiful little girls that we share. I lied and chose many things that were wrong and bad. You and I both know that I WAS all those things...awful, jealous, petty... I feel like things could have been a lot more for us if had made some of those choices differently.

I am mad at Anastasia, and Cain, and my mom and anyone else who ever said it—for saying that we weren't right for each other. Even if we aren't right for each other at this moment doesn't mean that we weren't ever right for each other or that we won't be right for each other in the future. I cherish the life and time I have had with you. A lot of times it wasn't easy but I did always think you were worth whatever I had to do. My life and who I am as a person have done nothing but become better and MORE with you there. I told you that I loved you each day because I did. I never once told you that and not meant it with everything that I am.

I would love a chance to have my son be a part of my life. And I will when the time is right. That doesn't mean that I want to be with Anastasia or that I want to sleep with her, or even see her if I could do it any other way. And when the moment comes and the boy is in my life I will need you to be there for me, not her. Even if you aren't with me, I will need you there.

I never made myself anything so that you would be able to say that you had it. What I felt then and what I feel now is undying love. My heart will always be yours if you want it. Any sacrifices that I made, I made willingly, knowing what it was and why I did it. I was only unhappy seeing you that way. I wish that I could have done that. I know you and I both need to become happy with ourselves to be happy with anyone. I wish I had done that.

Sweet Tabitha, I have no backup plan. Nor do I need one. I will go and be me, and in doing that I can make myself proud of me again. And hopefully you will be proud too.

I hope one day to be seen in a way that makes your eyes

light up like they do in moments of joy. You have been the best part of me through some of my worst moments and I could never have grown and learned and truly loved without you.

Always-

Rainen

(This letter was written by Rainen and he gave it to me during this time. I thought it relevant.)

010412

This is messed up right here. I am not deserving of this. I am not the beautiful vapid creature he needs. OK. But I can't keep up the intimate stuff. It's killing me very surely. We aren't together and I know I don't have to. It is too hard to be here and not. It is too much to think I can resist his smile and his touch. I know tomorrow will come (or tonight) and he will show me again why I should never trust him. He will play on every little thing I ever told him about my short rough life. Until I am curled up in my soft blankets on my fluffy pillows and crying myself to sleep again. Sometimes writing it down helps.

I will be through with the promise soon. That's all I can do. Wait for the promise to be finished. Oh, Rainen, why do you do this to me? Why do I let you?

--I kept going back to him and he keeps asking even now, for me to sleep with him. Clearly, he is crossing boundaries I set newly each day. I can't be everything for you anymore. Leave me alone. Please. Fucking please, already.

030312

You told me you'd come find me—me, the no one girl. Those words were so untrue. You knew I would need your comfort when my soul fell away from the rest of me. I cried alone waiting for someone real. I had a feeling my soul was gone. When I break, I fall. He thinks he is the king of everything. I waited for you at the end of that long-ass line. I think you can step aside. I don't need that kind. He will be here soon and then not want to leave me. I am his—whoever he is. I know I can call on him. He is with me everywhere I go and his touch so long ago marked me. If that's good or bad I can't even say. I am all his in the dark. I spend one more night (one thousand more nights) awake and by myself. I wish he would see. He is off in a dream he won't come back from. Maybe he dreamed himself beside me on that December night—3:48 in the morning. He brushed his hand across my neck and then I cried. I felt it, though he wasn't there in physical form.

I asked the darkness if he would come for me in the morning—if I am still here... he might.

--The ethereal experience I had made a huge impression and I am always sure he is mine whoever he is. I have heard more and more from the shadow as I call it. Ghost or apparition or presence...who knows what that is? I only know it pulled me from my cycle of self-pity and forced me back into the real world.

032112

I set myself up. I let myself down. I can't do it anymore. I am mad. I "leave too often" he tells me. He ignores me. I decided I was done. I am not able to walk away, yet. The promise keeps me here. I can keep myself a little separate, though. Save something of my soul. Obscene obsessions. People stare too much at my broken pieces. I think I don't want the pieces anymore. I learned my lesson. I looked for something for myself but I guess things aren't what they appear to be. He won't want me until I leave. I won't let him put it back the same exact bullshit way. I don't need him to be with me when I run and dance in the rain. I told everyone not to follow me because I was lost. I lead all those astray. Too many people are not going to stick with me. I don't want to become attached to the runaways.

I wrote about Rainen here. And the bullies who watched. I remember them.

040512

I walk a line no one has drawn in the dirt. That way when I cross it, no one gets hurt. I am alone. This isn't what I imagined. Why do I have to keep being me? Why do I keep running into a wall? Can anyone tell I am real behind the selfish show? Can you tell I'm in hell in time to let me go? Why don't you care if I am in pain? Why do I think his arms will shelter me when all he ever did was laugh when I hurt? I think it is easy for both of you to feel like a king, even when you have no kingdom to speak of.

--Rainen and Cain. Neither one seemed to grasp the importance of having a real friend who would have your back no matter what kind of douche they were being. I sort of feel as though people like that learn the hard way.

---Rainen proposed to me in January of 2012. I told him I would revisit after a year and answer him. Before we got there, he told me he didn't love me and we should split up. I created these vows for myself to prove I hadn't shut myself down for love ever again. I don't think I would use them but as a base they are true and not bad to start with.

040512

From Rainen--With this ring, I thee wed. With this lie, I tell you I feel love.

Too bad I got all caught up in that. I will not lie to my future love. Who says there will be one? I do. I will have one.

My words won't follow tradition at all, but tell the story in my heart---

Light my eyes and soul. Burn through me like wildfire. This could be something new... a fresh start. You will be the only one I ever want.

I won't always be the one to offer apologies after a fight. I will always hold my ground if I believe in what I am saying. I hope you won't always need to be right. If I tell you to leave will you stay and make me believe again? Will you promise to keep your anger away from me? I will take your words to mean the truth until you show me a lie. I will keep learning a new way to be. I will keep myself by your side. And I promise to keep no secrets from your heart.

Helluva way to know exactly what I wanted to say—just let me remember how it felt forced then and try to change that completely. I want to make the brand new me show the future man I want him. To show him I want to wrap my soul with the armor of his love and wake each morning in his warm arms. I can do anything now, but I know I will find a love just for me.

I am so pleased I fought that one each day and won. I do want love and I will find it. I loved Rainen so much I don't know what to attach the word love to, if not his face smiling at me.

040712

I wonder if he will see the fire and thorns. If my eyes will speak of the things I think only to myself. I always stayed true to myself. I remember the peace of the dream and I go there to feel healed in the still waters. I don't need to be alone with the dreams anymore. I fight too many demons in my sleep. Sleep doesn't give me rest, anymore.

--It seems weird that a whole list of people I knew should forget me so easily. I guess I asked for it by saying I was going to be busy for a while to care for Rainen and do all I had to. But how could I do more than what I was. And to be fair, I tried to work with several of them still. It isn't all my fault. They are at fault too.

052112

There are glimpses of light in the dreams each night. You and I share passion. Why does it seem like it never happened? Each bright morning reminds me of the words you say. How you never cared. I get up each day and look in your terrible eyes, only catching glimpses of your true beauty. I bear each small deception with a deep breath and surety that I can't change your mind, NOW.

Sunshine hears the silver song inside me crying out to be heard. I trusted you enough to whisper my secrets into the night, into your ear. Selfish of me to suffer alone when so many want to pull up a chair.

I am as lost as you.

I just wake up and keep going.

--Rainen could always inspire those around him to great deeds. I wish he could have inspired them to give a fuck about me. They instead found new ways to bash me and make sure I didn't come through this at all. Inspire the masses all you want. Hitler did that too. And Buddha. Could've went either way.

052412

Talk to me all the time. Why should I answer? I have nothing to say that could change a thing. What could you do that is worse than what I have lived through? You really believed you were the only one who could make it. My soul is fragile and my will is NOT. The night issues a permanent invite. The voices of those that loved me are both appreciated and full of truth. My life means as much as anyone else's. This isn't the last chapter, BTW. Tomorrow reminds me that life is what I make it. I will keep the ones I love and those who stood by me safe. I always do. I am triumphant. So, when you decide to leave for good, then I hope it makes you feel good when I don't try to chase you. Forget about my truths I shared with you. I am strong.

Why would you want credit for me? When I am always under such scrutiny. I need some peace and quiet and time for my wings to grow.

Queens and princesses alike, fear me. I don't want what you have. I want all the worlds. And I will have them while you sleep.

--For Cain. You should be what you like about this world. I don't know about revenge. I don't usually do that since I was a tiny girl and saw what it did. I think I could easily just do as the people all seem to and forget to be there when someone needs me. Which is never because after all, I see most hanging on to the illusion of perfection.

052712

How did you think it would be? Did you think I was so weak? Are you sure you are king of the world? I fell in love with you, but that was long ago. You sneaked me out too many back doors. Don't you remember? I did. Remember how no one saw you for yourself? I can't believe anyone would want a friend who would destroy another soul. I sure wouldn't. I laugh because you think you are going to get me to say some dumb thing that will assure you that destroying my life was worth it to you. I don't want to break you or your stupid marriage. That one then or this one now. I don't care if you are happy. In fact, I insist upon it! But are you happy if you want to do this sort of thing to me? I will tell you what the world will think. NO. The woman I am now must have love surrounding me each day. I must wake in the morning and be wrapped in safe strong arms. You won't be able to provide that. Ever. I could tell what you wanted, even then.

Let it go. I did. Or is that what worries you, Cain? I endured what felt like a thousand lifetimes of pain to make him well. All I asked YOU for was simple friendship. You talk a good game, much as when I was sixteen, and nineteen. But thirty-seven-year-old me remembers. Words are only words, and you never show me anything more.

--I was feeling hurt again...I often say things I can't say aloud- to paper. Ha-ha. And I figured he won't see it in print or care. But for some reason he cares what OTHERS think of him... wonder why I didn't hit THAT list...

052712

The wilderness here makes my soul sing. Life has been painful these days. I always felt lost. I saw a great deal of hate in my life. Most of it I didn't feel I deserved. I think innocence is a child's and you shouldn't ever fuck with that. I only wanted to run away to the woods and waters wild to heal. You had to make sure that would hurt, too.

Is this how you leave a legacy? Daughters are the future. You hurt those feminine souls you think aren't worthy, I certainly hope your own daughter isn't found by some man like you. It doesn't always work in your favor because I love you.

I didn't write off a damn thing. I fought and lived anyway. I tried to love and it was the BRAVEST thing because I bet many women would have given up, right there. I didn't care.

You don't want to apologize to me, then apologize to the women who will come after me. Or even your precious girl.

All I wanted was to be left alone. Your little games don't hurt me because I know what you are doing and it doesn't mean anything. Maybe I DON'T miss you.

--Rainen and then Cain. I can't be honest with anyone who isn't with me. I gave small parts of my story but not one got the entire thing. So how would you know?

052912

A word to myself on people and how I must get by—
Leave your sadness outside yourself. Decide right here that you won't ever let them get one on you. You have to fight,

somehow. Even if you don't want to. Let your crazy bubble up. The calm inside is helpful.

The biggest decisions are made in this time and space.

Tell him it's time.

Take one fierce step and let it all come down to this. When you let go at last, make sure you don't slip. There is only this minute. This, right now, is all we really need. Seize the precious minutes and seconds and do something great.

Before the priceless time is gone.

--I re-read and appreciate my wounded self of the past and how I stood through this trial and cried each night. I still made each day what it had to be for my daughters to be taken care of. I am strong. I always was. I didn't need a gang of stupid bullies to figure it out. Thanks.

052912

My dreams are laced with strychnine truth. My nightmares are full of sugary fake words. My mind doesn't see anything different than usual. I fight on the side of good in this. I just want quiet in my three a.m.'s I don't want to go to bed where I will have to battle for my rest. Instead of sweet dreams, I am the hunted guest. I draw down protection from my gods and pray that the light hurries. Is it dawn again so soon? I haven't had time to do anything but hate this night. I get up anyway. I force all the joy I can muster for this new day. I am long past exhausted. I can't stop living just because anyone wishes it. Even if I am beyond damaged by living.

--I got up each day three hours before anything was scheduled to keep myself on track. I would write for an hour and smoke while I made lists for my day to go properly. I had schedules for the girls and meds and food lists for Rainen and lists of what I had to do versus what I need to do versus what I want to do. Usually only sleep and paint and write on that one. Ha-ha. I would shower, change for the day, and have all my school shit ready. Fifty pounds of books and paint and all my work clothes so I could get ready at school after class. I had to walk a mile for a bus and then run to a train. Then I had to run to another bus and then again run for class when I got there. Very exhausting and I am so tired when I think of it, I am relieved to be here writing and sitting down!!

052912

I can feel the tide pushing and pulling at me. I can almost drink the moonlight and feel it pour out from all my wounds. I could never buy this clean feeling.

I walk in the shadows of this forest. I will easily forget what has been done to me. I can almost hear the stars' chorus. I feel the walk we are on entitles us to one more chance. Will you always go with me? I am surrounded by all the doors I have ever opened and shut. I can set myself free. You want me to give this horrible day a chance. You want me to forget what you said. I sing for my own soul. You can make your own damn music.

--I thought of Cain fondly even when he behaved reprehensibly. I tried to do as I did with Rainen and offer Cain a fresh start every time I talked to him. I never expected his honesty. I still don't. Lucky me. I am very in touch with the world and what it's like. I don't even have to read the news...ha-ha-ha!!

062312

I walked back into the desert, dark and pouring rain. I remembered who I was. It refreshed my soul. I hurt to say it, but I am not that girl anymore. Life brought me back. I couldn't help but appreciate my backbone and dedication. It was like me at sixteen but now I am wrapped in lightning and pulling the power of a tornado from my fingertips. That's when I knew-I am back to myself.

--I went back to NM to help my mom out. She had been

kidnapped and held in her apartment by a wacko tweaker for four days and beaten with a bat within an inch of her life. By the time they got her to a hospital, the docs wanted to cut off her hand and do all kinds of life support yanking and I was livid. Cleaning the blood was so reminiscent of the old days with George that I could hardly stand to do it. The smell of the place was so sweet and like death. I had to stay awake and watch out for mom because every time she drifted off, she would rip herself out of dead sleep screaming. So, I just sat next to her and cried a lot and held her hand while she finally fell asleep. I knew she didn't deserve this but I still warred with myself because shouldn't she have to save herself even once??? I didn't leave until she was all set up for moving and I had to make myself leave. I really had a hard time going to her. I paid for it out of my new credit card and it fucked my credit severely when I could have used it to save my family from the eviction and get bills caught up. I was so depressed and again—Cain trying to be there because he was sure I was there for a guy. I didn't care, I just sat there the whole night and every night I was there and cleaned blood off everything I saw it on. I mean everything. Pretty much. I did have problems with my mom but though I couldn't fix her problems, I still tried to care for her when I came back from Oregon. While I was in Oregon before I could come to her, I sat in a circle with my girls and Rainen and we prayed and sent our excellent positive vibes to her so she would at least live. I was so scared for her. Even in my absolute distrust and conflicted feelings, I never wanted this to happen to her. I love her while keeping her a safe distance.

070812 1240a

What can we expect of the girl who wasn't ever supposed to be anything? I would never feel entitled to you or your time. Never one dream-free night. Never a comfort from the nightmares when I wake. No one has considered that I live with them in the dark and then I wake and dream a new hell in the light. I have meshed the worst of the night's horror with the sorrow of what comes in the day. It burns to feel all these things at the same time. I must get a break from it, sometime.

--Cain. I told him that I knew what it was. He mistakenly thought I meant a love affair. I know you, boy. Don't ever think I didn't have eyes wide-the-fuck open. I am thirty-seven, fucker. Not sixteen. Go do your fro-yo Tuesday and scheduled everything. Go be into what you love. Leave me alone. I'll be fine. I never needed traditional shit. I love to blaze my own trails. Just don't think about me. It was easy before. It will get easier, too, I'm sure. You are sure to have little need of me. It's really for the best.

072112

When the first man let me go, he swore to care for his lovely girls. I never wanted to let them suffer for his broken promise. When the last man let me go, and swore to uphold his family, it was like I didn't give birth to them or care for them at all while he played with my life and heart.

The dreams I have had start to make serious sense. Sadly, I knew.

I sometimes wonder if I am the last real person in this place.

--At last I had the dream that tied all the others together and I saw it easily. I was disappointed in people I had always thought of as good people. Nice and of good fabric. I fell low in these months. I saw the older girls' dad, my ex-husband, make my oldest girl cry on her sweet sixteen. That is an innocent age when you learn who you can love and trust. She now knew she could never love him again because how could he love her and do that to her. I always try to keep the girls seeing their daddies as infallible and so I make a lot of excuses each day for the lies they tell and the simple ways they break each girls heart. I don't make excuses anymore. I ask them what promise was broken. And I make it happen. Who needs a dad. Not me. Not them.

072912

To someone in the future who will love me— (maybe I will meet my shadow after all),

Looking backward in my life I never worried about spirituality that much. My big brother died in 2002 and I started to worry about his soul very much because he was. He said to me while he was in his last few good months, that he was unsure how to view heaven since he didn't know if his good had outweighed his bad. While he was young and healthy, he did his share of running around and getting in trouble doing this or that as well as some more grievous things as he got older. I saw much I said little about. He knew I was aware and he knew I didn't approve. He didn't ever bring it up unless I wanted to talk with him about it. I tried to stay out of his personal business because that seemed to be the way we functioned as siblings. I loved him but he spent a great deal of time bullying me as a child. It complicated our relationship by making me the mom figure. I didn't take his shit and during the time when he pushed every boundary and mom and nana couldn't control him—I did. Not as well as all that I pretended, but I did what I could to make the little life we had a peaceful one. Me and my sister put up with every fool and madman my mom could find and bring home for a stepdad. Darius hated us both, feeling that my mom chose us two girls over him. Little did he know that nana wouldn't suffer the almighty boy to be raised with my mother. The girls, well now, we get what my mom deserved. I learned of his complex feelings later down the road and even after he died I was learning about him. I was bequeathed all his writing, which made me both sad and proud. My mom wouldn't ever read the things he wrote of her while she had the mental capacity to understand it. Chicken shit her. Always looking for a way out of real life. I guess I might be scared, too.

I was so depressed when I found he and I struggled with so many of the same things over our lifetimes. We were right there and couldn't be a help to each other because our mother splitting us off. He loved Charisma as his favorite sibling. She played whatever he wanted to and was a sport. Darius made life fun for her. Then there was me who could not do a thing he asked because he never said please. I did not fare as well. I was the one shoved into a corner and left there. I really didn't mind because they weren't really my sort of people. No one in my family really made sense to me. I was looking through the dirty lens of abuse after abuse. Still there was more bullying by my brother and sometimes even others. I didn't mind that, either. I found not giving a fuck for people who didn't care for me was the easiest thing I ever learned to do and I learned that skill young. I can laugh now because the people who hurt me always come back thinking it will get easier if I am low. It never does. Poor people. I have a lot of patience for world worn souls. But it isn't even weariness that takes them down that road. It's something else. Because I did make it? Because I will make it? Maybe. I don't know. Some things remain beyond my scope. Until I can understand the dumb shit people do better, I guess that just means I don't need to!

At least my brother understood what kind of person I was before it was too late. I feel like he made real effort. And yes, hell yes, it was by far too late. I know. But he got me thinking in new ways and thinking new things. I learned even more about religion than I ever had before. Which is saying quite something. I read and reread books that had given me little taps on the shoulder for the truth I read. I found I wasn't closed to any religion that stated you had to be a good person and you could not hurt people or force anyone to do anything.

I began to search out more knowledge. I found new books that were hundreds of years old. I found old books written in the great eighties. I sought all things that could teach me something about the futile life we live every day here on earth. I needed to see truth and beauty. Humanities truths are held within the most sacred trusts of religions. Humanities beauty is held in her dreams. I try to find sameness in all the people I meet. It isn't always easy. I find out a lot I never wanted to know. About them and myself, in the process. The person who ends up reading and knowing themselves from these pages will have to know love. Maybe not for me specifically, but for this world and the odd creatures that live here. It isn't easy for me to see the light at the end of this overly long tunnel but I am going to keep going no-matter-fucking-what.

I am tired. But I am going to keep going. I mean it. We all like to think of ourselves as heroes. But I MUST if I am going to make it through this.

081412

Another quiet letter. I don't know who will ever care or read it...

From this high up the old me is so small. Twelve stories are high when you are on a mountain already. I feel like I am more myself now than then. I am awake and tingling in my sureness that I am alive. I leave that all behind. I go ethereal distances to see that one. I haven't found him. I don't even worry about it anymore. Just look silently in the dreamscapes I can't remove from my head, no matter how many times I paint them or write them.

Sigh. I wish I weren't alone right now. I just need someone to smile at me and say that I am okay. I know it, but I need to hear it tonight. This place is scary and I don't know anyone.

I am back to not knowing if anything is real...

081512

I can grasp this. I did these powerful things. It's too much to expect a kiss. I just keep living and let loose an inner war cry. I feel like I can take to the skies with black wings and let the blue moon free the wild person I can be.

--I accommodated Rainen for the most part in his desires while we were in Oregon. I wanted to be angry but I couldn't. Just quiet and restrained. Practical to the end. That's me.

081512

I am out in the rain. It falls like whispers with the loving fingers of the fog. It wraps quiet little main street in its arms. I look over the multi-hued leaves under the muted street lights. I dream of the wild new life I will have for my own. My courage has been here all along. I am transformed. Feel this peace even now.

Walk with me aimlessly down the cool streets and watch the fog cover everything. There is magic here. I will never be unsure of myself again. Knowing I came to the woods and waters wild just like the poem said. This world saw and didn't care. I wonder what the world will do when I go back to the woods and waters wild with no more tears.

090312 0551p

Kelly,

Hi! I'm going to bug you until I get a letter back. You better get busy writing. Laughs. You are so stuck with me. I miss you badly right now.

I know I haven't been good about keeping in touch. I have been dealing with my mother a lot and Charisma, with her illegal endeavors to get mom a trailer, ANOTHER trailer. She is a big smart aleck about it too. Like I never took care of her little ass ever. I have been working our whole lives to keep this "whatever it is" together.

I know times are hard. They are here, too. Don't give up, cousin. We will make it through this I swear it. I have some things I am working on, too. And I know you never have to be alone with your big family but I often had to be and I hope you are doing OK. I miss you a lot. I think of you and pray and if there is something I can do for you, ask and I will do all I can. I hope your beautiful kidos are doing well. Kisses from us-hugs to you from me. I have to go out and work. Its daunting to me after staying home with the kids for so long. I feel lost and out of my depth. I really need to talk to someone but I sensed you kind of pulling away, like you don't really want to listen. I won't burden you with more than you can handle. But I do need someone right now. I wish I had you here with me. It's scary for me to be alone so much. I don't know how to do this, Kelly. I have put in like a hundred applications today. No one is hiring and McDonald's called me to tell me that I couldn't work there because they had QUALIFIED applicants with four years business restaurant management experience and what did I think with my GED.

I am tired and worried. I don't know how to fix this fast.

I love you even though you don't know how much.

Always—

T.

--There were like fifty pages of letters I started to her-but my cousin had told me how I wasn't there when she needed me, so I never finished most of them, figuring she would not want to know about me and my dumb adventure.

090912

I don't know why you bring out the crazy fifteen-year-old in me. I know what you are doing so why do I keep seeing you on the edge of my dreams? I don't think twice about romance. My life is not your woman's life. I don't wonder about that life at all. I think I am well suited for this life I made. I do love my life. I do love this craziness. It doesn't make me want to see the lightning in your gaze any less. Or make me unable to feel the wild thunder under my feet. The earth moves again and I don't care anymore. I know my fucking path.

I can be anywhere, Cain, and be happy without you. I am not pining for your heart like I was as a child. I guess by learning to live without you, I-CHUCKLES-learned to live without you. It's weird. But true. I can even admit I feel the love. Not for this new weird somehow sinister man you have become but for the once you. All geared up to do the big living and to be fierce...not meek like you think I believe or vengeful as you really are.

092012

Today I wonder if I have done something. Hold onto these days because of that one moment of joy I felt yesterday! I can find other minutes of happiness here.

Every time I went out into the rain and just walked for hours at night or even in the daytime if there was a free minute... (rare. Ha-ha.) I felt so bright and free. The rain did things for me that I could never explain. I don't understand it myself. I am excited I dreamed about someone I will meet. I don't really think I needed to know about him. Just that I would be okay after all this transmuted.

I have so much other stuff to do and it feels like I'm never done. I know these things I am doing are only on the to do list for a little while. It still sucks that there are no moments that feel like a break. There is always homework and art, and cooking and cleaning. I had to go to Safeway, a nice two-mile walk in the rain and with heavy groceries...with Rainen who probably shouldn't be walking quite so far. The good doc says yeah, he should, lazy Rainen. All that, so he could go make cow eyes at the pharmacy girl. Rolls my own gorgeous pale green eyes...

He didn't have a prescription ready, believe me I keep careful track. But suddenly, she has a script for him to get. So, I left him to gaze adoringly at her. Wouldn't want to stay in the way. I'm just the fat nurse. See, there is a reason yet that I don't dare to let you read these. What a yutz I appear to be.

He thinks I am "pulling away" and so he is sure to be with me anytime I leave the house. I might go nail some random homeless man on the corner, right? I AM lonely... cracks up and has to stop and wipe some funny tears. Yikes. Well he DOES smell like two-day old butt; however, he is starting to appeal to me with the kindness in his eyes.... And the nice smile he gives every time I walk by. Sh! Don't tell, I gave him a few bucks the other day. Rainen is a bit touchy about the homeless.

I do other things besides mother my kids and take care of asshole men who should have a real nurse so he can let me live my life too. The DHS people said I was eligible for a nurse but Rainen told them—get this— "No, thank you. I have Tabitha and she does everything." Wipes another tear away because it is SO funny and yet so sad. I do love Rainen or I would have smacked him. I am still contemplating it.

I can have sex with him. It is so nice to feel cared about. When I do, the world calms and he turns back into the Rainen I know... At least in that space and time we get along. I feel pretty wiped out, though. I wish I could get back to my same old self, all libido and major creative processes... I will. I will.

My poor darling girls, Ionthe and Iome, who know this doesn't seem like me... they come sit on my lap and hug me for so long and so tight I think I will break...they are my light. I am so glad I am showing them the value of promises. Even when they don't know I made the damn thing. Just because it is hard doesn't mean I can just break my word. I probably couldn't have kept my word this long for just anyone... Oh. Rainen the Kelsey. He is killing me. I love that fucker.

I wish I could just move out of here with my babies. Life

doesn't work like that though, does it. Laughs at myself. It always seemed like I could say anything to you and you would listen without judging me. I know that is patently untrue, now more than ever. But the letters do seem cathartic and I am not giving them to your judgy married ass anyway so what do I care what I say? And you for fucking sure don't, so I feel like it's all working out. I get a pretend friend and you get to ignore me forever. Ha-ha. It's all coming together....

And you have to laugh with me here, right?

You know, Rainen is sure I will marry him when this is over and act like nothing ever happened. I wonder what will happen when he finally figures out I meant every fucking word I said. I never gave a fuck for a ring. I gave a fuck for a life with him.

When you do read these—which you won't—due to the extreme embarrassment (and then the fire—don't forget the fire...), you will at least get a little laugh, I hope. It really is one of the finer studies in good irony. If irony were berries, we would all be having a lot of tarts right now. I make great tarts. Only takes two cups of irony berries. Laughs...

He is trying to tell me to quit smoking pot. Which is another thing he swore he would never do. I mean, let's break every single tiny promise, right. Ha-ha. I am not going to quit, and he can kiss my ass. But he wants to keep smoking. Laughing softly. I am sort of impressed with his lack of good sense. It might be the only reason I haven't choked his ass yet!! He should be examining that closely, and cutting WAY back so I have some more of the "don't choke Rainen" meds...

I have homework. I don't feel very peaceful but after homework I will go walk in the rain again and I will feel so much better. I miss you, asshole. Maybe. I don't know. Maybe I don't know what I feel when I think of you.

092312

"Whatever" is all you can say? Then that's exactly what you'll get. I can give you AT LEAST that. Take your anger, your screaming, and what's left? I don't know what else is there. I haven't seen anything else in a very long time. It's not true-- the you I saw during all those years of joy? Surely you couldn't fake it all??

The morning sunshine doesn't sting as much without your yelling. Life is sometimes a struggle but each day isn't supposed to hurt. You have taken my peace way too many times. I feel hope again. I took that back. My life is mine and don't you dare forget that, Rainen Kelsey.

092312

I wonder why my deities conspired so quietly to put a path before my feet. I am magnetized to this path now. I couldn't stay away if I tried. I felt like I chose it.

But something seems to quietly, proudly own us all. We go through life illogical, but soaking in our own favorite beauty as often as we can. We go through life loving fiercely our favorite truths. Even if they aren't truth.

092312

I had to search myself. I finally found a tiny piece of myself! It had waited untouched and patient all my life. I knew that bad people existed. I just watched them and tried to remain separate as much as I could. I never thought I had peace. I have been generating peace to the restless everywhere I went. I couldn't understand. I had the calm. I did it.

Evolution stretches us beyond our comfort.
3Days Grace-Burn

092312

This has been the bloodiest resurrection of the year.

The imagined pool I sink into at the end of the long ass night isn't healing like it used to. I don't run there to heal anymore. I used to hope someday I would meet someone who could just by their presence be able to thwart the nightmares. The dreams of which I am a reluctant part, no matter what. Unrealistic, but hoped for nonetheless. I am a dreamer. Can't change that.

The certainty I am alone hasn't bothered me since I was four. The tower I dream of served a real purpose while I was too small or defenseless to keep anyone away who didn't want the best for me.

It feels the same somehow... I sit in exile that I created to grant him peace. I love him so much I don't even want him to feel alone for one minute. While I wait I keep watch for omens and signs. Not like my mother. Like me. The simple signs of life that make you more magical by having witnessed them and the ease you feel while watching nature and its infinite cycles. These are real things and my dreams, though they make me feel at odds with the waking world, do not take me away from reality but make me appreciate it fully. Even when it isn't as I would like. I am one of the all-time champs at taking life for what it is, instead of what people say it is, or even what I would like it to be.

To me, it doesn't matter if you can see the metaphorical blood that covers me. If you helped put it there, you should be scared. Intentionally or not, you will for sure be made to pay. I love karma. I learned all my lessons, allowing myself to find my path to peace. You, oh, you. I don't know what happens to you. I hope your god loves you as much as mine love me. BTW-I have a personal savior. So, keep yours k. I once met Jesus in the Christians I have known- they DAMN SURE WILL let a baby go hungry or sleep in a car for weeks or do without clean clothes because their mom is a jackass. I didn't like the hypocrisy and I still don't like it. Love whatever god you like but do NOT think to wave your sword that says Jesus in MY face, for fuck's sake.

Written for jackass cyber bullies. laughs

092412

I feel like I have already died. I only wait for the day I wake and have been changed and then change my own world to be better. I want to keep believing and so I will. I forget myself in the little moments when I wake full of purpose.

092712

Too much to know and still do what I must. Too much to dare and still be proud of who I am. Too much to will my own happiness for once. Too much for me to keep being silent and not drift away.

--I felt like I was only half here in these days. I was so sleep deprived and worked too much. I walked all the time and I pushed myself to lengths I had no idea I could move beyond. I didn't sleep for days at a time during this. I was so entirely sad and deeply cut by people and their horrible ways. I didn't know people could be so mean. But there they were showing me every day I was crazy not to see them for what kind of beasts they really were.

092912

My most illicit words-truth-are written in the early hours. I allow myself to think of you only once in a great while. I know who you are and what you want. Silly of you to think I don't know you.

I begin the day lonely with my pen and paper and wonder about you. I found I don't need you to keep my hope. I can go on being bullied until you grow weak and bored. No big deal at all. You keep being the hateful spiteful child while I walk through this difficult time of mine. I didn't hunt YOU down. Remember that.

--I was pretty sure Cain helped the bullying, but no way to tell. Right. He played the entire time so what do I care. It seems sad and late to show up and act nice now.

100112 0934a

Cain,

My full moons aren't what they used to be...tonight I got a very nice and unusual evening with Rainen. Afterwards I didn't want to disrupt the beauty of the quiet. I really wanted to get back up and bug you. Instead I just thought about you. Figure it saves on the wear and tear my heart will get later from this. My texts were weird and its OK. Brooke was here and had some good smoke. She distracted Rainen with it. I figure she thinks I am horrible to him for no reason. See he is super sweet in front of other people. And she's a lovely young lady so it's easy to be sweet to her. I don't care who likes the way I am, anymore. Live it and then judge me, darlin.

Anyway. I was trying to get her help on clothes. Shakes head. No worries, right. I am not going to dress up to see you, anyway. I can't really get to the point where your opinion of my appearance is important. I know what I look like. I own several mirrors and consider them at least once a day ON PURPOSE. (So, don't lie to me...)

It was an OK night but I missed your good mood and sweet thoughts. Hope you had a great rest of the full moon night.

100812

It used to seem amusing to rip at my wings. Some people are blissfully unaware of many things. I guess I give off conflicting vibrations. I was scared but I ran to the woods. My soul has given all I have. If it isn't enough then maybe you can go somewhere you will have it all. You can't make me want to live OR die. I let all this be for a reason, Rainen. I did all I could to make you see how you were breaking me. I got stepped on with eyes wide open. I don't believe in being a victim.

I hope you are always so innocent.

10??12

Alyc--
My daughter who is sometimes my huge help and some-times my scariest weakness,

I know you are slacking off right now and think life will make up for it with easy answer at the last minute. It is sort of like you aren't paying attention to what's happening. I am very sad to learn of some of the things you are doing. You would be surprised about what I have learned of your rotten behavior and how fast some people will rat your little ass out.

I could have been the mother you wanted instead of needed and maybe you wouldn't have to start acting like you are bet-ter than me. Your father may be so very wonderful to you in your mind, honey, but remember who he is. He would rather focus on the new parts of his life and forget we ever happened, baby. I say we let him.

I don't want you to hate him. He's a human and we all fuck up. He fucked up big, though. I waited for him to at least be a human or act like one and he doesn't want that. I can't make the illusion any sharper for you little girl. I love you and I hope you are happy in your life. I can't make you do anything and I am tired of trying to get you to open your eyes. I am working myself into the ground. I am working harder than all the rest of you put together. And I am trying to save YOU all the work I think you shouldn't have to be responsible for. Do you think you can run right back into mom's good graces in one second? You are almost being like my other family, Alyc. I can only help you make this family run while I am here. If you guys run me to death, what am I going to be able to do for you, then?

I am not giving you this letter even though it broke my heart to write it. I am just going to save it and one day you will understand the promise I made to care for Rainen. He is more your dad than Carl ever was. And damn sure more than any other. If you can't be in love with the idea of your own mother's happiness, then maybe you need to reevaluate your life and your own karma, cuz honey. You are about to go to a hard fucking path and I wish I could fix it for you but I can't. It is not your judgment that makes me need or not need Rainen in my life. You don't know what kind of damage your dad did to my heart that Rainen came in and healed like cool water. It made your life in the beginning, at least, what I wanted for you and your sisters.

So, go do your thing. Be all the you that you can. I wish you well and I pray you make it through the hard times coming. You are always my very own baby girl and I am the only mother you will get. If you think I am poison to you, then go and find some better family. I had to, so I know it can be done. I just never knew you hated me so fucking bad. I didn't try to make your life rough, child. And I never would. I urge you to caution with this new freedom you seek.

And you can't come back to me with this same attitude. I know you have a lot of secrets and you think you keep them well. I know most of them, hon. And they aren't anything to get all hyper about. If these people cared, wouldn't they have cared BEFORE we left? Wouldn't they quit lying and make a fierce effort?

Sighs. I love you more than my own life and happiness. I gave up the only person in life I thought might really love me, so I could bring you a piece of that family I never had. I hope you someday appreciate it when you learn I did nothing for you to hate and everything for you to love. You are a princess. But you could have helped me instead of trying to hurt me every day. I am hurt enough, darlin'. I love you more than anything and I hope you someday see it.

Always your Mamma

100812 1243a

I may not want to walk in silence. I feel the wild song inside me pulling free. I won't walk on glass forever. This simple curse from my own dear blood can easily be removed. I called on universes in the early hours and I wept for one real soul to stand beside me. One simple soul feeling their own alone.

My young girls watch and travel with me. I must be always mindful what I teach them. I can't be any more than I am, can I? They can never see me be less... I must be more.

The rain still falls and the leaves still fall...

--I still wouldn't sing. I decided not to until I was done with the promise and away from Rainen. He hates my voice so much and here he is asking me to sing to him. Fuck you. Sing to yourself. My voice is best kept for only precious people.

100812

I had my eyes closed for a long time. You seemed to have malice in mind. Some days I was so sure. And other times, I didn't know. Don't bother yourself with worry. I will be fine with or without you. I always am. You are vain and think I want more than I should. I didn't seek you out. Your friendship isn't something you will give me-- no matter what I say or do. I was silly to think the best of this man. Some will turn dirty as fast as they can. I may not be a lovely lady but I still know who you are and I know what you find when you look at me. (If only you could see inside.) I have known all the little lies all my life. I catch lies with sad accuracy.

Laughs at this because it's still exactly true for Cain. Some things never change. There you go.

100812

Show me what's in your hand. It can't be anything real. Even though I am disappointed, I still carry on. You have some deep hate.

I died in the dream, sure. No more homemade disrespect. I get up and see the both of you saddened at my death. Is it that my moving on turned you both into animals? I hope you have all your perfection in mind when your last breath comes.

I didn't-couldn't-write either of you off. I held a best friend and a boy close, inside. It didn't matter that they neither knew how to keep me close. (So easy...)

Where did everyone go?

--Indeed, where did I go. Ha-ha. I had a dream long ago when I first associated with Cain and my then friend, Ann. They both got to see me in the casket and there were a few details I will leave out for my own privacy and comfort but I did see it come to pass and then it even made sense!

Knockin' On Heaven's Door--Clapton

100812

Who is that girl? She seems to be dark. I don't see any signs of life. She seems to be surrounded by death. I don't think anyone knows her. She hasn't even been thinking of herself. Maybe she already faded away and the simple fact is that no one has found the body.

You should have seen there was nothing else you could do to her. She wanders. I don't think she's lost. She had to arise and use all her courage.

Make no mistake. It was an act of high bravery.

--I had no one to pat me on the back and tell me good job. I did it for myself. I just found all the positive things I did in the day and praised myself for being so damn brave and fighting the way I did. I worked so hard. I knew I could do it, but

I found I couldn't keep everything going at once. I asked for help after it was offered and watched the way they acted. I determined it was just plain old politeness that prompted the offers and I should not worry about it. I just juggled as much as I could. I didn't expect someone to take care of me. I just waited on those who promised to keep their word. I am amused by my own faith in humanity. It always makes me shake my head and smile when they fuck it up. Just human...I say, and forgive. But skip their calls and texts, sometimes, right?

100912

You hurt me and I left. (You felt betrayed?) I ran away. You keep hurting me. I leave again. Now I am tired of running to places I don't belong. This time I will not run. I will find a place I belong. A bright and lovely life that waits for me and my little women. I say goodbye and carry on.

Rainen.

100912

Do I fear this? I don't fear anything, anymore. Your lies were expected and right on time. I waited with gentle knowing for you to see. I was so pleased to see your beautiful face and hear your beautiful voice. When I hear him talk shit about you, I listen only with half an ear. Doesn't matter what he thinks, anyway. He doesn't know your ice blue eyes in the late nights and he doesn't know your beautiful, impossible promises that meant the entire world when we were young. You didn't need a come-on line. And I knew I wasn't beautiful! I didn't care. I only needed a real friend and a real person to be on the other end of my text. We don't really have to talk. I don't need to hear about your extra stuff. I just need to be connected to a real-life person who cares.

I am quiet now and reflective. I wait for the day you don't need me, anymore. I know it's coming soon. Who will I be when it happens? Will I be ready to never see you again and to go all the way away from you? These are cloudy days. You don't wait for me and I don't think I want to wait for a man that will never be mine. Is this free?

I ask and answer myself. Yes. I know some intrinsic truths about myself that I didn't know then. One is that other people's approval made me do dumb things. I fought- always thinking I had to fight. I knew I didn't want anyone I can't TELL with. I am finished trying to see the pov of the other person. I know what it is. Doesn't make it matter to me.

Nothing Else Matters-Metallica

101012

Do you get sentimental in the earliest hours of the day? Do you fall apart even when they say you have no time for that? Listen to me. You can do whatever you want to. Life is open and alive and a process. No one is perfect. Yet each of us is. Our energy and lives reaching for each other constantly and unapologetic. Three thirty-eight may have some special meaning for someone else too.

I am joyful for the autumn rain. It falls and bathes some of the old scars in silver drops of magic.

Are you sure it's THIS soul you want?

Theoretical shadow. Presence. Thing. Whatever.

101012

There was something about that time of year. The autumn came with a quiet chill that barely frosted the ground. We walked hand in hand breathing clouds of air in front of us. My fourteen-year-old self could smell the rain that would come later that night. I became sad as I walked. I recorded sounds and colors and the expressions on your face that I just knew I would look back at later in life. It's as though I knew then how much I would despair in the future while I was on my path. I secretly wished to store the beautiful memories... some of the first nice memories I got in my short life. I pull out the memory in October. You might never think of it on that day (the 22nd) and I don't expect you would, but I need those to get me through this. I need every good memory I ever had... I could never forget them. You could never be forgotten, despite the bad feelings you still have.

Cain.

101012

I walk alone while you pretend you do. There are a million miles between the two of us. Here I am complacent for now in my unhappiness. While I keep a real promise and not to just anyone. To the love of my life. To the only man I wanted to be with forever. I will cry a few more times and then realize its futile. I always know how you leave me behind. I know it will happen again. And this time I won't think twice about it. I guess I am a little bulletproof... stupid superpowers.

Cain.

101012 0104a

I bet you don't know that I still hand write long ass letters when I don't talk to you for a long time. Nice of you to say you were proud of me. I have really come through hell here and I think I deserve the praise. Even if you might not believe it yourself. Mostly I work hard all the time to make everything flow smoothly and I get quite a lot of noise about how I am not doing enough. I stay up till four in the morning trying to get it all done. My kids do their best to give me the free time I need but they are just kids. I try to not put too much work on them. I do love them with all I am.

I hope your issue, whatever it might be, is dealt with quickly and you get back on track. You sounded stressed out. I flipped a tarot card for you. OK three. It's tough to get much from one. Don't think I can't multitask and talk to you when I am doing something else. I will always be here if you need someone to listen. I don't judge. It doesn't help. Ha-ha. I was going to the post office on my middle of the night walk. I had to mail Ann's stupid letter. Why I still try so fucking hard to be friends with people who show me every day I am not worth it to them, I will never know. Yeah, I do. I would hate for anyone to feel like I feel most of the time and not have an ear when they need one. I spoke with my mother's new man. In jail. Ha-ha. It is ironic that after all these years, she finally goes for a simple guy with no alcoholism or coke habit. Just a pothead. Ha-ha. That's irony-rific.

Mom wanted to send Jerry's uncle Hank to get me. Laughs. Funny. She doesn't give a shit. She thinks I have money. That's funny to me. If I did, would I make it available to her? Probably, but not with the knowledge it was from me. She hates me and yet she loves me fiercely when she thinks I have money. Meh. Whatya gonna do. Some people. In any event. I told her to skip the cavalry. I didn't need them in NM obviously—I learned this by the way they wouldn't talk to me or be near me...--so why do I need them now. Oh, yeah... I don't.

Oregon state motto: She Flies With Her Own Wings. So badass.

I read cards with the Brian Froud Faeries Oracle. Your cards are:

- Nelys-27
- Sage-19
- Singer of the chalice-12

Card one is a card of inner transformation. The stuck becomes unstuck. You may find an opinion of yours changed and it will never go back. Card two is one that speaks to wisdom. Hidden knowledge and patience. Organize and simplify. Tradition is valued but change is needed. Judgment applied with wisdom and mercy. Card three is revealing a sense of trust and joy. Patience again. Creativity and miracles require an openness to them. Look them up if you want. The deck is easy to purchase about anywhere online. The ISIS book site is a good one. But I doubt you want to go to that much trouble. Lol.

I have to go load a bowl. Jeez. I am relieved that my procrastination and tiredness didn't make me stop the college thing. It was tough to get it all squared but now I am back and running well. I was twisted up into knots over the mess. My neck has been so tight I can barely turn the goddamn thing. I have no time for doctors either. They will just give me some idiot pill that will zonk me out for days and make me late to class. I will have to keep on doing what I am doing and just fuck it.

(—052317 0932a I drew all the strange flowers I see every day all over these letters. I hope the book people let me keep my illustrations and song lyrics. They make this book real to me.)

I was going to tell you about the little esoteric experience I had while I was in NM before I decided to come to Oregon. I don't know about that now. Maybe some other time.

Something good.... something new and really nice...taps fingers on table.

What else is interesting? I have over-gardened my house. Ha-ha. It's beautiful, now. My kids say I am hoarding plants. Ha-ha. Makes me crack up. I have some hoarders in my family and it made me laugh to think about how full of plants my house would have to be to get an intervention. Laughs my ass off.

I don't think me talking about college should make you not want to talk to me. If you really want something, you just have to do it. Even when the circumstance doesn't provide for it. You have to fight. And I know you don't need the college, but if you are mad at me for going, maybe it's because you still want to go. You are quite brilliant and I don't see why you couldn't. There are fifty million ways to get something you want and if you are working hard, you just work a little harder. Ask me how I know this. Sarcasta-face. I think if you wanted to, you would.

So that was a long letter and I know you won't read it. But please be well. I do care a lot and miss you and hope you are as badass as usual.

I am not bitter, a little sad maybe... after all these years I am still here for you. You could just talk to me. I want to go tap you on the shoulder and say wake up.

What can I do to convince you? Probably nothing.

Bye and be good.

101112

I don't hold this day close anymore. I remember it, though. In its entire shittyness. Emotions left unchecked, and unspoken. They make me fall apart. I start again. I start to breathe and try to forgive again. He does too. He begins to move on to another girl. I hope your new sun will forever stay bright. I hope she never flickers-- even one time. Or you will stop your worship and leave her alone too. I am at home in the cold rain.

Rainen. For him and the new girl.

101312

Finally. He said it. His lies and his real self struggled free. Finally. When he comes to me contrite and ready to be mine again, I can say goodbye. I dreamed his new woman. I saw them. They were getting married. Thank gods, it wasn't this bitch.

Rainen.

101312

Here I am, the girl of his dreams. Don't you dare worry about me, now. I was present in the desert all those desolate years. Now I am lonely in a new place. He is so happy to give me another option—try to be close to Mr. Far-far-away. What a sad day. Always wonder when the ball drops. It drops further each time. He hopes to break me but I am not as breakable as some think. But if he has breath, he will try. I was robbing me of my magic as much as he was. If there was no love, then there can be no tears for him, then. My smile lasts.

Cain.

101312

Is this the new betrayal? Funny. Are your lies let out? My fragile heart is something you don't know about. I asked the right question. And your words stayed with me reminding me of the real reason you were here. I saw the lie. I knew. I let you have your three strikes because I am a fair person. The cold blooded me you heard about is another lie you would rather believe than ask about. I wait for you to get finally bored enough to leave me alone.

Cain.

101312

There is wild in the rainy air. It brings a spark to me that I didn't have before. If he loved me he could never hurt me. He's been in love with someone. Go be better than me. I don't mind. I have carried on.

Rainen.

101412

I fought for your love all those years. It seems second

nature for me to bow to your wishes. I can get the love you feel I don't deserve. I know someone will love me. I deserve arms around me that let me know. You could have been free all those years. I never would hold another man if I knew he wanted away. I am getting back to happy. You may have to see me be happy, too. Hey, it could happen.

Rainen.

101512

It took many miles to come to this path. It took so much of my precious time. I didn't write off the simple world. Though I was done wrong over and over. Can I still breathe even trapped here in this promise I must keep? Then I am not chained but free. Can I see myself as I am? Then I must still be me. You can think I am weak or dumb, you know little truth. My life may seem joyless to the king of the liars, but I am full of great stores of knowledge and power fuels me onward. You want to be great? Walk the millions of miles I do before you let your pettiness speak words you will regret forever. You don't know anything about me at all, do you?

--Cain really pissed me off when he apparently got ahold of my letters I wrote as a suicide therapy exercise for my psychologist. I have done the damn project several times and I hate it. I never finish and I only manage to get it so far before I tire of it. I spent a lifetime suicidal. No letter project is going to fix me, now. I deal. I cope. I do my thing. I make it. Can't ask for more. Anyway, he asks me repeatedly in my time since the Facebook message if I have "written off the world". I always laugh. Long ago, my fake friend. Long ago. And, never, no matter what.

101512

I wake and greet the rainy morning with all the smiles and joy I have within. The sun seems far away in the desert. I am glad to be where the rain grows something wild inside.

--This is my shout to the devil. I forced myself into feeling good feelings so when I was done with my promise I would be able to feel those emotions and know what they were. I don't like being thought of as a victim. I don't lay down and die for anyone.

101512 0813a

You laughed when you asked me if I was giving up. Is it funny to you that I am sad and alone? Cain, you are a douche. I will never change my plan for you. Even if I DO go back. You think it is joyful shit to hear about my pain? Shakes my head and remembers who you always were and who you will always be. No changes now.

101512 0941p

I am here in the now feeling all the different emotions. I know I am alive. That's good. He comes off the meds and looks to us to make the comedown easier. We are here for him totally. The girls all take turns tickling the back so the nerves have something else to think of. I make him a nice chicken wrap with his favorite Oregon berries and avocado. He is much more mellow today. We do love him and we try to show it. Sometimes it's difficult for us. We are all working hard here. I also tell him to get ready for physical therapy. That is the kicker. We have to do it. On the bad days, it's more impor- tant. To keep momentum. So, we take an hour long walk in the rain and though we are both tense, we calm with the walk and he starts to feel endorphins ten minutes in. He is glad he came. The rest of the day is a joy.

I don't even notice today—is it walking through the falls first leaves in the beginning of the new rain? I hope that some friendship will appear but then I notice I am hanging out with a pretty decent guy. I am a creator so I get up from the ground full of fight. I will never lay down and die. I am going to the trees and stand under the canopy while the rain falls silent and peaceful. I will stay in the rain if I can. I can't walk away from the magic inside me no matter what.

--Just written to try and stay positive. It makes a difference to be able to spend intimate time with him and remember who we both were.

101512

To feel the rainy grass under my bare feet under the moon. To hug four sweet girls to me in the mornings and smooch their little tousled heads. To wake knowing he is healthy and can do as he wishes now. To understand my friends and give each of them what they needed from me. If the world is to be written off, it won't be by me. These are the reasons I get up in the morning.

Opinions on me vary. I didn't ask, so I don't care. I do want to be able to see Rainen off to his happiest life. I don't know what his real feelings are. I guess I never really will. And I don't even want to anymore. He has his path and I can't walk it with him. The days are so random. I can't stay on this roller coaster. He loves me then he hates me. Yikes.

101712 1219p

Do you know the steps to this dance? Real at last! Soaked under that moon- soul singing as loud as I can; with no voice. I am all heat. I move and you don't know this woman. Finally, the moon illuminates me from the inside. The stars sparkle and I watch them swirl around me. Do you know me? Singing a siren's song, you haven't even heard. The enchantment is the desert heat and the coastal rains. Freedom, reality, and joy. You didn't even hold me for one moment.

--My reminder to myself that Cain would rather hurt me than be my friend and I should do well to remember who he is at the root of him. Yes. He helped. It cost though. Didn't it.

I suppose, most of the help I get is that way. Cost me heart, soul, mind, and body....

101712 1231p

The universe is ready. The truth is a gift I will tell with love. And create beauty. It is what comes next...

I decided long ago when I began to write that I would be the same me. Telling truth with tact and discipline. So, when I wanted to lie and say I was awesome, I could step back and say—no...I was just me. I succeeded and failed and did it all my way. As to anyone else, I tried to write them honestly and still let you know why I loved each person. I do remember being at Multinomah falls with Rainen on our ten-year anniversary and being so happy to be there with him and my girls. I remember him taking us hiking in the forests and to new parts of the city and showing us what he liked about the place. He did so much for us by taking us there. My girls learned and grew. They were always learning at his knee some new thing. He knew how to carve well and build things of total beauty. He knew about the places the beauty hides in plain sight. He knew things about me I never saw until he saw them. I wanted to always see myself in the light of his eyes. He had so much heart and soul to him. He loves music. He loves to show us new music so we can grow and share and change with him. He let me see some things I didn't know existed.

Including my own independence. Forced on me, but no less beautiful. And now I have to go do my thing while he goes on to love some other girl. As much as I want to say I am a good person, my heart is so tired of hearing things I can see with my own eyes as false. It is hard to forgive him. I am still working on that. I loved him so fully that I am working through this writing with my soul ripped wide open again. I can't even talk to people I know right because it is tearing me up. I have such a hard time trusting and especially someone who says they love me. I have heard some mean things from people who say they love me. Things designed to work like a razor.

I want to paint the full picture of my love for Rainen because in the beginning it was a great goodness. It made me feel and be real after the marriage ended.

I won't sit and be mad over the way my marriage to the ex ended. I wish him well. I do hope the new wife will bring him joy and they have love, everlasting. So please just be happy, Carl.

I even wish Cain well all the damn time. Laughs. I know he was out to have a last revenge on the stupid little girl I was... but I don't hate him. Opposite for sure. I want him to be well and have love and joy and peace. I believe that comes when I leave though. He won't decide he is sure of me until I go. But that's to be expected. And I don't know if it was love for him or love for Alyc that prompted me to go with Carl. I wanted her to be a happy girl. I knew a dad that loved me would have been what I wanted and might have made me slightly happier. But I wanted Cain to have his dreams and when I left, it looked to me like he got them. So, what else is there, except to wish him well and go on about my business. I didn't even seek him out. I knew better than to do that.

My...self didn't raise no fool...laughs heartily.

And Rainen. Oh, my gods. How to reconcile those emotions. I worked through so many and still I am every fucking day. I don't only think of the bad times. I am a sucker for the good times we had. I remember every day I woke in his arms. A special and separate joy each day. I remember feeling safe and loved. I remember the romance in his kisses. I don't need it if its false especially, but it didn't feel false. I felt it. So, I hope some other girl gets to feel like that with him. I do want him to be happy. I will not begrudge him the woman that CAN make his life what he wants it to be. No, Rainen, you don't get to change your mind, now. You committed to everything you said, every day you said it, and all the things you said you would NEVER take back. I don't need an apology. I never wanted one. I wanted a fucking thank you. Also, an acknowledgment of the great thing I did by keeping the promise when I suspected you were using the entire thing to have me there. I am a wonderful keeper of promises. I am joyful over that at least. I did love you every single second, Rainen Kelsey. I loved you with my whole soul and I loved you for exactly what you were. I never wanted money for itself. I didn't ask you for flashy shit. I drove our stupid van. I wore my clothes as inexpensively as I knew how. I just wanted your love. And it wasn't good enough that I gave all my years now you want me to give you some more and prove I am a damn idiot. Well I love you. I can only say that isn't going to happen.

I am so tired! I just need a break to move past this and be who I am. all of me. Not just the things you say I can do or with the people you say I can do it with. I am not a girl in a cage.

See. It was true. The submissive often controls more than he or she thinks. By him taking trust and abusing it, I learned I could take it back. And he can't ever have that control again. I am not the same girl.

I don't want to be either.

101712

Do you know the steps? I always have. I am real if nothing else. Running around soaked and barefoot under my moon singing. I never opened my mouth or made a noise for all my joy. Silent songs are sometimes the most deeply felt. You never even bothered to know this woman in front of you. I brought the moonlight in to help see myself better. The stars twinkle in my sky. You never even touched me, though you think you ruined it all. Be sure you don't miss the moonlight.

--Cain's. I didn't want him to think our relationship was ruined by him. I did my share and Rainen did his before old

Cain Benedict ever got there.

101712

I went back to that same old dream with the tower. Only this time I saw a huge wasteland, very desert-like and intense with heat. I can also feel the wings I never felt before. I can only see blurry dark shapes in the dream. I wonder if others in my dreams can see the wings or if it is just me.

The wasteland area in this dream is crisp and ready to catch fire. It takes hours walking in the vicious heat to see waving grass far off in the distance. I can see the grass parts into a path showing me the way. Since it looks like the only way, I walk it.

Wild things obviously live here. Silence seems to be the only noise I hear. I walk extra slow and careful so I don't make a sound. Though, I think I am the wildest creature here. I reach a stand of trees behind the grasslands. I can tell that the forest is cooler and the heat starts to fade. The forest seems wrapped in a fall change of colors. I have walked for hours again by myself and now I can see the sun falling behind the trees at last. The moon rise is the only light. I feel an urge to keep going, like the night won't be long enough to accomplish whatever goal I have. Finally, I can see nothing but a huge barrier that seems never ending both in height and width.

I can hear crying, but I can't seem to process how to get to it. I wake with a feeling of dissatisfaction.

101812 0133a

The stolen child was too wild by the time they noticed she was gone. Others looked on and wished bad things would make her less special, less intimidating to their sense of simple self. Honored dead look on and wonder how long she can last before she is ruined. Where does it leave a child that never could love to fight? She knows things they will never learn and she wants to share with a world of greed. Faerie rings every-where but magic seems lost.

--I wanted to convey my feeling of alone and felt rather persecuted by bullies. It was wearing on me at this point.

101812 0115a

I wonder why the people I knew are so angry. What did I do to them except leave them when they wanted me to go? I had to raise myself and even I know that is wrong. Behind my eyes are depths no one can seem to brave. What do I do when the masses start stupid wars they can't win? I will just live and watch them fade away just like before. I look out of my green honest windows at what I am given. This is a path like no one else's. No wonder they are acting stupid. I wouldn't know what to make of me either.

I will find someone brave enough to love me. It may take a minute, but I will. I know I will.

101912

As I drift into that same familiar dream, I watch a person falling from above and it scares me. He is plummeting down onto the cold wet grass around the wall. I feel like a pale-skinned, rain-soaked gargoyle, heavy, like stone weights me. I can almost see in my mind the wings I would have to have since I am hovering above. When he lands, it makes a very loud noise. I am almost certain he didn't make it.

The windows in the tower are black. This dream will be dark. Its OK. I am used to this same old dream. The man doesn't seem to be anything special from what I can see of him as he stands and dusts himself off. (Tall...) He is walking around the wall looking for a way inside... He could see some-thing shine from the sky, as he fell. He is figuring out, he only sees what I want him to. The back of the wall is so tall, no one could see over it. It seems to go on and on to the sky. He isn't looking for anything but the shine he saw from the sky while he fell. I am surprised he is alive after the wicked fall. I am intrigued by this weird person who has shown up in this dream. It is usually dark and lonesome. I feel resentful and curious at the same time.

There are weeds around the outside of the wall. It is a terrifying place outside, wild and odd. I know what is in the tower so it doesn't scare me. The man is looking around in some serious confusion like he knows I am there and he senses I am not going to help his ass. He fishes around sort of half blind in the weeds looking for whatever the object is that was so bright from above before he started falling. He keeps looking up like he knows I am there. He seems to think whatever he is looking for will gain him entrance to the tower. What does he think he will find there? A princess? I am so amused by this idea, that even in my sleep, I laugh. All he hears is a huge scraping metal noise from my strange throat. He is scared by it, and this amuses the me-creature even further.

While I watch him silent and invisible from above, He finds the silver object. It is a silver handle to an old-fashioned and worn-out looking screen door. He seems surprised and delighted, at the same time he is sure he is going to get carried off by the me-creature. He keeps looking up and although he can't see me, he is very scared of that metallic laugh he heard earlier.

I continue to watch; I'm sure he will grow tired and go away at some point. He seems very interested though, and now I begin to get serious.

The wall is not open, anywhere. There are holes and bricks missing but there is no real way inside. The screen door, which a moment ago, seemed a real find, is now a source of scowling consideration by the new person. He sees it isn't any entrance, but a way to the vault door. The vault door is as impenetrable as the sky-high walls. It seems to shine ridiculously in the environment. He isn't daunted, just wary. Something good must be in the tower, if he is meeting this much resistance. (I keep asking—what does he think is in there? A princess?) In the dream, I fly up to the top of the wall where I observe him trying to open the vault. He uses his strength to try and pull open the fifty-foot-high door. Unless I open it, I know he wastes his time. I still don't see anything that makes me believe he is worth letting in. I can't see much with the creature's eyes. Just his form. I can smell his bad cologne, though.

The ground is very inviting and I can see the things he can't with his normal vision. There are bleached bones littering the ground. I can't see many of them, but enough to know there were others who came.

I am still watching him. He sits on the ground and uses an old bone to draw something in the dirt. I decide to leave the man alone and go back to the top of the wall. That is where the dream finally ends. I hate stupid metaphors and symbolism. Really ruins the badass dream.

102112 0112a

I almost texted six or seven times but I don't really like to feel dumb, so I stop myself. I am dealing with you rather well, I think. If I thought you would ever read these, I would never have written them. But it is honest conversation, even if yours isn't. Rainen decided five days and fourteen hours ago that he didn't want to be with me. Not just that, though. He said after the very first doctor's appointment, the first year we were here, that he hasn't loved me in ten years. I guess that is why you were waiting around. You went out of your way to ruin my relationship. When you knew I loved him with all I had?

That's fine of course. I get it. And look at that—I guess I am better to have found it out now, rather than after I might have married him. I am not dumb. I won't ever be dumb enough to let you back in, though. Doesn't matter how long you play the game. I am so sick of your shit, Cain.

It's stupid that at my lowest, you would think you mattered to me so much. I never would have done one THING unless I knew he didn't love me. I still must keep the promise and no matter what, I will. I do love him. And you are a weird and emotionally stunted man to think I would want to try to make anything with you work. You hurt me too many times. You are married, dummy. Pay attention because sometime soon, karma will be looking at you. Bet me.

I am sorry I didn't live up to your expectations with regards to running and begging you to take care of me. I asked certain things after you promised them and watched and created a more complete picture of you. You are so full of shit, your crystal eyes are changing.

--I had an affair with this man in the summer of the year 2013. I didn't ever think I would get with him. He was married and spoke some real words of truth that night. I knew he was thinking he would hurt me and then see what I did. I weighed my decision. Rather than follow my own smart advice, I gave him the bat and let him go. Chuckles.

He thinks he is good. Was it a dog party? In all my fat glory? I guess maybe I sought any contact that night and that is why I don't feel like I should apologize. That would mean it was wrong of me to seek humanity and comfort after the words Rainen said sliced through me. I will not apologize. I will say I didn't want to ruin a marriage and I didn't. I didn't want to hurt Rainen. I did, though. He proceeded to play the "I can hit harder" game. I have learned a few things over the years, though. One of them is that I can take a lot. No. No victim lives behind these eyes. But a hurt girl and a girl who can also decide for herself what to do. Right or wrong.

It sure didn't give me any feeling of worth. I felt like I should go inside myself and repair my damage and work towards being well someday. I knew Cain would leave me to it when the stupidity was out. And he did. I wished that he would have shown one minute of real compassion. But it is sometimes too much to ask. I won't ask anymore.

102112

I think about two fish fighting each other always. It is futile for a crab who will retreat rather than play. Lucky me to read in his eyes what he couldn't tell me no matter what: the truth.

Cain. He notoriously lied. I expected no less.

102112 0150a

Hello. Nice of you to text me randomly at two am. I am not really flattered. Next time, DON'T.

Cain.

102112 0212a

He says I am nobody. I am someone, though. He thinks he can put me in pain. He can't. The one who can, did. He thinks he can make me do something I don't want to. I am free. I can walk away. The rain can't wash him clean of this sin. If hate could bring you back, how powerful must your feelings be, Cain? My soul is still beautiful. Leave me alone, blue-eyed revenge.

102112 0223a

A blessing for those who weren't raised better than to fuck with a good person...

I hope your life is rich and full—inward and outward.

I hope you and yours want for nothing.

I hope your children are blessed.

I hope love stays by your side always.

I hope your work is rewarding.

I hope your life is fulfilled.

I hope you get your fondest wishes.

I hope love never forsakes you.

My blessings for those who forgot me every day until they needed me.

I loved you and wanted nothing but the best for you all.

Even if I don't make it, I never wanted you to hurt.

102212 0233p

Is there a new life I can create for myself? I am brave. I can step forward now. I just let those people and their tiny meaningless opinions drift away. Let it go, Tabitha. I don't think I ever expected to belong. I wield fire with abandon and laugh because you are all scared of the flames.

I can say the words and not hurt anymore.

I am alone.

102112 0235a

"Dance within, without, but only with me," whispered a dream I could not see. The loneliness became too much. When this man told me he loved me, it sounded true because I wanted it to be. I never found the dream even though I searched. I found comfort in the rain like I always did in those days. I used to believe those words. It seems like there should be something real somewhere. I will find it.

Rainen's.

102112

It is very easy to forget about any princess who doesn't acknowledge her meaningless crown. She had no kingdom and no prince. Time forgot her easily. She wrapped herself carefully in layers of silken protection and waited for the day to emerge.

Magic is what it is, as well.

102212 0420p(ha-ha)

I feel like I gave up long ago so I don't have to feel disappointed anymore. You came to see what you sensed. That I was in pain. It can't be that entertaining to watch me be in pain. Too much bullshit from all of you—"friends". I retreat far away and I feel like that is the best choice for me. Make another attempt at life. Make another attempt and another and another until it works. No one comes for me. I feel like I didn't expect them to, so I am the same as when I began. No worse off...

Why worry?

102212 1131p

Sometimes this place is paradise. There are still days I need to be in the desert. You bring me to a long-ago dream. Change it around to a specialized hell. Sometimes faith can be a fucked-up vice. I came here not knowing how alone I would feel. (Hold on no matter what. Don't scream.) So love is a vice too. Too much life to get rid of it now. No matter how good it might feel. To fall in the water or to jump in the fire. I saw it all. You thought I didn't. I may have to steal my peace. Doesn't mean it's right.

102212

Finally, it's raining. Cain. You should tell me what the hell your damn game is. You DO want me to text. Laughs. What the hell is with you? You already think I am out to get you. Even though I kept all my stupid info away from you so you didn't have to read it or be confronted by the stupid shit I get up to. I am always here for you but I don't have to wreck myself to get love you know. Are you narcissistic? I don't have any minutes and I won't waste money on that for a while... Sorry, I'm not ever going to be sorry.

102212

The sun rises behind those dark clouds outside. The leaves are the brightest of all the falls colors. One night of sexty weirdness. (or whatever Texas wants to call it.) I know who I am. The day may be new, but since he acts the same as the asshole I am already with, what's the difference? I wonder why I wanted to believe in him?

Anything saying Texas on it is Cain's.

102712

I used to look at Oregon as a bit of a paradise. I sometimes wished myself back in the desert I called home. I went to Oregon not knowing. I held on no matter what and I loved you as I wanted to be loved. I've lived so long and there is only so long to go. Nothing can be as beautiful as peace.

102712 0649a

Here's yet another letter from the edge of the world,

Since I won't be giving any of these stupid letters to you, it doesn't matter what I say. I become-sadly-able to write both fluidly and often. Ha-ha. That's funny. You seem to think I still lied about Alyc. Serious sigh. I didn't. it's not something I would lie about. I am glad you have some things in common with her, but I don't lie about parentage. My shining example mom lied about my dad all my life. He lied and she lied. I would swear on a stack of bibles if it meant anything. I just don't want to hurt my girls at all. I determined long ago that my girls would never find a reason to ask.

So why would you try to get me to a far-away place? I don't enjoy traveling. I also have no urge whatsoever to visit Vegas. That was mom remember? I am a totally different person. Woods and waters wild, Cain. Pay attention.

I think you decided long ago to be an ass and that's why

you were sure to let me know how you are. All good I suppose.

As I made my way outside to take a walk last night, you quit talking. Talking to you is obviously not a good idea. I like more general conversation. I don't really get impressed with all your vacations. As interesting as all your stories are, I believe I will stay where I am. I will take my vacations later and I think I can wait and go places I love. I don't need to worry about going to Vegas or any other damn fool place.

Would be nice to be able to talk to you like you are a person that gives a fuck but I understand. Your behavior when I try to talk to you about important shit going on, lets me know that I shouldn't. I won't. I mean, you say you want to be my friend, It is obvious you aren't looking for that either. Which suddenly makes me sure I shouldn't talk to you at all.

It's OK What I must say sounds dumb on paper anyway. I don't think I will worry about it. You CAN be a real asshole.

I made a real promise and I wasn't trying to welsh on it. I understand Rainen's pain and all that. It doesn't excuse his raunchy behavior, if that matters. My word is good and soon he will see that. I know why he came here and I know why he will leave. I also know I don't want to go back to NM. I can't predict what happens next but I had a dream in which I was moved back to NM and Rainen wasn't there. I know what it meant. One day I may explain it, if I can stand to.

I did try so very hard to make him see who I was. I guess he won't see it until he sees me all finished with the weight loss and the self-improvements. Great. Another shallow Hal. Just what I need. If someone offers you a shadow of your dream, sometimes you just take it and run. I knew he wasn't mine. You can't own people anyway. I just wanted to claim some real emotion and to feel what having a family would be like.

I don't even like to think these things, let alone say them out loud. He is going his own way. I think now that he has a pain-free existence, he is worried his life isn't all it could be.

It's raining heavily out there right now. Cold as hell, too.

Nice. The walk I took last night was full of leaves all bright and thick throughout the town. There is this one street that has many Japanese maples and the whole street is flooded with the tiny dark red leaves. It's so pretty! I wish I could give you these letters I have written. I know I won't though. Stupid to attach sentiment to a name on the top of the paper when I know what you are. And its damn sure not "Dear Cain."

I feel sad this morning, even though I shouldn't. I wanted to talk to you or anyone really. You would like to think I broke up with him and all for you. I didn't and I never would do that. I dreamed the situation before it happened and then it did. I don't know if that's me making it happen. I fought for him. He didn't think I was worth it. I find those words coming from the mouths of the people I love way too much.

Laughs at how no one reads my stupid letters anymore.
T.

102712 0735a

I hold this relationship up to the moonlight and examine it for flaws. There! Look...I see that I wanted him too much. I wasn't the damsel he wanted to save. There! LOOK...he didn't think I was worthy of it.

I am pale in comparison. I was just a friend he thought was too insecure to leave.

The flaws are many. I don't think I can weld these cracks to hold again. Life can start for me at last. New and full of bright new ideas and people I don't know yet. I couldn't come out of the breaks any more whole than I am. Life is filthy and on fire. Like an old tire burning, I don't want to get too close. I don't want to talk to him in case I TALK to him. Silence is better than his anger.

Rainen's.

102912 1210a

Here I am again. Writing little stupid notes, you will never read. I hope your weekend is great. I always sound like an ass when I talk about myself. I don't know why. I don't like to for that reason. Oh well it's been going on for some time before you ever came along.

New subject: college. Midterms, for fucks sake. I am not nervous. I feel I will do well. Change subject!

My friend Brooke was so sweet—she got me all into jello shots. Chuckles...I know. Where was I, right? Having babies, I guess.

(No close on this letter. Probably I get bored or more likely sad, thinking of how no one will read them.)

103012 0558p

Who am I now? Not the same little girl I was, I have walked alone. Dreamscapes of black streets and frozen cities. I wished and cried and looked... I can't see how I have made it this far. Seems sad to trade beauty for truth. I can only be myself. Who else could I be?

110112

Today has magic. It leaves me signs. The poetry in me pours out. It calls me to the fog. November is my favorite here. There is a wild energy in me. Do you feel it? It's hard to contain. I have to hold myself back from running into the cool night—so much to do today. Even though nothing is ever written in stone, I will let it be what it is. Just for you. Sigh.

Cain.

110112

Today matters, I understood this long ago. I didn't want to

let go this piece of time where I felt truth. I knew within me somehow it wasn't true. it was a short time. I came out of the dream and into some new future I wasn't comfortable with. I can't let selfish desire for a feeling so brief and beautiful consume me. I am too often like this.

Rainen's.

110112

There isn't any gentle that can ease me, now, fellas. I am finished suffering. I am not the same girl and I am not waiting on these jokers to decide I am enough anymore. I don't know love, so when I find it at last, I will be surprised. The rain just keeps coming down. It sparkles silver, like my amusement at the funniest three boys in the world.

Carl's, Rainen's, and Cain's. That's funny. I hope it annoys them to all be lumped together. Chuckles...darkly.

110112 1146p

Another letter you won't be subjected to.

Aren't I thoughtful. I am going to the coast. One way or another and probably by myself but I AM going. I love the Oregon coast. What I really need is to see my stupid brother.

Psychological dilemma...

Why DO I keep writing the letters? I have established a way more solid friendship with the paper than with you. You might not care, but old Doc Schaefer would give me badass brownie points. He would be mad for an entirely different reason... "Give the letters to him. What's the worst that could happen?" I can hear him say it. Ha-ha. It's very hard for me to talk to anyone and you used to know me way back when I was more myself. The choices I made weren't always mine to make, but I tried to do the best thing based on what knowledge I had. Brave new world with such wonders... right. You can't go back, though, right? You don't want the letters until I burn them. Or publish them. Laughs at irony.

Firefly—Breaking Benjamin
Cain's.

110112 0132a

I miss some part of me. I am tired and wish for joy. Some feelings don't come with a goal. Some feelings don't come from anyone else. I close my eyes and blow the little spores off the wish maker... (Please Universe, hold my love for me. Give it to me in a brighter day, when I can love him with a whole heart.)

Somehow, I made it this far and I am okay. The world is tinted an ugly color right now, and sunrise seems far away. I just need to let it go.

110112

November is lovely here. Cold, foggy, and crisp. No one is out to enjoy this beauty, so I am invisible. It feels nice to not have to hide. Sometimes, even with my healthy body image, I feel like people are looking and making judgments. I don't care so much. We are all humans. We all have things we would improve if we could. At least I have lost one-seventy.

It feels better to leave my self-consciousness somewhere else while I am free and walk in this amazing weather. I am composing poetry in my head and looking at the natural signs all around me. My energy is high and I am carefully controlled. I hold so much inside. But I remember easily that nothing is written in stone. Just let it go and be you, Tabitha.

Blessed Hellride—Zakk Wilde...gorgeous, talented sonofabitch.

110112

I finally found all the lost pieces along with my strength. I have been starting to make myself feel the little joys again. My good feelings are returning. It wasn't from anything else—a person or a goal I met. I wished I were ready for the good things from the universe and I was. The new life is started even if no one else sees it. I moved when the universe said the time was right. I will get back OK. The world doesn't feel so lonely and this sunrise feels easier. I just want to go somewhere else and live without that sadness ever again.

110112

I built myself around other people's happiness for as long as I can remember. I imagined my walls down and here he came to see what was inside. He had no right to ask me the questions he did. He has no right to my body, my soul, or my thoughts. I gave him access to my friendship but he wants to own it all. Married as he is. And silly because he is happy in his vanilla life. I am no easy flavor—rocky road—all marshmallows and unexpected caramel among the chocolate smoothness and bright pecan crunch. Laughs to myself because I see the attraction. But I won't give everything to anyone like I did before. He should know he is not tricking anyone. I don't want to be second place and I won't be. I used to love you, Cain. USED to. You are amazing in your audacity. I might be busy keeping a well-meant promise to a long-ago love (Rainen), but it's OK if I wait patiently for a REAL love, instead of this— whatever you would call it.

110612 0652p

I am a coward from way back. Or was it that people did damage and I lost my courage from the pain I felt for so long. It wasn't my fault truly. But now if I let the courage go, it IS. Black white and grey are the only colors in which I can paint myself. I can take myself into the light but I am more comfortable in the night. I want to dance in the moonlight, again. I don't have to fail. I can do anything I want to, you know.

110812 0659a

The new day pulls me along with its newness and dark cloudy skies. The leaves are all brightly fall-flavored. One single night of unfriendly texting... him hurting me to make sure I felt the hate he had for me. And I did. I made a mistake. I thought he wasn't a horrible person. He showed me. I can't even be mad at him for being exactly what he was. It's too lovely a day to let his far away thoughts bother me.

I know who I am and what I want. From his own lips, he can't POSSIBLY provide what I need.

This new morning greets me and says, "Tabitha, I can give you rain. Isn't that what you wanted all along?"

Yes.

Cain's.

111012

I can't find gentle people. That worries my soul. People who hurt others and cause suffering smooth my rough edges as nothing else can. I am not the same girl who arrived full of that desert heat and flowing warmth. Autumn pulls a tight cloak around my shoulders and assures me that I do not need gentle. I grew and thrived in the harsh desert... why can I not grow here too? I don't know what love sounds like when it answers in the dark. I feel a sparkle from the universe that makes love irrelevant and makes ME what's happening here. I can do anything. I never forgot that. I did rise and grow in the desert. All the things in the desert bloom and give beauty to the wilds. It does require some rain, though.

111012 1053p

It was a black day when I realized you wanted me to leave so you could feel like a victim. If I had only known...I would have certainly obliged you.

What a silly notion that someone would see me--really see me—and decide to stay. No love for a gypsy. Damn Bea for raising me in all her hippie stupidity. It turned me into this. Not all her fault, I suppose.

Love seems to elude me and I don't feel bothered for once. Rainen's.

111312 0338a

Let the beautiful joy of love flow in and fill your simple soul. The new life waits in there somewhere. Against your better judgment, share it with the wounded world. Never regret walking with purpose. No matter what direction you find yourself heading. Your soul brought a great energy to this chaotic world and filled a soul with happiness, even if it was only for a short time.

Don't close yourself off from this ride. It feels and hurts and heals. I do these things, too. We will all know some perfect moment of truth in beauty in our own reality. Remember the beauty and keep it close. So rare.

111312 1154p

It's hard to feel this. It's probably harder for you to step out of the stupid world you live in. Is it? Is it easy to look outside yourself? I would like to know. Be uncomfortable for one solid minute. See what comes for you. Maybe you can feel for me, having to live that same awful moment forever. Maybe it will open you. I can fight for my own honor. I don't care if anyone believes I have any. I will always fight for myself, since it seems the kindness and goodness I have done is quickly forgotten.

Rainen's.

111312 1158p

I woke today with a song full of sadness on my lips. I stood at the top of a cold hill and felt myself invincible. It took the darkness awhile to find me. I ran a long way. It shouldn't have known how to find me. It manages to hunt me. I asked for some relief in the 3:38a.m. morning. I remember all the NO ONE helping me through my hard times. I didn't dare ask you for the arms around me—even if it was just a simple comfort in my darkness. Your love could never be mine. I learned that when I left. I hope when I offer my hand to one suffering in the night that they will appreciate my comfort. Even if it is a small one. I am always here. I sing through the pained verses and move on to the courageous part of my song. The part no one will ever know about. Wow, it does hurt, though. I can still manage a smile for

Whoever you are—keep looking! The loneliness won't last forever.

To a person I have never met.

111312 1253a

The one big word is "IF". If I did this or that?... if I ran and hid... if I felt honesty...if you didn't hide behind your lying eyes... if all the people I knew would quit hiding behind their lies... I get too freaked out to deal with it. Now, I say when. When I went through the hardest time--oh, yes! When I stood and fought for myself and my dearest. When I find one honest person willing to share knowledge with love. When that day comes I will let the world know.

111312

I listened to the noises of the rain that night. I heard the woods calling me home to somewhere I would belong. The woods don't know me now. I haven't danced in the November frostiness. I have to kick the leaves and watch them fall silent-ly in the rain. Then numerous thoughts crowd me. The woods offer me escape. You try to pull me back. I'm only here for a short time. I am learning to understand. Perfect moments don't usually happen for me.

Mine.

111312

I gain strange perspective on loneliness while I walk down rain soaked dark streets full of falls leaves. I don't own him. Thankfully he can't own me anymore either. I want him to want, need, AND love me. All three.

I can find my way. I never needed a map. The old me did die.

To honor her, I kill the bad things that hurt her. I'm a new me. More than I have been this past year. I went forward into a new dream. I knew I would be happy.

Rainen's.

111412 1111p

I can speak to the stones around me but they don't hear. I don't turn to anyone these days. I know I can't live inside myself anymore. My walls are torn down. Doesn't mean you see it all. Hope has not forsaken me. I am feeling like I should let it be. And so today, I do.

Cain's.

111412 1208a

I can't catch my breath when I think about the entire story. Our love was golden and full of light and passion. Was it just eleven or twelve years of disinterest? Who cares about me and my pain? I am less than you because you measure your worth by different standards. I say good. I don't want to be worthy if I must judge myself that way. Keep your judgment I hope you don't get cold in the dark night with your judgment as your only warmth.

Rainen's.

111412 1251a

This was too much too soon. We rushed like idiots to our doom. My love was not what you wanted and yours meant being someone I'm not. You remember the girl you used to love? You thought I would believe the devoted words you gave when I saw your eye follow the next new thing. You couldn't see the real me and I stood real and alone behind the windows to my broken soul. Love or not—it hurts too much to sit behind the windows and wait. I can't do this anymore. To you or me.
Rainen's.

111412 1226p

Let the little girl watch from behind the curtains. (She is me—she tells the sweet girl I would be that it is silly to trust you.) She watches the hero become the demon again. He pushes me under the water. Same as it ever was. The water doesn't help. The day is louder and louder. The night won't be an easy one. All this shouting and rudeness will put me right back into the bad dreams and then I will be never-ending tired tomorrow. How can you know, when you don't even care? I'm too tired to throw something at you through the phone and tell you to go away. I start to talk about how my day was and you go away at last...what a relief to be alone. I don't need extra hateful. I have full servings.
Cain's.

111712 1017a

I don't need to be set free by a man, but I did need a friend. I sheltered myself through the times I needed someone worst. How strong am I? I still have hope.
For the world.

111812

I think I will survive. I mean, I still breathe, I still walk around with all my former purpose. I still have tasks which call for doing, whether I want to or not. I walk around within much of the time. I feel like I am laying inside in stasis trying to wake up. I keep waiting for some day that hasn't come. I feel like I waited long enough. Is anyone listening?

--The days were bleeding into each other and I was very alone and dreamlike. I mean, I had no way to tell what day it was except I kept a planner and phone on me at all times. I could never tell when I slept if I was awake, or when I was awake if I were asleep. The days blurred and I cried in random places and spoke to the fewest people possible about the most inane chatter I could think of. I tried to keep my girls away from me because I was so out of it. I started sleeping in one hour increments. I didn't dare to sleep longer or the old nightmares would creep back up. One hour was restful and kept the dreams away. I didn't talk to Rainen except in dire emergencies. He would still try to hold my hand and be supportive sometimes. I would get angry easily when he touched me. He didn't realize I was back to protect-Tabitha-mode and had no other way to make it through emotionally except to distance myself. Touching always bothered me when I was young because no one did, unless they were doing something wrong to me physically. I stopped letting people touch me. I smiled a lot to make up for it but I felt it didn't matter. I just had to make it through this. Somehow.

I forced myself to let go with my girls. I would sit on the floor and hold them each one after my worst days and just rock them or pet their hair or just talk and try to be normal. Whatever that was, I can't say. My touch was the only thing that separated me and Beatrice Ross in my eyes. She didn't touch me unless someone was watching and it would make a good impression. There was little love for me there and I wanted to show my girls another way to be. So, I constantly hugged and smooched them. I tried to say things that would matter later to them. I really wasn't sure I would make it because of the stress. I was so out of it. I can't even convey the spaced-out way I was for the six or so months here. I felt alone.

111812 1152p

To himself-

Whoever you may be. I saw your card again in my reading today. All the way back in NM I saw your card. I can't be sure who the hell you are since my judgment is so skewed. I should have been able to tell who you were, immediately. But when you do arrive some future day and I am not a child anymore, will you know me? I may not even know you. Sometimes the universe in its infinite stupidity, or even possibly infinite wisdom, expects too much of me.

The shadows?

111812 0206p

You can imagine that I am cold or calculating. Whatever makes it easiest to push me away. You in your infinite ego think you are better than me. You show me over and over you can't be trusted. You can lash out at me when you are in pain and maybe I will feel as bad as you do. Instead I go to my calm place. My "coldness" brings you to a boil. (Is that what makes things boil? Cold?) My love has always been worthy. My heat will inspire passion. My voice will be loved again. Pretend I am cold. What I will BE is gone. I don't have to keep dealing with it, do I?

Rainen's.

111812

What do I do when I am no longer loved? Who am I that someone should love only me? I have been your option for so long, I don't really want to live with your cruelty anymore. Rip out the piece of shit you call my heart. Just please kill it now. Don't worry over the details. A great deal of life is perception. A horrible awful and stupid truth. The hate hits like a Mack truck and I just live with the pain. On and on it goes. When will he stop? Never. I see that now.

--I knew Rainen would keep up his "I love you, I hate you" game until I snapped. I decided I would never let him see me slip again. This is when I became cold, mean Tabitha again. I still completed every task including sleeping with the man that didn't really want me. He just wanted to prove he could still have me when he said so. I did everything autopilot and didn't even say ouch when I was hurting. I just took whatever came and then wrote in the night. I stopped responding so much to texts and instead wrote. It helped to pretend Cain was real, and though he might have been a real person where he was, he was quite unreal to me. Therefore, he became just a name on the top of the paper to keep me writing and being alive. He doesn't know that lending me the name was all I had really asked. He didn't even have to text or talk. I didn't really formulate words well unless I was writing. Even then, I was faded and tired most of the time. Maybe it would make him feel if he knew. I wondered about that. I don't mean love but maybe remorse or some other real human thing. Shakes head and knows it doesn't matter now. I just hope he knows when to say when. It seems the masses are having trouble with that one.

111812

You horrible man. I begged you to stop before it got here. You swore you wouldn't do this to me again. You saved it all up. You unleash it in torrents to make yourself feel like the big man. I am grateful to know I am thought of as stupid. You (and him) can just stay away from me. I am sick of being so sad. Never one damn moment.

--ANOTHER fight over Cain. I tried to explain to Rainen what he was doing and how it was dumb to get worked up over him, but he did anyway. The fight shattered my quiet. I shut up and Rainen finally GOT that his yelling wouldn't ever touch me again. He began to understand how things were going to be and I think it humbled him a lot. He quoted words to me from this fight time after time. I stood by them, for they weren't defending Cain, as Rainen always thought, but myself and my right to do as I like. My freedom. It doesn't matter who I talk to. I am a human with that right. Just like Rainen always has free access to his women anytime he likes. Goose and gander honey. I will do as I like, Rainen. You can't stop me anymore.

111812

His warm embraces are meant for some other girl. I keep wanting him when he doesn't want me. I keep asking all the wrong questions. This day will go down in history. Who knows what, but something broke. Maybe it's my soul at last. Now I can finally say goodbye to him.

--Girls girls girls. Chuckles. Rainen of course. I think he embodies the great leader with his one great fault everyone thinks I should forgive. Laughs. It was not once. It happened too many times and I don't even care now. Have at it, son.

Three Days Grace "Pain"

111812 1236p

The horrible realization dawned when the levee broke. I am grateful to whatever higher power that in her wisdom knew. The dreams kept coming and life kept happening as the dreams played. I cheerfully stopped torturing myself and stopped waiting for him to realize I'm worthy. I am worthy of magic and 3:48 a.m. songs blasting in my ears just because it's my favorite. The facts don't stop the aching. It didn't even MATTER whose invisible touch it really was that stupid night in the desert. It's senseless to wonder. I am alone in the dark holding my empty breath in the quiet. I don't want anything from him. I know I'm done. It doesn't help.

Led Zeppelin "When the Levee Breaks"
The night visiting shadow.

111812

Let it all go...I just blow my breath out, neutral. Let the "love" go. It serves no higher purpose. Let the pain go, as much as I want to say something. But I am special. I can take peace from this. I just put it all aside and no one even noticed!

Tina Turner "What's Love Got to Do with It?"

--I was very lonesome for anyone I could talk to on these holidays. I wished everyone I met joyful times and made my house full of cookies and turkey and love for my girls. I finally stopped thinking anyone was going to notice me or my need and let it all go. I began to be joyful and walk again in the rain and weather. I always found joy in the rain in beautiful Oregon. I never wanted to be anywhere else. I need that rain. I don't know why.

111912

I am twirling! I feel the cold rain do its dance on my skin. Elements push and pull, leaving marks in places no one will ever look. As I twirl, I think about how the dreams are in full speed now. Small details change but the basic premise is the same. I dreamed them and there they went. Sometimes it's a spoiler to live my life, but I guess the mean surprises are easier to deal with if I know how it works. Laughs at myself and others.... I am leaving the lights in my eyes on and the fires in my heart bright because I am a fierce woman and there is a man for me. Even if he doesn't know that its him right now.

My mind always goes to the night in December. Shadows.

112212 0100a

I live too many days filled with an intense fear of escalation. I can't let his girls see him in such a furious state. It will kill some of their love for him and he needs it more than ever now. I am the bad guy. It's a familiar role I play. I can do that, even if it fuels nightmares later. Ask anyone, I am a monster. Yelling like an idiot.
Rihanna "Monster" feat. Eminem
Rainen's as usual.

112212 0112a

I don't think you felt the darkness I felt. I think you believed me easy to have. I don't need to seek out men at midnight. They do come to me when I want them. Goodnight. Sleep well. I wonder if any of them will ever get it right.
Cain's.

1124/25?12 0235a

I didn't know you thought I was a bitch. Everyone you spoke to knew. The pain I was in meant nothing since the darkness you endured was me. I guess I held you against your will all the years of our "love". Now I guess knowing makes it easier to let you go. It would have been easier if you had just told me. I would have let you go in a minute. I always wanted to see you happy and it makes me terrified to think I was the reason you weren't. Someone waits for you and I know she will do you better and keep your heart away from bad people. You think you are home in the rain but I know you are missing some girl from the sun. I can walk away from this too. It may kill me but I can do it.

Creedence Clearwater Revival "Have You Ever Seen the Rain"
Rainen's.

112612 1050p

I used to miss NM so badly. I miss the good times I had there and the good people there with me—before they changed. It's too painful to think about most of the time. The good meets the bad and it overcomes me. I fill my day with everything and anything to keep myself from feeling and thinking. I wish I could talk about the things that keep me sane.

I keep thinking about Multinomah Falls.... sigh. It was lovely! I do wish I had had a moment to sketch it or have some real picture time. But the girls did love it as much as I did. It was way worth it to see their little faces light up under that amazing waterfall. I will have to try to go back. It was a peaceful moment. I have always loved waterfalls.
TLC "Waterfalls"

112612 1100p

I just kick open the door. It's open wide one more time. I don't think I can let the world in anymore but I will try. Why would anyone want to come into this weird place where I try to be me? There is always a fire burning and its usually me. Humanity teaches me hard lessons I knew, but am used to.
Certainty does hurt, but at least I know exactly who I am and exactly who you are.
—John Meyer "Waiting on the World to Change"
Cain's.

112612 0159a

ANOTHER lost letter to someone who will never read it?

No one wants to read these letters. I don't blame anyone. But that's probably why I keep bringing it up. I need someone to read them. They chronicle a time when I didn't know in honesty if I could get up and walk away.

I don't have a good mamma who wants to be a part of my life when I need her most. I don't have a sister who knows I am low and comes to check on me. I had to for her so many times. I don't have a husband who is wonderful. I don't have a friend who cares. So yes. I pretend you do and write you a letter that you won't have to read. Someday I will be all finished with this episode of my life and I will start a shredding party. Maybe I will cry and get it out a little. (I feel so much for Rainen, who rips me apart.) And while I am shredding paper that was only ever mine, I will laugh at how no one reads my letters anymore.

Everlast "I Get By"

Cain's.

112812 0351p

This is reality. Trapped in a weird world where love hinges on if I take up for myself or not. Is there even a choice? No. How can "we" be happy if I am constantly shoved on a back burner. Insignificant because you like me?

Ugly. And I am. I don't care about the superficial judgments because I am changing in the cocoon of this reality and I am becoming more than I ever was before when I was "pretty". I can manage to walk away each time still looking for the important things in life. Like quiet peace. Can't seem to find truth in peace at the same time. Maybe you won't get beauty from this honest girl.

I find this all VERY significant.

Don't Bring Me Down...--Electric Light Orchestra

Rainen's.

112812 0402p

I have been remaking myself, crafting a finer version of myself—inside AND out. Far from the prying eyes of the judgmental. I am trying to let my old skin fall away from my soul. A day will come when they look for me and can't find me. I will probably be too busy to see them.

I have a generous spirit. No one could meet my eyes as that kind and overweight woman. Truth fell in with me some time back, though. I became sort of invincible. All I ever had was my will. All that time when I needed someone, I couldn't find a soul to care for mine. It became my custom to go right ahead and not need a damn person one. Once upon a time doesn't happen in real life, but I will be more than the indifferent souls thought I could be. I bet no one knew how strong I was. I sure didn't.

Firework—Katy Perry (for me to boost myself up a bit. I was LOW.)

--This was a scary one. I sat in awe of this for so long. I didn't even write for days because I was scared of how I quit living for everyone else and stopped caring about how anyone was doing. I stopped worrying over Rainen and I started making myself spend as much time as possible with the girls. It saved me. The girls were the only and best reason I woke and did what I had to do. I didn't want to see anyone. I saw people all day long and dealt with them all day but never had a solid, honest interaction during this time. I was drifting in the clouds and moving only automatically. The girls raised my heart and made me feel. It was hard to bring myself back after this but I did. Rather Alyc, Ionthe, Iome, and Lily did. I am a blessed woman to have the will and the heart to keep looking for reasons to be when there looks like none. And even doubly blessed to have these daughters of mine to look to for joy and light when I have none of my own. They light my way. It has never been too dark with those four little stars in my life. They make me real.

120512

Last letter to you.

I can't stay in this place forever. What is it all the prag-matists say? "It is what it is." It's a crappy saying, you know. There is a reason I hate hearing that so much. It is unrealistic of anyone to believe that's all there is. I can manifest other things if I want them badly enough. Alice had the right idea.

I was making a grill cheese while texting you and it leapt onto the phone causing chaos and butter to be all over the phone... it was a sign to let it be. I did. Have a good afternoon. And bye.

Ode to My Family—Cranberries.

Cain's. Who else.

120512

Trouble in mind. These are grey days when the sparkle seems distant. The faeries will find me if I sleep. They torment my gentle dream with visions of things I don't want because they aren't mine. I didn't seek it out. The balance found me.

I think everyone has a place to run when it all falls apart. It's strange to me but it seems normal for everyone else. I have some issues with the concept. I feel like if I had that sup-port I would be OK. I wouldn't be myself though. I really like the person I am. I have managed to keep a hard ass promise through this bullshit I have been dealing with. Online bullies suck and so do most of my friends. Ha-ha. Nah. I don't give those people nearly enough credit. I mean, they are all going through something even if they play like they aren't. I am glad they were there for me. The few that have been. And I keep trying to be there for them. A lot of the friends I had don't know that I always send prayers and blessings their way. I re-member good times we had and how they behave when I am going through something of my own. I do want them to all have good lives and have what they want out of life. Even if that's just a cold beer at the end of the day. Hell, I look forward to my sweet bowl... no judgment here! I encourage them because it sucks to have no one to encourage you. They all have support systems that give them this so they don't think it's important to have me doing the same. Shakes my head in disbelief of their shitty gratitude to the universe for getting to have that. Well, it's because I had to raise myself. As my lovely aunt says, I was raised by wolves. I am a savage, I suppose. I tried always to be who I am while being the best I could be at what I set out to do. I appear flaky. I think. I am not though. I have a desire to do everything on my little list and I am so close! Like 15 more things to do...Including keeping this promise. Then I can start a new list full of things far more adventurish. Chuckles because I am a plain girl but my tastes are different than I thought. It should be fun. I look forward to that so this is easier to do every day. It would be easier if I didn't love his mean ass. Why can't I stop even though I know he wants to hear me cry? Man, it would be so cool if I didn't want his love so bad.

Rihanna "Love the Way You Lie" feat. Eminem
Rainen's. Again.

120612 0114a

I don't know the name of the invisible apparition that came to me back in the desert. I don't know why he put his hand on my shoulder and made me feel scared and loved and ready for change all at once. I try to kill the little hope that lives in my heart that it was real and it means something. That year was so hard for me, I thought. That dream where I walked through the snow by myself was a true one but more symbolically than anything else. I wasn't ready for it though. That was true as well. I remember to play a little. It helps me to stay exactly who I am. It's all that gets me through.

120712

Hey you.

I wrote more letters than I thought. I'm making a bonfire. Some of the poems are good. But you can't read them.

Lean On Me—California Raisins

Cain's... I threatened him a lot, but truthfully, I knew he wouldn't be reading these letters or poetry. They are all my most personal things.

120912

Burn the letters!! YAY!! Fire!

You are trying to make me insane. That was a long walk and I was not sorry I took it. I am so far away right now.

I wonder if you do think of me. I mean besides when you throw darts at my picture in your garage. Right. Ha-ha. I know. You "don't keep pictures of me". I get it. It was just something funny to say. I am glad you called. Even though you only did it to stir up shit with Rainen. And it worked too. I know how proud you are when you do that. I guess I am just not as tough as I need to be to deal with this situation. Bullshit. Sorry. I am. I just get discouraged. Its wearing to fight all the time. I should probably quit writing to you. It's soothing and creates this false sense of security with you. Aren't you glad you are my best letter buddy? Ha-ha. I tell you things in the letters that I don't tell anyone. It's funny. Because I know you hate me and have this crazy mission to see me be unhappy because of the little weirdo I was when I was a kid. I didn't mean to hurt you. I really thought you were already attached with E. and needed me to leave so you could get on with your exciting new life. So, I did. I couldn't see making you give up all your dreams for me and my daughter. I am sorry. I didn't think for one minute Carl loved me. I saw very fast that I was going to be doing everything with the baby myself. He would never even come home. I had to try to do the right thing for that precious girl. But I quickly saw what was happening and I didn't like it. I never told anyone. I had to be an adult when I was still learning how to be a child. It was not easy.

Rainen has been randomly going through some of the writing because I think he thinks the way to solve this problem is to be married. Oh, my dear gods. I will lose my shit. I am close to hyperventilating if he does. I don't want to marry him anymore by far. He thinks that is why I am cranky and he can turn it off with a ring. Holy shit, it's like he wasn't even HERE for the last two years...That last marriage was so awesome and wonderful that I can't wait to do it again. Ha-ha. Not really. One piece of paper fucks you up to where you must spend the day in co-parenting classes and at the courthouse with them and outside the house away from the new boyfriend so the he can show off his new girlfriend to you. And don't forget he must always first talk shit to you about how worthless you are. How he hates everything you have ever done or said and how he is right and you are stupid.

The judge at least didn't think I was crazy. He told Carl HE was stupid. I was a good woman and he was throwing it away. Ha. Yes. That was the goal. Chuckles. Newer, blonder and older.?? I don't wish him ill. Anymore. I forgave him. I wish him all the love he can wring from life. But I think we can all agree that Carl is a dick. (Amens and hallelujahs all day long from all parties knowing him.) I watch marriage fuck up one person I know every day. That's a rough statistic but I see it. I didn't like the servant I became when I was married. I wanted to be loved and wanted. That's a noble goal, not a dumb one.

Change that subject already. I kind of like walking with you in the rain. It was nice. Like I was boldly walking around with no Rainen and not just that but talking to a strange guy, too. Laughs. See that intimacy thing I spoke of? It matters. I keep the positive feeling of you being there for me when we both know you don't care to be. I will get over that, too. I keep your words on steady constant repeat. The really mean ones--so I don't be dumb. Don't worry. I am grandly excited that you are having fun in life. I am sure you are glad when I am having fun, too. Laughs. Not really. We both know you aren't, right?

You know my mom and her predictive skills. Well, she told me before I left for Oregon that you would come back into my life in my thirties. I didn't even like her reasoning but I listened. She is often correct, unfortunately. I know this is a bad thing we are getting into here. You do too. And if you're doing this to be a dick—I have to tell you I think you are- I will certainly not be attached to you when it does happen. It's funny because I am very romantic as a person but I just know better with you. Rainen says I romanticized you and it is what made him not want to be with me. I don't think that's true. I think I never did even once start on any path without my eyes being fully open. This one is no mutherfucking exception!

However, I did keep this box of stuff from our earliest time together. My sister kept it for quite some time, but I was going to Oregon and the box had to stay. Well, its trashed, now. I did go through it and Rainen had to know what it was, so I told him. It was funny because he was so sure I was not going to give you the time of day that he was cocky and told me to talk to you. What a jackass. I knew you would cause me no end of trouble. He was mad I hadn't thrown away the box before. Who knew you would reappear so in his face? I figured I had never seen you and I wouldn't. I didn't attach a significance to it. It was my choice and I lived with it...

I always used to be so myself when I was with you. I was different then. You don't know you made a positive difference in my life but you did. So, kiss my ass if you have bad intentions. I still think the good in you is there.

I hear Rainen in there muttering darkly. I have that effect on people sometimes. I better go do something quieter since this pen is obviously too loud for the nighttime. I am rude and keeping him awake with my shenanigans. Have a good night, Cain.

Riot—3 Days Grace!! (I would so throw my king size panties at this band anytime... laughs because I can see the panties hitting the lead singer upside his gorgeous face and his neck making a nasty snapping noise when it jerks backwards under the impact...NO!!! NOT MY 3DAYSGRACE!!! Hahahahaha!!!!!)

121012

Stupidity is a late-night tryst with a man that you already know hates you. Stupidity is an early morning conversation that you know will end badly, even though you have to give it a shot. Stupidity is running 1700 miles chasing an impossible dream of love that wouldn't be, no matter what I do. Stupidity is believing magic will balance the account and that your goodness will matter, someday. Stupidity is the unending joy I still seek. Stupidity is grasping at straws. Stupidity is calling on friends who wouldn't be there for you back then or now. It is loving when you know you are not loved.

Too Bad—Nickelback

For Rainen.

121012 0656a

I guess I live within myself so much these days I doesn't occur to me to try to be here when Rainen wants me to be. I am there way too much already really. He does hate me, I guess and need an outlet. I don't think this is it.

Yes, I believe men should love their daughters more than life. Surely. But not to the exclusion of their mom. I am not so super that I can stand to feel left completely out of my own family. I am so tired of staying up all night to do anything I want to do but can't because I serve the family all day—work, school (so I can work more...), homework for the kids and then more for me, and Rainen's physical therapy and insurance bullshit. Doctors/dentists for kids. I haven't been able to do that stuff for myself... I am exhausted.

It's OK. I am a happy soul because I know this promise means something to him and even if not him—to ME. I can love the moment because I am sure it matters to the rest of my life being lived well. I can love Rainen from here or NM or China or Antarctica. It won't matter where I am, he didn't love me. So, I can be sure that though I think of him often I won't be miraculously loved at the last minute. It seems dumb to me to stay with someone when you know you don't love them. You could be happy and chose instead to make yourself and now the person you lied to miserable for that many years.

I don't believe in princes. I watched Disney with little joy as a small child. I saw the last-minute saves and the wonder the girl always showed at her rescue. I laughed because the girl always screamed and someone showed up to save the day. In real life, it works amazingly different.

REAL PRINCESS TECHNIQUE: I would calmly assess the situation and then decide what was the best way for shit to happen. I would then try to make that future happen. Very difficult for a child who knew nothing. I looked for ways to quit being the adult, but always I was back in charge by the time responsibility was needed. I really hated being so alone. But I managed then. If I had to manage that much on my own at four, then what could the rest of life possibly throw at me. Just this.

I believe in only the people I can count on... chuckles softly. Me. I didn't get a chance to rely on people who took that seriously. I tried to turn everyone I met into a reliable person but I found that wasn't something I could do. It made life seem hopeless at times. I had to create my own joy. I did that for myself.

I have felt better these days when I look back and remember how things were. I am pleased with my integrity and honor in the face of Rainen's little revelation after my hardcore promise. He didn't think I was going to keep it after "that day".

--Letter was Cain's. I quit writing it because I knew that I couldn't keep going when I was so sad already. I didn't want to talk about that really. Sure, not with Cain.

121012

It is a dark night, crisp and chilled. I walked around town and felt the mist fall on my grateful cheeks. I thought of calling, but didn't. I knew you didn't want to hear my voice that night. Or maybe even ever.

It's a dark morning. Still at eight o'clock. I can feel the quiet. The cloud covered greyness is affecting. I walked with my face upturned to the drifting clouds. I thought of you and did nothing. I knew you were just like before.

It is a clear and frosty evening. Almost three o'clock in the morning. Last night I felt that stupid shadow back again. He touched my arm. I know why I hang on. Your quiet still puts me in my place, right?

--This was written with Cain in mind but seemed to drift from him to this shadowed creature. I can't often feel anything real from Cain. He doesn't really want to be attached to me. I don't blame him. I must seem a cool wreck to you. Ha-ha. Good. It doesn't matter for all intents and purposes. I am invisible...ha-ha. Like a ninja.... laughs a dark low laugh.

121012 1109p

Take a brand-new look at this problem. I don't know what to do with this stupid stack of letters. I don't think I should give them to you. I need someone to read them. The only solution is a book. Then if you happen to find it, cool. I am going to count on others reading it before you ever know it's in print. I was going to save a copy but I can't really send it to you. I would feel bad, even if you didn't. She never had a thing to worry about but she wouldn't like it that it's so much you either. If you don't think I am going to slap a word to you in there somewhere, you are crazy boy! No killing trees. I love writing and paper and trees. I love earth and don't want to kill the inhabitants. Trees or animals or whatever. I eat some animals still but my little Buddhist is a vegetarian and she is helping me to do better. I love her so much. Confetti party reprieve. Ha-ha. Only because of dear and sweet little Ionthe being so forgiving when she is in a mood to be. She softened me up for you. Damn. I should have waited to think of her sweet little face... I knew it would bite me in the ass.

I did tarot readings at this party. It was supposed to be a paying gig. The woman didn't pay me even close to what I was worth, nor what she agreed was a fair wage beforehand. I don't care cuz it was really for Brooke. I love her so much and I would have done it for her, anyway. She's a kick ass little gal. I got in a huge fight over that party. Laughs. I wasn't even gorgeous or anything. I am old and plain. I don't mind my looks. They aren't a model's but they are mine. But some guy was really hammered and he took a liking to me.... maybe. I confess I suspect Brooke... I redirected him. To younger and more available females. Shakes head.

I need to quit writing you letters.

jenny8675309—can you believe I forgot the band?? I blanked. Shit. I am getting old. Possibly too old.... I heard it earlier on the bus and now its stuck in my head. Tommy Tutone is the band ha-ha. I usually remember them right off the top of my head. Not anymore, I don't... laughs because I am losing my shit while I grow older. Meh.

Cain's.

121112 0151a

Hi! Whoa by the way! I didn't know that after I went through and tore up a shit ton of the letters there would still be so fucking many. Fifty pages??? You shut up. I am crazy. I know you are thinking it. And maybe I am. You can't read them if you don't say nice things about your crazy friend. Chuckles quietly. It might take drums of gasoline to burn all these letters. I miss talking and hope you are doing well.

I Miss You—Selena Gomez

Cain's.

121312 0217a

There's a monster waiting. Watch yourself, right. I am a born survivor. Every time I bite my lip I feel this cold. Let me be today. Maybe the shadow is thinking of me in the desert and wishing for me. Or maybe not...

For myself.

121412 0743p

I am proud, alone, and cold. Strength means little at three o'clock in the morning. I can only run so far. Maybe I should stop running and give the monster what it wants. Set me free on wicked wings. Ready to be exactly who I am supposed to be.

--Rainen's late night "wake and fight" thing is getting on my nerves here. I am a strong person and I took so much for him during this time. I was trying to keep the man alive and well and ready to care for himself. He acts pretty helpless in the overall scheme of it. But I know if he is ready to spend all day on the trimet then he is for certain well enough to care for himself. And then he would come back and ask for a meal, like I should be ignoring how flushed and happy and excited he is. Yeah. Make yourSELF a sandwich, asshole. Or be hungry, you bastard. Sticks my tongue out and flips him a bird too.

I still make the food... I am trying to be there.

121412 0731p

The cold pours down with reckless drops. They reach for

my face. It's a perfect Oregon evening. The warm smells of pine and fires being burned in fireplaces. The rain is demanding. It whispers all night for me to go and dance in the dark. I pull myself up and go even though I am tired. I dance and it makes me alive and happy for the first time in so long. The rest will come later.

--I couldn't stay in the house on those rainy nights. I felt if I wasn't out in it, I would die. So, I spent a lot of time out in it. I guess Rainen thought I had a boyf. Ha-ha. That's funny. I sort of wish I was the sort of girl who could just toss the whole idea of Rainen out. It isn't that easy for me. But it is OK. I will not be sitting here in this awful situation waiting on him to leave forever. I will be free of the mess soon. And then me and my angels will go do something truly remarkable. I am ready.

121412 0337p

I am drinking some nice, quiet wine right now. I have a great solution to the letter writing. I will write them. Damn. I mean they help. Maybe I WILL make a book after all. Then we can all laugh over it, later, right? I will laugh loudest. But I don't have to keep them this way. Sigh...yes.

--Decision on keeping the letters and doing something more with them. For Cain. Who can't read them unless I put them in a book and write it under a fake name. Which I was going to do anyway but it's sort of hilarious you must admit. In an ironic way. Still. I take the funny where I can get it these days. Even in irony-tart form... those goddamn irony berries grow thick in Oregon!!

121412 0534p

Some relaxing and loving never made anyone feel bad, right? We all have a few of those moments in life. I need a break from the fucking stress. I am trying to keep my heart away from Rainen while I take what he DOES offer me tonight. He looks at me with those eyes and he focuses his attention on me fully. It is amazing to behold! He makes me feel like the only girl in the world. (There is good in the world. Just because he is going to treat you like shit tomorrow doesn't mean there is not good in the world. So, let it go. You will be fine, Tabitha.)

--He always wants me but in this space and time it was so difficult for me to keep it all separate. I had the hardest time staying true to myself and not having the passion. It was something slight he could offer me while I sat there and suffered. So, I took it. I needed him and his hands and his arms around me and his lips on mine.

Little Wonders —Rob Thomas.

My other obsession... hears the faint noise of a police bullhorn—"Miss Ruslon, put the king-sized panties down!! We know you are responsible for the incident at the Three Days Grace concert and we are taking you in!! Put down the panties and step away from Mister Thomas!!" Laughs so hard...

121412 0722p

The letters seem to make me want to talk to you now. Which is silly after all. You don't like talking to me or it at least disturbs you immensely. My own stupid response. I keep forgetting you don't read these or know me or care right now. You are a misunderstood creature sure, but... I guess it doesn't matter, anyway. Tonight, I have handmade many Xmas gifts for the girls. It's some cute stuff. I have nothing to do while waiting for the term to start back up. I guess I'm going to go make some damn cookies or something. Maybe Christmassy brownies.

I am going to take these letters and soak them in alcohol. And dry them. And burn them. And bury them. And then I am going to go stomp on the dirt over their grave. Ha-ha. Bye.

Black Horse and a Cherry Tree—Katie Tunstall

--I sometimes hated myself for even trying to be a human with Cain. I knew he wasn't who he claimed. But then I also felt a distinct need to write these things down. I knew he would turn out much like before. Treating me like I meant nothing and his little wife and life were so much better and so much more important than me. Well. Perhaps in his eyes. But I don't live in his eyes. Anyone who doesn't see me as wonderful and amazing and like I am the most important girl in the world is a douche and can't possibly have me. Even YOU, Cain!

121512 0108a

I am running ragged no matter what season it is. Too tired to search. Can anyone hear me? I am never near enough to hear the universe's quiet whispers outside. My shouts sound like distorted echoes to my ears. Lend me your ear and I will lend you my heart. That's a shitty trade though. Silly for so many reasons.

Take Another Piece of My Heart—Janis Joplin

--Felt like I was trading my own heart for his shitty and only sometimes love. Which is what I believe to be called "NOT LOVE".

121512 0102p

A part of me wants to stay the same sweet girl I was. I don't know if it's true, now. I never felt left behind. No matter how thoroughly everyone I knew ignored me. Let them see what that is like. The book of me is being written.

121812 0244a

I stand on the dark edge of day. I choose, today. A moon sparkles behind the cold December sky. I look to the coming rain clouds, breathing gently. I don't want to disturb the storm in any way. Those magic drops of white geometry begin to fall into little drifts. I am ready for the snow. Now I can sleep.

--I slept so well when the little town was all covered in snow. It snowed eleven inches and it was the freshest and most lovely thing I had ever seen. And then it started raining and it melted off in like two hours. But the whole place was as beautiful as I have ever seen it. The flowers didn't even die. It was magical. I wish I could share it with someone...

122112

I guess the world didn't end. Kind of anti-climactic? Maybe you had a nice solstice anyway. I'm sure you don't notice the moon like I do, but it doesn't mean I can't share myself in the letters-of-no-reading. Ha-ha. I made my awesome sugar cookies. The girls are already cookie-ing it up right now. I have a soft spot for my babies. I finished three pairs of earrings and several bracelets for the girls. They are all so different that I can't give them all the same thing. I got their individual interests and the earrings look great. So that's good.

I don't think I will bother you today. I mean other than the letter. I used to chase around people who won't do the same for me. I did quit. I had a dream last night--normal. It freaked me out--normal. I don't remember the rest of the dream besides the freak me out part--not normal. I am too old to be awake at three thirty in the morning. I'm tired still.

To Cain--but really just talking to myself--like always.

122312 0753p

That touch of grey has spread to my eyes. I feel faded and dusty. This winter's rain can wash me new. I don't know why I believe that. I don't understand much of my conviction. About love either. I feel like love is heavy. The weight makes me think it isn't a good thing to do. I have nightmares of things from my past but I am trying to believe.

--I hadn't had that dream in at least eight or nine years, but when I went to bed last night finally, I dreamed of George standing there screaming all the same shit he used to when I was a tiny girl. I don't repeat the words here because they are all stupid and untrue. I know my worth and I always have. I just hated waking to Rainen yelling straight out of that horrible nightmare. At the end of that dream I am running away and can't move. It is a horrible recurring thing. It has never been triggered by Rainen before. I guess his arms used to comfort me from this dream. But he is a part of it now. Not the part that offers relief.

122312

It's a long road I walk. Full of sharp and deceptive turns, it's trecherous. I had to sit there all that time for a promise made from my simple love. Don't tell me words aren't powerful. Promises take so much time. Can't waste the time doing nothing, though. And he still spent time trying to convince me he had lied when he said he didn't love me. The lie occurred, but I didn't see what it mattered which lie. One carefully crafted to save my feelings for ten empty years, or one masterfully told to hurt me the deepest way possible. One a ten year lie and one a split-second spur of the moment lie. I still watch his eyes to see if I can read the truth there. I can't tell anymore. I shouldn't have to.

--I was reminding myself here of the time I had and the time I told myself to utilize and use for my growth and change. And man did I. I got my brain right even if the rest of it wasn't as good as it could have been. I made my lists and checked so many things off. I am so proud of how I used my time then. I am a real woman and a smart one. I knew what I would be doing for the rest of my time.

122412

All your issues get worked out, one at a time. Thanks Tabitha, I appreciate it. Shakes my head and understands that "thank you" will never happen.... It's precious how we both ignore me, like me and my problems will go away if ignored long enough. I really need someone to be there for me, right now. I need you, Rainen, to be there for me. But you can't do that.

I get it. Your sadness is greater and your grief more pressing. Your soul and life is much more than mine are right?

Why am I less than you? Why don't I deserve tenderness and joy? I reach out with what I think is kindness but you don't believe me. I can't keep fighting with you. I am about to be lost forever.

Let It Be--Beatles

--I did talk and try to make him understand what he was doing. He was so unreasonable. I told him to keep his meanness to himself if he hoped to ever have a chance at getting back in the girls and my life. He really couldn't be bothered to think beyond the stupid girl he chases around. If he chased me around like he did that whore, he would notice a marked improvement. Laughs. But the difference is—he wants to be with her and he thinks he can fall in love with her. I am so sure she can keep him. I mean... until he figures out she doesn't care about him. Just cares about feeling superior to me for some reason. I don't care what she thinks. I knew who I was then and I damn sure know who I am now. I never will let him chase me now that I see how far he let me go.

122412 1009p

Darius-

Merry Christmas. Like you care about that wherever you are. Chuckles. Happy Yule Moon, too, while we are wishing you happy, pointless holidays. I miss you, asshole. No one knows how to talk to me since you are gone. I am stressed right now, but obviously, there is something working on me right now. It sure doesn't matter to me what—except I am tired of working on myself and being worked on by the universe. I think it might be senseless to place hope in something flighty like love. I have noticed it is a disaster, mostly. You know, Rainen is a helluva guy when he wants to be. But right now, all he wants is to make me miserable. Man, Darius. I don't know why I always love so hard! I don't even care if they change. I just keep understanding and loving. It sort of feels like by now he should know me and way better than this. I am sure it will take serious shit to get through this. I just hope at the end he hasn't said and done too much for me to take him back into my heart. Maybe he already has. Am I selfish? I guess at the end of the day, I am supposed to be alone. I hope I can make myself reach out again when I am done. I love you, big brother. I miss you and I know you are there, even when no one else is. I am so tired, Darius.

010513

No one wished me a happy end of the world! Buncha super rude desert people! MY end of the world was great, by the way. I drank a little Red Rum with my sometimes friend Brooke and a few of her friends. Young crowd but fun to hang out and relax a minute. Sweet of her to drag me out of my house and expose the world to me. HAHA!!! Actually, that right there wasn't very nice at all! Chuckles. I hung well and had a decent time. I sang, we smoked way too much, ate great food, walked all over the west side of Forest Grove. We listened to Brooke's iPod and didn't even worry over cops—no one seems to on New Year's! Chuckles. I think Brooke is trying to make some of these boys hit on me. I almost picked up a dude completely without trying. Which says something for the guys here (the fine-ass, sweet Oregon guys here...mhm.) OR Brooke is trying to make me get out there and be dating? I don't think that's a good idea....

I should quit writing these fucking letters. They just remind me, now.

Like a stone—Audioslave song for Rainen

Letter is Cain's.

010513

Today's sun will rise hopeful for life working out after all. No suffering can cool my love. It isn't love if it makes you want to die. The hatred was all you and no lies. So, I find beauty in this release of your long held back emotions. Whether for her, or for me. I will take your truth and let you feel it. Perhaps the best gift a true friend could give.

You used to tell me that if accused of a crime, we should all have the joy of the bad act. And do I follow this rule with the sweet Oregon boy who seems to want to know me?

I have a soul too, Rainen. I didn't sit in any cage for which I didn't have a key. You can betray all you want, I just don't think I am like that. The strength I never wanted to need reminds me I will make it. My inner child seems to be stronger than the men looking out at me from behind hateful eyes.

Nevermind--Nirvana

--Rainen's. Laughs because I wanted to be around this sweet Oregon guy. He was nice and very handsome and he sort of pursued me even when I told him it was a bad idea. Sighs. Some things you just have to keep to yourself.

011613 1138p

I must shake my head at myself because what am I doing? Writing a fucking letter. I guess I can wonder this way without hurting my own feelings. Laugh if you want but I don't have three hundred buddies running around waiting to be useful to me. Or helpful. Or just being human. I wish I could have seen you one more time. I never meant to not be there for you when you needed me. You never need me--so you see why I am confused. I think you have so many friends—I mean real friends. Ones you talk to—that you don't notice whether I am there or not. I need people in my life too. I guess I can find some right. Too dumb sounding. But I am a good person you know. Despite being a little weird. I like being weird. I just wish someone would realize what exactly I am. I am not the jerk you all think. Fucked up place in life to be with the full knowledge of you and what you are about.

Learning to Fly—Pink Floyd

--It was amusing for me to read this—I felt like I should have said, "Hey big jerk! Please look at me and see I am not a big rude jerk!" Laughs... he really tried to be helpful but he wanted something for it, didn't he? So, I feel like I am going to pay him back if it takes the rest of my life which it won't. And then I will see how long it takes him to get ahold of me then. I won't make it easy and he thinks he can find me anytime. Maybe he even can. But I imagine a huge electric gate and a large guy at the front entrance and a nice big, mean, trained dog to make sure we all stay honest—those things could make it not matter if he finds me. I never wanted to make my life this complicated and I plan to make sure it isn't. Even if I am not with Rainen, it doesn't mean I can't find me a guy who isn't married and who will try all the time to make me see his love. I can do that. I can love this wacko from anywhere and not have to put up with his bullshit. I learned fast who he was and is. I am no dope.

011613

I imagine a terrible thing. I wake up on that day I am called upon to take the house back and care for everything like I used to. Rainen is here but he doesn't say, "Hey, Tabitha, good job getting that interview and kicking its ass. Good job going to work when you haven't in so long. Good job not dying of stress while you waited to hear back from them. Good job, Tabitha. You did it. You are officially taking care of things. I am proud." He just couldn't do that. The BOSS congratulated me for having balls to go back to school while dealing with all I was. I guess that made me proud. I start on my birthday. I asked Alyc to keep the entire day quiet-when it gets here... If he can't wish me a good first day of work, he damn well doesn't need to fake a happy fuckin birthday. She promised.

It feels like a bad dream and I am walking through it feeling the enormous dread. The bad thing is, I know I am awake. I think it is time to go try to sleep. I am so glad I got work. It was killing me to know I was the reason we weren't going to make it. I may get to start earlier if the boss gets to boot the girl she says doesn't work. She will put me in with some good hours. I am so lucky. My girls are going to be OK

I spent the entire night after this awake and crying out of sheer relief. I wanted to be able to deal with this stupid situation. And finally, I got to show this place what I was made of. Steel.

Fly—Nicki Minaj feat. Rihanna

012913 0932p

Poor Chuck Norris...

He sleeps in his Bruce Lee pajamas tonight, like the squealing fan-girl he really is. Couldn't be sure, but possibly he had a black eye. I did kick his ass badly. As I took off the foot part of the ninja-footies this morning, I giggled because I knew you were unaware somewhere in Texas. Laughs a little.

I hope your day is good, I have had a very exhausting day but that's having girls for you...laundry is endless, ha-ha. Don't worry I saved some of this same joy for tomorrow!! Creates a fun activity to bitch about tomorrow. Not really. I LOVE laundry, that's the funny thing. I really like to make everything shiny and smell good.

Brooke wants me to go dancing with her. Ha-ha. Not good to go out with girls like Brooke because I will always be older and right now heavier than the girls around me. I have my own thing and I am not down playing myself in any way but its true right now. She is lovely and much younger. I don't dance. I am the DJ. I mean I can dance. I just choose to look pretty when I do it, so I will wait.

Don't laugh. Mom dances and Charisma dances and well. I just always let them be the center of attention since they liked it so much. Laughs.

It's about to be hard as hell. The surgeries are imminent and I feel like I have trained for a decathlon all this time and it is sort of anticlimactic. The physical therapy is only covered for two visits and that's put it on me if it's going to get done. Once he gets started its OK. Rainen won't start if someone doesn't make him. Then its wheelchair time or even worse. Lots of bad pain and I haven't taken care of him so long to watch it fall apart. That's a huge part of the promise you know. He must be better than before so when he looks back he will know. Chuckles with no humor. Cain, it's too hard to not think that way even though I am doing this to keep him well for his kids. I am not trying to make him love me. He doesn't and I can't change it. I am OK knowing that. Really. And you, as well. I know. I know it all.

02??13

I saw you in this dream I had last night. Your face was turned away--waiting impatiently for me. I just knew who it was. You, there, like you belonged in my place of peace. We both know that's not true.

A little bird sang in my ear while I walked to my door. The bright sunshine washed over me, taking the chill off. I saw a bird flying around loving this moment and himself. He drank deeply of a flower's hidden joy. The light glanced off the glass on my door. I felt a cool breeze pick up my dark curls and blow them back. I can still smell last night's rain. I look in the door and there you are. Standing by my counter and leaning on it like you should be there.

I was almost mad when I woke from this dream. How dare he pretend all this time and then show up in my dream. I know who he is and I know he isn't the man I thought he might be. I don't need to worry about being what he needs...remember man. You are married. Go back to her and stay the fuck out of my head.

Pretending--Clapton

020513

Just keep sparkling, Tabitha. He is going to hate you either way. He is angry and fearful. Let it go. I don't have to watch him rub what he believes is my dream in my face. Laughs because he has no idea who I am. Disappointing. If he would have played his cards right he really could have worked a number on me in the name of revenge.

You let the precious word love run around too much. I know you don't love me. I don't think you ever did. When you are fifteen, the world is different. You won't evolve. I don't care because you will go home to her. I must grow. Change. Never stop learning. I missed who you were. But maybe that was a lie too. I hope you remain happy and keep the stuff you value close.

Cain's. Meh. Nothing else I can say.

021113

Why can't you say what you mean? I guess if you want to sound dumb and lie, then go ahead. It's easy not to know me. Also sort of fashionable. I will continue to grieve until it is fully buried. Somewhere this man sits with my name on his lips and my soul on his mind. And it's not you. Or you.

I spoke of the future love I knew I could have. Not Rainen's or Cain's. Which are both unattainable. Inglorious fucks.

021113

I have dreams of backwards places where darkness comes in all colors. I found souls there, but they are not seeing me. Then I take a closer look and see that the wrong souls are behind their faces. I walk around glancing into unfamiliar faces, puzzled at this strangeness.

The highways are in all the dreams, because of dear old mom. I am not going anywhere but I am lost, nonetheless. I can't even search for the other while I am lost like this.

--In my dreams, I used to find myself visiting all these crazy places I never have seen and I knew I was looking for something important. I felt like I was arriving just too late or way before I was supposed to. But I usually woke tired because I stayed in the dreams so long, if felt like I had had no sleep. I spent nights grateful for these dreams versus the nightmares. What a relief to be able to have a plain dream of SORT of normal things. Me looking for my own love is a nice way to spend the night. Laughs.

Lonely, but nice.

021213

He is only a man. He is a hateful person and a special love. I am well-placed within his iron grasp. I am not pleased to be tied to his kiss. It feels like he owns my soul. I have loved the darkness too long to fear it now. How do you say goodbye to a dream?

Rainen's.

032013

Can't take my will	my will overcomes
Can't have my all	my all is too great
Cannot break this soul	the one that you thought ab-
sent is strong	
Will not make me fall	my rise is on

Spirit low, heart locked away. Pulled myself to safety. PLEASE no more fights.

All the time I gave that autumn seeking love. Now just

walk out of the deep and into the rain. Can you bring me back?
I wish for love. Maybe I do have a soul.

For Rainen

032113

You always give my love to someone else. Is it stupid for
the little girl inside to show him my heart? I know he only
loves perfect creatures. Not me. It was too easy for him to walk
all over me.

--His first surgery was in the week following this writing.
The time I did spend around here was so busy I had no freedom
to write or even to sit down some days!! I noticed the writing
got spotty and short as I re-read the pages I had and saw the
spaces of blanks. The spaces here were filled in with napkins
from the cafeteria and envelopes pulled from my purse while
sitting in the offices of whichever doctor it was this time. I was
so exhausted. I would get up early and run around getting the
girls food for the day ready and then making my lists of the
things the girls needed to have done by the time I got back
from Portland and the hospital. This was both a relief and a
trial, to do these surgeries at last. I had to make sure trans-
portation for us was arranged. His mother came from NM and
sat with our kids that day. I went after getting Rainen settled
and i.v.s started and I stayed up on the tenth floor and looked
over the outside city wondering what I had ever done to make
the universe hate me so badly. I sat there for hours praying
and holding random magazines I sometimes read and sometimes forgot I was holding. Sometimes, I cried while I walked.
I would drift in and out of the real world. When you are waiting for the nurse to call you in the concierge waiting area, everyone looks at you and they have this sympathetic look on
their concerned faces. But they don't know I am warring with
myself between hating him and wishing I was done with this,
and loving him and praying he makes it so his daughters will

have him forever. I just sat there so out of it from staying up nights with him trying to manage the pain with hot showers for his back and rubbing the back muscles with all my special oils and giving him his meds and my herbal teas and trying to keep him from shouting as he could feel the spinal cord turning corners inside his skin. I never wanted him to be in pain to begin with but he didn't listen when I brought up college versus construction until it was too fucking late. Why could he not see I was taking care of him, then, too? I wished those nights I had anyone to talk to. I was so alone. I just wanted to go home and fall into bed and I knew I couldn't for another day and a half. I had to walk all over that hospital to stay busy enough to not think. I paced and halfway watched TV. I had to walk. The people on each floor knew me very well. I knew the cafeteria girls from sitting there so many days before for tests and CAT scans and things of that nature. I sat with a cold glass of tea and let it melt down and threw it out. I just needed something to do while I worried over him and how much I loved him. The doctors from all floors were kind and saw I was completely out of it. I heard more than one doctor tell me to go home and get some rest. Ha-ha. No. It took hours to get there and I couldn't survive a trip home and make it back. Plus, what would Mary do with me not there. They didn't know I was so out of it already from the years leading up to it, that no one night could ever make me rested enough to make a difference. I sat and read all the medical journals on the surgery he was having. I remembered the tools the good doc had shown me and how steady and sure and real that doctors hands had been when he shook my hand that morning. Had it only been six hours since I spoke to him and he shook my hand? Then he had gone in to cut Rainen open all the way and remove pieces of him and put him back together. I had received a call from the floor nurse at three and half hours and then again at seven. The doc wanted to haul ass while he had him open and do the most he could. Rainen was doing well; his vitals and all were well. He was a miracle and I had been taking good care of him, she said. So, they kept at it for another two hours and he was put into recovery. They told me he would be out cold for another five hours so I sat and waited some more. I wasn't allowed in the spine ICU until he woke so I walked some more. I went down to the bottom floor and walked outside. I smelled the night blooming flowers and felt the cool rain. I watched the sunset and went back in. I walked down endless corridors looking at and not seeing any of the beautiful art on the walls. I smiled at endless nurses, doctors, patients, and staff. My smile was a hollow thing and the people all looked at me like I was a ghost. I felt like one. I wandered back up to the top floor and sat in the very silent hallways of glass. I prayed some more to any gods who would hear me. I talked briefly to Rainen's mom and reassured her with all the enthusiasm I could muster. She was satisfied and I was done with having to sound so chipper. I was sure to tell her they would call when he woke and let her chat. I moved every ten minutes to a new seat so I could take pictures of the beautiful, indifferent city. I admit I cried. I didn't know what to do with myself. I called down to the spine ICU and asked after him every hour and a half. I wondered if he was going to be walking soon and how I would deal with having to do everything for him again. I spoke for a moment with Brooke and she was a positive little gal. She sensed I was not in a good place and she went on her way too soon. I wished anyone else would text or call just to distract me from the waiting. I knew it wouldn't happen today.

I went out on the tallest balcony and from the top of that building I saw the city lights and the forested mountainside I was on. I was scared and at the same time not even close to scared. I am a person fearful of heights. So, standing outside on the tenth-floor balcony was a brave thing for me. Or even, I thought later, a stupid thing. I felt the huge winds from up on top of the mountain. It is super high anyway but right at that moment, the tall building made me feel like I could touch heaven.

I didn't even feel fear for the first time in my life. I just stood there in the dark where no one could see and let the hot silent tears just run down my face. I thought of all the times he had wrapped me in his arms and kissed me awake in the morning. I thought of the days I had given birth to his daughters and he had looked at me like I was an Amazon and he was in awe of me. I remembered the times he had stood up for me when Carl had been thinking he could play around with my girl's food money. I thought of all the beautiful nights I had spent in his bed and his arms. The evenings in front of the fires when we had thrilled at the passion we had together. I fixated on the times he rolled around and wrestled on the floor with my daughters and had them all laughing and screaming in fun. I went back to the times we spent in the forests and wilds here in Oregon. The beauty of the leaf fall at Henry Hagg Lake and how proud he was to have shown me that magic. The morning he told me to close my eyes as we pulled into the parking lot as we got to Multnomah falls on our ten-year anniversary. And how he led me into that place like he was taking me to a sacred place. I remember opening my eyes and having the breath taken right out of me. I had to grab his arm to steady myself. It was the most peaceful, awesome and lovely thing I had ever laid my eyes on. I thought of all these things and I remembered back to this morning when he woke all mad. He told me he just wanted to make it through the day without having to fight. I didn't argue or anything. Despite watching him text that little red haired hooker he always talked to. I was sad when I got into the anesthesiology room and he was looking fearfully around. I went to him and held his hand while they got his needles and i.v.s going. I tried to make him laugh for a moment and forget the bullshit we had been fighting about all this time. I showed him pictures of the girls and their funny texts with his mom to wish him well, like it was no big deal. We all acted like it was no big deal even though the good doc had already told me the risks were huge

(60%) and he was doing basically an experimental surgery. He was so damn good he convinced us all to be worry free. Rainen knew better and he remembered the first experimental surgery and the pain he endured. He was so tough and he could do it. I knew. But I was the fine line between him and everything else. So, my calm was both heartening and necessary for him this morning. I hoped that I would not have to hear any bad news and it brought a fresh wave of tears while I contemplated the man. Finally, at four hours after the surgery had been complete and he was put back together, the floor nurse called and said she did not have a clue why, but he was awake an hour early. I should come see what was good today...

I went to the elevators and sagged onto the wall while I went to him, grateful I was alone in there and no one could see how ragged I was. I texted Mary and the girls. I walked in to see Rainen with eyes wide and bright and he was laughing at something the nurse was saying to him. He looked at me and he looked well. The nurse was sitting him up in bed and he was doing it by himself!! I saw the gown fall away from his back... the incision was from the bottom of his neck to the very top of his butt. Eighteen inches is what the entire thing spanned. I never had seen anything so weird. The incision wasn't stitched!! It was glued together and tiny like a pencil line down his back. The good doc was running through to check his fine work and he was jolly. He said Rainen came through like a champ and I had done a great job taking care of him and doing the therapy he needed. He was looking at me strangely, probably due to the way I looked. I must have been some sight to see! Up for two days and bags under my eyes and no makeup and red rimmed eyes.

I know he pulled me off to one side and began a lecture on the whole "how can you take care of someone else if you don't care for yourself" thing. I smiled my most radiant smile and took his offered hand. "I can handle this and I have been handling this. I have myself all under control and I have the situation well in hand." I made sure he saw my most confident side that moment. He did relax visibly and he shook my hand but then held it for a very long time-- longer than needed. I made sure to be extra reassuring to him so he would know Rainen would get the same fine care he had been receiving from me the entire time. I told him how much Rainen had been doing to perpetuate this recovery before the surgery. And I spoke of his family who even now was texting to see how he was. I also showed the silly get well soon pic my girls had sent to speed his recovery. I took pix of Rainen and sent them to his mom. I took pix of the incision and the first walk he had out of the bed. He was only awake for twenty minutes before they put him on a walker and moved his ass to walking!!!! I was never so surprised but with Rainen I knew he could and would exceed the expectations. Being such an overachiever, he didn't disappoint. So, we rejoiced he was well and had only the "little" surgery left. One more time under the knife for the tailbone since he was going to need specialized machinery to make the back work like it needed to after all the titanium pipes and bolts they had put in today. I was relieved and as I sat down in the chair by his bed to let him walk, I nodded off. I woke and Rainen was looking at me from his bed and told me, "Tabitha, you made it possible." I just couldn't control myself--exhaustion or something else entirely--and began to openly cry which I hadn't done in front of him in a very long time. I didn't say anything at all back to him. I just wiped my tears away, mad I didn't control it better and looked at him. I got more pictures for the girls and his mom and then I pro- ceeded to hug him very lightly and take his small kiss. I told him then I was glad his surgery was easy and he was a mil- lion-dollar superman. I smiled and left to go take the six-hour ride back to the house until the next day when I would come get him prepped to go home. I walked out of the front doors of the hospital with a feeling of triumph, but a feeling of loss as well. I didn't know what to do with the entire day. On the ride home, I sat silent and looked out the window so no one would try to talk to me. I was fragile like crazy and didn't know if I could make one more polite conversation without breaking down and ruining my night. As I got close to the house, I felt like I would never be able to get the house in order and make sure the girls were all good. After the almost mile walk, I didn't know what could get me out of bed tomorrow but I knew I would get no rest. I spent the night after putting the screaming meemies to bed weeping and wondering if he was going to text me. He didn't say anything after he found out I made it home. I wondered if he was talking to someone else. I assumed he was. I just smoked a bowl and let it go.

041413

Cain-

Helluva way to say what's up. You must've been PRETTY drunk...All the way up to "L, M, N, O, P..." Impressive. Not very much going on. I know you don't want to talk about the surgeries. They went damn well. I did everything right. Now it's all up to how much I can motivate him to stay moving. I can. He hates me already and so it's easier. How shitty that truth is. *wry grin.

I hoped you really wanted to talk to me. I am feeling bad. I have forced myself to keep going but it is not as joyful as it used to be. I still see the rain all the time, and the girls keep me going strong. That's a positive way to keep a smile. Nice. They really are little lights in this dark time.

The second surgery is tomorrow. It is the easy, short one. Only six and a half hours instead of eight and a half. And only a tiny incision on his side versus the eighteen-inch one down the middle of his spinal column. I am annoyed because I barely get to see my kids and the stress keeps piling up. I wish for a little escape but meh. Who needs a break. Not fucking Tabitha. Chuckles... I am super...um. Yeah, super nerd? I think it will be fine. Just have to get through this. I CAN fucking do this.

I can't imagine why I am writing you another letter I won't send.

Heavy—Collective Soul

Bullhorn squeaks and the nice officers voice comes through again, "Miss Ruslon! We don't know who keeps bailing you out of jail, but you must stop visiting these concerts with intent to murder by king-size panties!! Collective Soul is a nice group of boys and there is no reason to harm anyone. PUT THE KING-SIZE PANTIES DOWN!!!"

041813 1107p

Hey. Sort of crappy day. Nah. I got a lot done. I just wish I could get some sleep. Or anything else I want to do. Guess that's everybody on planet earth though, right. When I get done with this, I will be taking a permanent vacation. You know. No more stress and no more bullshit from anyone. Oh, I mean it, too. I am visualizing this situation being finished and the beauty of my life returning. I keep it in my head or I don't think I would make it through this. This is rough, you know.

Home visits from officials from the insurance making sure we aren't mistaken that Rainen had two insanely huge and life-changing surgeries. Rolls my eyes. I am pretty beat up from this ordeal. Can you imagine if I gave you these letters? Jesus Herbert Roller-skating Christ. I bet you wouldn't read them. I wouldn't give you the chance anyway. We all know what the real deal is here. Shakes head....

I am tired enough to sleep without the dreams, I hope. So, goodnight.

I Can Feel It Coming In the Air Tonight—Phil Collins

04??13

I wake abruptly after the bad dream later that night, and

tiptoe to check that he didn't pull the eighteen-inch incision on his back in the night. But he is sleeping a righteous sleep. I close my eyes in the doorway and wish for one day of peace and quiet. This is my silent minute of hope in my day. There is always an eruption, but I can do nothing about it. Why worry? I inhale slowly and quietly and begin again. Breathe very deeply and focus my intention to keep this promise. I can care for him until he is whole again and able to do it for himself. No matter what it takes. I can make it through this. I always make it. He is a fucking asshole. But he wasn't always and he might revert to good- Rainen in the future, even.

Why do I love him? I remember all those things; his green eyes flashing in the dark when he turns to me full of passion... the early morning when he sleeps and looks like a beautiful angel... the way he lights up when he sees I made his favorite lunch or dinner... the way he smiles full wattage at my girls and how they all catch fire as well. It is a beautiful thing—just remember and keep going, Tabitha. You can do it.

I can. I know I can...

041813 1119p

He makes me real in the moonlight. You even make me want to dance like I used to in the rain. I finally began to understand myself again. To understand the nature of my love and what I am doing here. I learned what pain is and who gives it. Also, why I do or don't want it anymore. I learned to grow through it. Something pulls me towards a new feeling I can't name. Into a new strength and will. I can keep looking for a new place that will take me far away from that step father —somewhere he can't go. I want to be outside myself and free again. I sat too long in the darkness until my changing green eyes are seeing clearly. I see the truth of who everyone is every day I am here.

I always thought you embodied the truth and beauty. But

you lied too. I can always tell when someone says something contrary to their nature. I am a silly little prize that neither of you wants. Just wants to say they had me and helped ruin me. Strange. Or wants to be immortalized in my art? I don't think too many of you will like the images you create in my head... laughing... too bad you weren't brave enough to be my friend for real, weird creatures.

I can't sympathize with the devils anymore.

Laughs because I lump them together and I know it will annoy them both...Cain and Rainen.... My favorite reasons to run to the rain... at least Rainen will maybe appreciate where I was in this moment...

Double Vision--Foreigner

042413 1250p

What's going on with you? I am just listening to music on YouTube. The best I can without listening to something someone else picks. Ha-ha. I wonder why I write these letters sometimes. I am weird. I know. Thanks, because I know you were thinking it. Hard copy of Tabitha being bored. That is the real reason I don't send them. Too much for someone like you (so adult in your strange way) to deal with from someone like me (a wild creature).

I am not texting you. And you won't talk to me, so we are sure to be OK, then. Right. I guess am just whining while I wait to smoke a bowl. Yesterday was a little high stress. Usually when you text, I talk about it. I just don't feel like talking about this thing. Really don't.

I know why you don't talk to me. Trying to prove you SO don't need me. Well it worked. I believe you. But I didn't need you either. Remember please. I have myself and I am badass no matter what bullies or jackasses say.

I texted. Shakes my head...

042413

What will bring me through this...what do I call it?... A trial? The aftermath of the promise? I can't imagine since I am apparently not even close. I hope I am ready to walk away from him when the time comes. I got myself a pair of boots but it's more of a motivational tool to help me remember to be myself. you know...those boots are made for whatever... I feel courageous and afraid at the same time. Sort of confusing for me. Life doesn't have to be gentle, but some aspect of it should be. I try to be that for my girls, at least, though I am sure one or two would say I epically failed. I hope I am even half successful. I know I don't see a lot of gentle but could life just slow for one quiet moment and let me breathe? I won't run away. I have things to do and miles to go yet.

A simple sunset helps me to let it go. I sit inside my beautiful bubble with a view and remind myself to be grateful nothing really touches me. Except the tiny grimy little hand prints of my daughters of course...sweet little chocolate prints all over that bubble...laughs at myself.

A door slams shut (-please, not so loud!). My vision drifts. The angry shouts shatter the peace of the moment. Violent clouds quickly bruise the sky. It won't rain... it's OK though. I keep the peaceful vision and let this moment go. I will bring my peace inside and soothe the angry and hurt man until another uneasy and simply broken truce comes about.

Breathe Tabitha. You were born to keep this promise. Even if he decided last minute he wasn't for you. Remember the love you both did feel, because it makes this promise easier for you. He needs you whether he knows it or not. Let's just get through tonight. One more night with him at least.

Just Like a Pill--Pink
Rainen's.

042513

Fresh hell grown locally. All organic hate...mmm...no preservatives, must use it NOW. But it still lasts years. If you use it right. I can't. I am tired. I need a break.

Home—3 Days Grace

Same date

I don't want to force love. I look for those that want to love me. These two. Both with a mean streak towards me. They will hurt me. What they are doing cuts the face of this night.

Walking On Broken Glass—Annie Lennox (Rainen's.)

I Hate Everything About You—3 Days Grace (Cain's)

042513 1205p

I am unsure why he spoke them, so far, but yes. I heard the mean and painful words spit out at the back of me from behind the door. He is scared to confront me and I would be too. I am no meek child these days. Why, if I am a burden as he claims, does he ask me to stay? Must be easier than starting over. But I AM beautiful. I chose to change and he didn't like who I had to become to make his dreams come true. Now I become a faded relic. Someone he used to know. Crisis will come when he sees the newer version has problems worse than mine... and she isn't going to work on fixing herself like me either. It takes a long time to find a woman of my bearing. If he even can.

Stronger—Kelly Clarkson

Loco—Coal Chamber

Bullhorn's familiar squeak and nice officer's voice... "Miss Ruslon-we are aware of the new terrorist group funding your bail from jail. The BBWTP or big bitches who throw panties is not a lawful group and you will keep being placed in jail until such time as you put the damn panties down and quit trying to kill prominent band members! Please take heed to our warning, Miss Ruslon and don't harm any member of the band Coal Chamber! JUST DON'T DO IT!"

Rainen's.

042913 0148p

The dreams had told me all about the darkness. I walked in those same dreams searching for something I was increasingly certain I couldn't find. The tallest windows in this dream frighten me with the prospect of becoming more. I am alone but I am not afraid. I am comfortable by myself. The dreams were true but they didn't tell me much except that I am going to be alone because most people I interact with can't tell the truth with any degree of tact or realism.

Lonely No More—Rob Thomas

--I give a laugh from the seat I am in now. Alone doesn't seem so bad sometimes now. I don't really care for his attitude now, much either. He was sure he didn't want me here while I wrote this page and I see no reason to jump to change it now. I wish he could have loved me as I am. I damn sure had to adjust to loving him for who he is. Of course, there could be no compromises for someone so rigid in his attitude.

I was unsure if this writing was even to become a book until 2017. I didn't know if I might still burn or shred the lot of this. There was so much of me in these simple writings. I couldn't bring myself to destroy the real me and what I learned when I wrote it. I am hoping someone gets something from this. If one person feels encouraged or less alone by reading this, I am successful. Smile and take my solidarity, okay? I mean to help heal the torn bits of the wild world, somehow.

043013 0100p

There is no break after the ignition. No comfort comes when I learn all about you. You shouldn't have bothered me. Make fun of the magic that attracts you back. You try to take my peace. I am dealing with other things. Maybe later.

I can forget just as easily as you. Even in losing my one

love, I learned, I can't force anything and I don't even want to. You should never have messed with me if you weren't going to at least try to be a true friend.

Small Wonders—Rob Thomas

Cain's.

043013

No one anywhere. No light. Nor perfect dark. No one to care. No sight. No simple mark. I was alone. I won't be much longer. I am silent. I will be for a time. My walk brightens and my step lightens. My soul grows and my body dances under the clouds.

What I Am—Edie Brickell

For myself only. The funnier thing here is that my soul grew and my body shrank... good irony, dammit!

050313 written for Rainen for his thirty-seventh birthday.

Your birthday is NO LESS SPECIAL a day because of what-ever is going on in your life. Remember the day you were born isn't only precious to those back in your childhood home. We love you and think you are the most amazing man we know. If I hadn't known you, I would never have found my personal worth. I could have at many points in life quit. When we lived on Fitzgerald Place, you told me that if I weren't with you and my kids that your lives would change badly. It made me think and rethink. If someone like you, so special and loving, would miss me, it would change my mind on many issues. Even if I can't be with you, I did try as hard as I could and then expand my capacity so I could go further. You are worth the effort. Your heart is beautiful. You will never stop meaning some-thing beautiful to me and the girls. I know during this, it isn't a comfort. To me either, Rainen. I am still acting dumb and jealous and I am working on that. I will try to keep it to myself.

With love for the man who gives us so much of himself—

Tabi

Sharing the Night Together—Dr. Hook and the Medicine Show

--I always needed to go and be with him. I wanted to start over at the beginning. I can't of course. But I will remember that time. And hope he finds something like it sometime. And that I do too.

050213 1158p

Back to basics. I put my soul away into a nice little box so I could continue to live this and not just kill every little part of me listening to what's wrong with me. All the previous damage looks like a little skinned knee. Chuckles.

Fragile things need bubble wrap and tape. Ha-ha. I picture my weird little soul all wrapped unrecognizable and strangely shaped in bubble wrap and tape... that is sort of funny. Rolls eyes because I am so dramatic.

Apologies. This isn't all I can do. I can do what I need to and still mark shit off the big list. I am already down from seventy-six items. KICKING ASS! Silently appreciates my own personal power which brought me further than faith, hope, or love. (Self? Very awesome, self. Good job, there, honey. Ha-ha.)

Back In Black—AC/DC

050317

I stopped writing because I finally felt the futility of worrying about him. I don't want to hurt him. That is the difference in us. A bully never needed a friend like me. I don't want to cheat nor help him to. I can't give a backstory that makes us all love this man. I was told my mouth should be shut.

I always figured his mom did an okay job raising him. I bet she would think I was a stupid risk to take. I agree. People only show up when they know for a fact that you are down. I don't care if I am there for them or not, since none of them remembered me till too late to matter.

Unforgiven--Metallica

Cain's. Who else.

050813 1212a

I can't get a response after that ass-backwards conversation...Jesus, that was stupid. POLITICS?! Really. You have no idea what my house is like. So, don't you judge me. Maybe the best thing is to go ahead and quit talking to you. It was going to happen sometime. Might as well be my fault. And it did take a while to get to the real feelings about me, but now at least we have it finally. I wish you well.

Man, I knew answering that Facebook message was a bad idea.

Goodbye, Cain.

Let It Be--Beatles

050813 1225a

You think less of me because he broke my heart. Because I love so wholeheartedly, I am less than you?! Laughs at your ass-backwards logic. I feel like you are just trying to make he and I mean nothing because you found your life boring and love unfulfilling. Is that real? My purpose doesn't serve you and I don't care. I didn't delude myself into thinking you were that love, Cain. Don't worry about me. I always make it. I am amazing!

Amazing—Aerosmith

These old guys could probably appreciate big panties.... They know to duck I bet! Hahaha!!!

050813 1235a

I don't like to need love. I want to leave it behind like my childhood dreams. I can't let those go, either. Put me some-where peaceful. I want to forget who I am. Just drift and do the things I know how to do.

I can't be perfect, Rainen. No matter that I don't care to be. I can't make Rainen not matter, Cain. I valued the experiences we had together, see. Rainen made my life special long before he made it hell. And you don't want the things I want, Cain. I can't resolve that, except to leave the both of you where you need to be: Where you are.

Epic—Faith No More

Both of you leave me alone, k.

051613 0630a

What a beautiful morning. It's all rainy and dark outside. Mm... something had to go my way, right? It's not important how wonderfully or unwonderfully the day is already going for me. I wish I could keep the dreams in check somehow so the truth of things didn't INTRUDE so forcefully. Though how they are managing to affect him right now is beyond me. But it's like he knows exactly what I dreamed, though I didn't say a word. Neither did I write it down; some things are too weird to put on paper. It is just too much. I am sure you have no idea what I'm running my...pen about now. Laughs at that. It's sort of funny. Better that way.

I am off to the library to fill out applications and get a school project book for Alyc. I will certainly be boring the rest of the day. Ha-ha. I don't get very exciting most days anyway, but today I am extra boring. Chuckles.

I shouldn't be thinking of you at all. Knowing what you think about me. Letters? So too much. Cynicism is bad and so pointless.... life is uncertain, I wax philosophical. Sorry. I really am trying to be a better person, whether you know or care or see. I have worked on myself for so long that I am tired of me. Ha-ha. It seems stupid and "My Name Is Earl-ish". I know. I can't disagree with the overall premise though. Life is short and why should you regret one single thing if you lived well and tried to be a good person to others who need you? If I think through my decisions first, then I find no room for self-pity later. That's why I don't chase you. I know you think I am some desperate housewife but you have no idea. I am the least desperate housewife you ever met. I know what I am worth—PRICELESS.

You know the hardest part of being a better person than the last year's model TABI 2012? It's shutting my damn smart mouth. Nobody's perfect. Me least of all. I don't expect it from other people or myself.

Inspirational "Eye of the Tiger" (Survivor) music comes up in background...I am the master of myself. (Evil laugh.)

You on the other hand can't complain because you have what you want. I think you make it hard for yourself because you like a challenge. You should chill out on the risky business. Make your life how you want it. Growth doesn't stop because you are getting older. It should intensify because of your life experiences. We should get better as we go, no? I am taking a bash at it. You should try it. Do one new thing you haven't tried and one old thing you know you love each day. It enriches the day. Or if you already are, then how are you bored enough to keep fucking with me? Laughs hard...add an activity, son.

Yeah yeah-you goddamn hippie, Tabitha. Laughs.

I must go look at jobs again.

Let It Rain--Clapton

051713 1255a

I can't believe you said those things to me. I mean, I have heard it before. Why would you want to hurt me, as happy as you are now? What a friend you are. I knew better than to deal with you at all. Well, no accounting for the one sucker born a

minute. Ha-ha. Laughs because that must be...I don't see any other suckers here-- so you must be talking to me!!
 Riders On the Storm—the Doors

051713 0445p

Felt like texting you but don't worry. I caught myself. I remembered your May is super busy. I figure I have one more child and ten more things on my to do list than you each day and I seem to have time for you, when you bother with me. You are sure I will keep running around worrying over what you and yours are doing. I am sorry but that mostly seems boring compared to my to do list. What a piece of work you are, Cain.

I also have five physical therapy sessions to do with Rainen each day, which is harder than ever now. I have to touch my ungodly-hot ex and talk to his cranky ass with all the love I have. It isn't easy at all. I wish I knew how to make this easy. There just aren't answers to some things. Life=harder than we think....

I also had to make red enchiladas. Yum. The only time things seem right in this pacific paradise is when I ruin it with my yummy Mexican food. Mm. I miss the hot chile. I guess I will go write something else. Something someone will read. Chuckles.

A pen pal from jail would set me right up. Ha-ha. I joke, but several of my friends are in now. I miss both the ones I know of. They are good kids, both. (Be nice to see my big brother. ...Speaking of jailbird buddies.) At least they might read my letters and maybe write back. If I had time to go visit Lee and Rick, I would. They are good guys. Blue-eyed and sweet Rick came into my house and brought music back for me. He always looks me in the eye, treats me very well too, even though I am heavy. That fucking matters when people won't look at me most of the time. Wise old soul Lee always has something funny to say and he is intelligent about some stuff. Sometimes he makes me wonder if he is ever going to grow up. But they are both young and they will find their path. I am always thinking of them and worrying if they are OK Those two made me really stressed out and I always thought of them as my family even though they neither one wanted to be, I don't think. Laughs. I sure hope they are OK and do well for themselves. I always talked about taking the two of them with when I took off. Shakes head. They won't want to be there but I am still rooting for the both boys. Good guys and will for sure do great and amazing things.

I Remember--Madonna

051713

I spend too many nights letting the day bleed into the next. Yesterday's fight comes full circle and I know I have to let it fucking go if I want to have a good one today. My heart is beating tiredly. I want more than this. More than a man who looks at every girl and disregards a fabulous creature like me. I want a man that can't resist me. Hey! There are dudes out there who like bigger girls. And I won't be this way forever. I am working my ass off—literally!! Chuckles hearty like because I am. Two ten is a lot of weight to lose.

FAT-210lbs=still going....

I want a man who won't stay away because he can't. I know how to love. I did it with the fullness of my heart. I dreamed the rainy day I find him. I know it's got to be soon. Waiting is. And waiting is the hardest part.

I've been having dreams about a man I saw from the back or blurry from the side. I dreamed it was a rainy day and I couldn't tell where I was. I mean, no way to see if it was Oregon or somewhere else. It was raining like crazy and I saw him turn around to me a little and he said, "Hey!" and I looked at him and knew he was looking for me and I was about to meet the man I was supposed to be with. I felt it plainly. My heart was beating so loud and erratic... I woke with renewed vision. I knew-- just KNEW-- I was going to be OK and I could make it through this and anything else, to get beyond this last eight years. I just wanted confirmation I would be alright, though. Love is sort of secondary. It just seems when I get tired of fucking with it, here it comes to fuck with me some more.

051813 1208a

When your eyes met mine tonight, the thought crossed my mind. I love him, I thought. It shouldn't have. I was enveloped in my sadness. All I ever wanted was to be loved. I am being patient. I am waiting for the rain; beauty I CAN attain. The weight of my life is too much and sometimes I set it aside to remember how to dream. Those who see the fire in my eyes are too scared they will be consumed. I don't know if there is anyone who can look, love and not burn. I don't find any guys who are willing to be brave and love me. I feel like it's fine and I can wait as long as it takes for the real thing. Despite being tired of waiting.
Burn—3 Days Grace
Girl On Fire—Alicia Keys
For Rainen.

052013 0331a

Three o'clock returns. I am alone, a condition to which I grow accustomed. The demons in my dreams barely let me sleep. Then reality wants a piece of my sleep and dreams— what's left for myself?
Make more and more demands of me. I won't cry for you anymore. I don't see what is so special as to make me do this except that I want to. Sleep well, arrogant sonofabitch. You do more damage and then tell me I am broken too badly for you. After you satisfy yourself that you have tamed that inner me,

so totally yours. Note to you: I hope you are never lonely at three o'clock in the morning. Though I would be THERE for you.

No More Tears—Ozzy Osbourne
Break—3 Days Grace
Rainen's.

052013 0346a

I shouldn't be sitting here this time of night writing, thinking, or hell, even be AWAKE! Laughs. I could just tell you what's going on, but man- I don't wanna. It's so too much. Sometimes I don't think things are moving fast enough. WHAT?! Tabitha is impatient?! No way!! Chuckles silently so I don't wake the sleeping Rainen or the babies. Damn small apartment. I laugh because it is so stupid to keep a promise to someone behaving like this. He enjoys the 3:55 a.m. fights. I need sleep so fucking bad but I cannot get a minute for it. I have three and a half hours and if he wakes me up right after I go down, I just shake for the rest of the time I'm in bed. I get up and shower with no sleep and do school. I can't believe I am passing! And all my kids are alive and Rainen even—there's the miracle. I am so fantastic! Makes muscles and kisses them. Laughs hard at the picture I make in my head...

Why, in other topics closely related, do you feel the need to "smack me in the face" as you put it? I offended you for some reason? The possibility that I am a democrat upset you that much? Can't help but crack up and sort of loudly guffaws! I am not a democrat. But still. That's a little excessive, Cain! I am sure I am missing something obvious. Was I caught taking too much shit again? Snarky look and flips you off...

I hope you took time to plan something nice for the mamma of your pretty babies. Women everywhere are making a wicked contribution to your life. Thankfully, right? I am sure you did. You always were thoughtful. She surely deserves it.

And of course, your own sweet mamma. Whom I hope is well. Like it matters what I hope. Snickers... MMM... Snickers. Laughs.

I am going to go sleep. Hopefully.

Rockabye—who the hell did it—a nineties one hit wonder... um. I'll think of it. Very low and slow cool rock...damn. I really AM getting old. Or I smoke too much. Or both. Yikes face!!

Cain's.

052013 0341p

Ah. A godlier hour. I have a Starbuck's in me now and I am feeling slightly better. Like saying I have religion in me. Lol. Oregon understands. It really is supportive by putting a coffee shop on each block... what if I am too tired before I get to the next block? Did you think of that?! Laughs so much. And sees some people hit several in a row... how do they sleep? Laughs hard... they must climb the curtains at night!!

It's an OK day. I bought myself a cute little dress. It made me feel a little better about Mother's Day. We won't talk anymore about it. How's that? Laughs only a small laugh.

Did you really look at a new truck? I bet it wasn't even blue. Probably red. Ha-ha. Do I know you? Good shit. It was a dream. Not concrete. Laughs. And you are one of the funniest dudes I know. It really had to be the opposite of the color I dreamt, right? I know you too well. Color in dreams is symbolic, asshole.

I must go make some stir-fry and write my freakin mother. I don't know why I do. She is never in the same place twice and she is not going to write back until two months later at least. I know her too well also.

--Cain's. I had a VERY bad Mother's Day. I didn't know what to do with the early mornings... badness. Rainen was in a mood but I did manage to keep my up attitude. I chose to turn it around and make it a much better day. The dress made me feel so pretty and happy. The girls made me so many little doodads and hung them on the wall and just loved me and made me feel appreciated. Even if Rainen cannot seem to. He was looking at me differently after the dress-like he forgot I was a female again, and I reminded him. The rest of the day was a win even though I messed myself up by sleeping with his hot-ass when he clearly wasn't interested in all actuality. Laughs. Doesn't matter. When he puts all his attention on something it is so fucking hard to not love it. He is a magnetic force and I have always had a hard time not immediately falling into his arms. Sighs.

052013 0400p

I walk tall because I am worthy. I am brave and strong, today of all days. No matter what he has done so far or will do today to make me cry. I wear my silken robe of gold and blue and green. The mother within me smiles and pushes herself straighter and her chin prouder. Feel the moonlight set free from my soul. Dance in the rain and love who I am. A wonder. For once loved by four little faeries and beautiful in the cloudy night. ALIVE.
Rainen's

052113 0500a

Cain—
I will NOT wish you a happy summer solstice. The magic of the moon may be unfamiliar to you but it is a moon of high fertility and sexual awareness. Potent magic happens this night. Usually the more natural the magic, the more powerful. Human magic is the most potent kind. I usually do blessings for my friends. I am always thinking of how to make life more joyful by being in the moment of wonder. I also ask, but I won't ask YOU because you think I am full of shit. People like

that can't usually get these things to work. I think you must want the magic to work. Because like I said, natural magic is best. Beltane feels like Christmas. I had myself quite a wonderful holiday one year and I am a believer ever since. I wasn't supposed to be able to have babies after Ionthe. Yet I had two more. I think due to the magic of the season in which I wanted to conceive. It's weird and all that, but I saw it work. Makes the world happier to have sweet love.

Now. THAT is what your dumb ass gets for giving me the democrat bullshit the other day. Dick. You shouldn't need to bully me if you are over me. Shakes head.

I quit walking on eggshells to make jerks happy a little while back. Sorry you missed that. I valued this struggling friendship but I believe I am the only one. So, I guess I don't have to tell you I don't want to hear any more of that "I wanna be with you so bad" shit. It isn't authentic, Cain, and I would know authenticity if I saw it on your face. I promise.

Sleep well. I am about to move this day along. Sighs.
Don't Close Your Eyes--Kix
052313 0322p
Hey Mr. Willpower. That's funny.
(That's all that there was on this entry. Cain's, obviously.)

052313 0420p

Magic reentered my life when I felt my most lost. I woke and stayed pale. I couldn't leave. I wait as I have always waited. Alone. I felt him. So far away and yet right there with me. That one moment. I cried bitter and heartsick, and wished for more than I allowed myself. Make me real, make me feel. A spark catches.

Not for Rainen or Cain.

052513

Hey.

I would wait for your text but what's the point in that. We are all kind of on edge here. Rainen is coming off the mega whomping dose of the meds he was on for six months. It isn't the drug, it's the amount! It's shocking. He should not be able to walk around with that much narcotic in him, but he does. And I wonder if the huge amounts of acid he did in the oldie days caused him to be like this? I mean the viscous way he is being... It was a spine surgery. They took him apart and put him back together. I don't know what that does to someone who has huge amounts of acid in their spinal column. I am a little worried the flashback never ends and then he is like this forever. He was so wonderful before. I am scared he will be mean to everyone and have no one and he is a good person. He needs love. I wish... But. Well. What can I do? What MORE?

I am glad I didn't get weak and let you read these. How much more of me is there here than everywhere else. A lot. I am sorry, too. You never asked for this part of it. Just keep your sense of humor. You always had a good one. And some of this shit is funny- you must admit. Though I paint myself in a strange light. I try to let you all know me well. The good and bad.

How can I possibly miss you when I haven't seen you or even know where the fuck you are? I don't think I do. I think I miss the memory. I don't know. You don't miss me much, either. Laughs. Shrugs.

Why did you just text me? I hate that vibe thing you do. Can't you leave me alone?! I don't want you to. I do need the contact but I think it's a bad idea all the same. I do care about what happens to you and yours. I hope everything is like I never happened. I am sure you go to lengths to ensure its so. As I do.

Tangerine Sky—KMK

Squeaky bullhorn turns on. Officer Awesome is ready for me. "Miss Ruslon, these young potheads have done nothing to deserve the giant panties to the face that you are about to throw! These kids are good boys—think before you act Miss Ruslon!!!"

Cain's.

0525130809p

That same spark of magic I have been looking for pulls me...it's three forty eight. I only feel beauty from the rain. I know that a shadow is somewhere feeling for me. Where the hell is he?

I wish I had closure on the shadow and I don't. I still hear or feel things from him but I don't know how to gain anything more from the clues I have. I will keep looking. I know sometime the day will come when I wont care anymore and I will let the entire thing fade from my mind. I cant let pretenders stop my life anymore. How could I resist writing about Rainen? He is full of light and energy. He is amazing. How could I resist writing about Cain? He is a good person and he holds some strange attraction for me. I am sure they will both go on after me and do great things. I think that's the best thing I can say about either of them after the way they both behaved.

Rehab--Rihanna

06??13

You have to force the feeling. Force my hand. That's great work, Benedict. Can you force a little bravery? Can you be courageous like I am? I don't hate you. I did see you coming a mile away, though. It made me smile, to think you find yourself so clever. I didn't regret my choice. I found out much from it. I knew what you were. I knew what I was, too. Alone and worried about the future. I just needed one person to smile and say, it's going to be OK. But I didn't expect it from you. And that's a bit of luck of my Irish. Laughs hard. I'd say we both dodged bullets, right? No one wants to admit they are a hot mess. I admit it and embrace it. What else is there? What do you do? Try to hide it. Shakes head. You know I am your friend. It's not a big deal. We all need to talk it through sometimes. Doesn't mean we want to run away necessarily from the situation. Just have a free moment to be our inglorious selves. Right? Well, when you are ready to be normal... Ha-ha. That's funny coming from me.

Chuckles because you are funny as hell. You had your teeny little revenge. Aw! How cute and so adorable! I would keep showing me pics of your kids so I don't do any revenge-ish things of my own, right... no one finds me capable, even after all this time. You screwed with my family, why shouldn't I screw with yours?

I guess because high school was a LONG fucking time ago and I am thirty-seven not sixteen and dumb. If you were over it and beyond your stupid pettiness, you could have had a great friend in me. Well. Be happy honey. The story you told said one thing and the actions you showed me were not congruent... stay away from me. I don't need a married guy. You keep on not calling and not texting and I may just forget all about you all together! Ha-ha! I do care. But.

I will just keep being myself and doing what I am doing. Thanks for the...hm. Whatever you wanna call it.

Bulls On Parade—Rage Against the Machine

Crowd of protesters with huge signs that state BBWTP on them...crowd chants "THROW THOSE PANTIES!!" no officer awesome today...

Cain's.

060213

Hi.

Maybe I should spend two or three days on the phone reading these stupid things to you. Waits an appropriate amount of time to ensure you are scared... I would never. I know how bored you get. Hard eye roll....

Random thought for the day: I want to go stay at my coast. It is so pretty. I wanted to go back since I left the first time. By myself I could draw and read and write—AT THE COAST. Dance in the rain on the beach.

Later. Plenty of time to see it again.

Umbrella--Rihanna

Later on...

Wow. He proposed and rescinded and re-proposed and re-rescinded. I said no, all of it. I wanted to do this in January but he made sure February and March and April were so... bad. I am down-playing that hugely. Smiles at my under exaggeration...

It probably won't even be like this when he gets finished healing. I can see him getting more reasonable every day but I also see him going out to see other girls. I guess it wouldn't matter if I did want him. I am too tired to deal with it. He doesn't realize I need to get away from him. I can heal.

I am about to shoot myself in the fucking FOOT just to have something new to focus on!! He is coming off huge amounts of Oxycontin. It isn't easy because he used to be addicted to them before. But he was all kick ass go-getter and took himself off. Just like he is now. And I am so proud of him. He doesn't know how much in milligrams that was! 1500 milligrams every three hours. Leveled off handfuls (In my hands anyway.) Every three hours. No one would have believed it, but the doctor said he knew what the fuck he was doing. I shake my head because he came off them just as smoothly as he did in NM. He doesn't like to be anything less than present. His daughters are so important to him. He wants them to see him be a hero. He is every day but he doesn't think about those tiny things. I don't care how much pain you were in, you were still a human being and it is very important to stay grounded. He wouldn't do the mindful meditation shit. It worked, though. When he finally came around and tried. Instead of yelling and getting my ulcer all acting up. I am fine- no victims live here, but I am saying, "People, be aware before you open your mouth. Shit is not OK to say."

Love Hurts--Nazareth

Cain's. Sort of Rainen's too, I guess.

060513

Morning. Seems like I was so far away I needed to pull myself back inside somehow. Early morning hair-wrecked smile because I saw you in that dream I had last night. I don't know what the fuck you were doing there. Standing with a bunch of mean looking people in the way off distance this time. You were looking at me and I saw you didn't seem amused while they laughed. I wonder what that was about. Then later the same night, I had another dream about you standing in your kitchen. But it wasn't your kitchen. It was a much older kitchen. And the town was Denver but at the same time Artesia. You threw a bar stool. I didn't see anyone else till later. I saw a blonde girl who was a little rubenesque and she gave you quite a look. You looked at her and stomped back into the house and slammed the door. There were other people but I didn't see them up close. Anyway, I am sure there are personal things to the dream that I did not notice and then there is the connotations to me vs. to you. You know how dreams are.

I don't think it will be as easy for me to say goodbye as it will be for you. I say too much shit that doesn't need to be said to someone who isn't even aware of this me. You don't have to think about me. Laughs...Lucky you. I try to keep this all to myself so you don't have to worry about attaching. I know it's easier for people to think the worst of me, so I let them. It's fine.

I am going to have to bake some peanut butter cookies. It will help me to not text if my hands are doing something.

Butter must be colder by far. Sighs heavily...

I hate the entire children's dad thing. It's biting me in the ass. I can't deal with that jackass, Carl. Why would I, knowing how he feels about me, ask HIM for help when I know he doesn't give two shits? But as a dad I never saw this side of him. Sort of hurts to know he doesn't care if I am doing all I can. His kids do without as little as I can possibly get by with, but still. Shakes head. I am grateful to you for making sure you do what you can to help. I know you have a family and care about them first. I would expect nothing less. But you have so many in your house compared to him. And he does NOT a thing. It IS kind of you to ACT like you care anyway. Dealing with him means dealing with Rainen being all riled up again. Over what, I don't know. Rainen is still unreasonable about Carl. He thinks I give him too much time with the girls and too much of everything with the girls and he abuses it by not giving a fuck. It's true. I did. But to be fair, right now I think he hates all men (of the male persuasion) if I talk to them. Rolls eyes and says when to all this stupid crap.

Daughters—John Meyer

I say fuck it and throw the panties before the swat arrives...

060613

This hope curls around me and makes me feel warm for the first time in a long time. I feel solid for once and peaceful. I do have a calm personality and it does extend to my home. It is much better than it could be...pain makes people crazy and I know without me—Rainen couldn't be even THIS calm. I know this. I am proud and started exuding this calm all the time so he can remain mellow. My talents are impressive. I am happy I reminded myself of my strengths in time for it to matter. Everyone seems calmer today.

I can take my quiet stroll through the forests and think of someday doing so with a man that wants to be nowhere else and only with me. Not a dream but a certainty. Thank goodness for my inherent calm. I am grateful.

Take It Easy--Eagles

061413 0608p

Where can I go that feels like home? I really don't know what that feels like since I have never had a home. I think I set myself up right there. All places seem foreign. How will I know when I find home? I may be lost. I want elusive peace. Beauty of a true home. Love that lasts. I needed love to be real. It was the last thing on my long list. Love.

You-Breaking Benjamin

061413 0238p

This is a dark hour. I have little patience. I keep living and have no feeling of purpose behind it. Waking up to hurting because of that fucking promise. I have to breathe and remember the reason I made this promise....his hands and mine working in our gardens... his hands smoothing my hair while I shook after one of the dreams... his arms pushing everything evil away and keeping me warm and dream-free.

The beautiful bubbles of colorful illusions shatter. All of it disappears when I see your eyes clearly considering mine. What does this matter? Do you ignite in the darkness? No. I can't let go and dance this one.

--It was a rhetorical question, Cain. I know you would never go so far as to catch fire. And sure not for me, darlin. You are far too practical. Grins. See what I am saying? I know you aren't for me.

Sober--Pink

Rainen's and then Cain's.

061813

Looks like back to pen and paper. Did you really want me to bug you on Father's Day? I figured your people would have something planned. Me and my girls always make big plans and do banners and cards and paintings and poems and all that wonderful shit. Plus, cake and dinner and all that beautiful stuff. I love the day. I never had a dad and I determined I would not let my girls do without a dad. A good one. And Rainen is. I am happy he does such a good job. He dotes on them and spoils them and loves them. I usually go out of my way to thank the fathers both but you know how that is. If they don't care if the kids eat, they might not be the father... Maury says...Carl, you are NOT the father!!! Yay!!! He jumps up and down, and let's Rainen do it. And when Rainen absolutely can't—fuck it! I am an awesome dad. Laughs. Rainen's getting back to good on that front. Makes happy faces for them and wry ironic grins that are just for me....

I must give back for that. His karma is good for the kind of dad he is. I spend too much time worrying over other people and not enough worrying over my stuff. My kids are always number one. I do love them. Though my writing seems to focus on me, there is a reason. My days are focused on any and everything else but me these days. Where can I go and let me out? Paper. That's where. I sure hope you can see how I am trying to stay smart and not develop feelings for you. I realize you just wanted to peek and see if I was all fucked up like you hoped. Well... yeah. But I am getting it all where it needs to be. I wouldn't worry about it anymore. Don't let me cross your mind. I think your wife is a fabulous woman and deserves full attention. So, go! Do that!

Funny you call me a prude. How would you know? You don't play this stupid game well enough to convince me I can trust you. I don't know if I ever will. You scare me. So, I learned to respect the feelings. I am usually right. I relax when I get all trustish. I can't get far with sex without it. Sometimes a freak orgasm but usually no. I wouldn't worry overly about that k. Just go do your thing and I will go do mine.

Speaking of trust-- See, I knew your sorry ass was part of it. Grilled cheese happened that damn day because Rainen wants time with me anywhere he can get it. I am accommodating for the most part because he is chilling out now days. If it means dinner must be smaller and less wonderful than usual, he will take that quickly. You are a dick. An intrusive dick. I need some major space from you. That worries me that you might take liberties with other people's privacy. I hate people who feel entitled. Don't you.

Bullies who feel entitled. Bully-dicks. Bully-dicks named Cain! You don't get to feel mad I call you on it. Since you aren't here, ha-ha. I can say what I like.

I am glad your truck deal went well. and did I fucking call the color or what? Laughs so fucking hard --- actually makes my fat-ass sore to laugh that hard.... It's sort of funny you think I attach a lot more stalker feelings to you than I do. It wasn't an instant love connection. So, it worries me that you say the words so flippantly. I was really trying only to be a friend and have a friend. Its OK you wouldn't unless I helped you to gain revenge on any man I might have loved. I will be happy whether or not you are around. I don't know if that is the reason but I figure you felt it would hurt SOMEone to see you hurt me. BAHHAHAHAHAHAHA!!!!!!!!!!!!!!!!!! Now THAT was funny!!! I can't even stop smiling. Carl had it in for me for years. While I was with him even. So, no. I can't get worked up over it now. I would have been friends with any one of the exes I had. Not the creepy type of friends either. Like the type that hurt someone during sex on purpose and then act like it doesn't matter and they don't need to apologize for it. It's sort of dumb, I admit. My own stupidity. What else am I to guys like you and Rainen? A great hate-fuck. Shakes head. I would worry, but why. Love is supposed to be wonderful. Sweet. Feel good. I want that. And I will have it. Maybe not right this second, but I am attracting a lot of things from the universe that others thought I couldn't get.

Beltane this year is going to be different than other years. I want to invite someone different to be with me for the holiday. I am sure I can find more gentleness for myself than this.

Abracadabra—Steve Miller Band

061913

I wish I could talk to you. I wouldn't say what's on my mind anyway. It is comforting, your pretend presence, I guess.

It's a big city full of two and half billion people.

It has been a lot to get used to here. I am usually by myself anyway so I know I can do it. Alyc is about to leap into adulthood. Then my other kids will. I will be by myself before I know it. I will be in a quiet house. I am sort of not knowing what to do now. I can't explain myself. I want someone just for me. I should be used to this but I don't care. I deserve love.

And not some half-ass love. I can find that by throwing a rock. I think I will just wait it out. No big deal. I got it.

Cain's.

061813 0109a

I am alone and sitting with a very old coping mechanism. I usually smoke to keep calm. Tonight is different. I may have a nervous breakdown... This year I get to watch Rainen get ready for a date. He is preparing me and just being a great guy about it. I am so fucked up right now. My birthday isn't for another ten days but I am getting myself mentally ready for this. Happy birthday, Tabitha. Your gift is the gift of "I don't give a fuck about you..."

I don't know how I am going to handle this. I don't think I am doing all that well. I need to talk to someone so bad, but I guess I sort of don't have anyone. It's a damn genius who thought of paper. You know that's right. I might not make it if I don't write. And do a lot of deep breathing. I am too emotional over this already. This is no way to treat me. He could have waited. *shakes my head because that would mean he was being soulful and thinking of something that was not himself. (Please go be selfish and I will be fine.) Right now I know he needs to do this for himself. Shit.

He could have said his feelings changed when it happened and he would be happy RIGHT NOW instead of stuck here with me. I am no fool. I let anyone go if they say they want out. Fuck. ANY MUTHAFUCKER. No matter HOW much I love him.

Hello To Heaven—Temple of the Dog

--To no one in particular, just had to get the words out before I freaked out and lost it.

061913 0747a

I am drifting and everything appears to be erased. When the sun rises, you are already dressed for battle in your armor of hate. You have been lying awake since seeing her rehearsing how you can make my cry. If I have learned anything over these years, it is that I can cry all I want and it doesn't matter to you. So, now, I don't care if I cry, either. There isn't even a slight sense of conscience at the words you spit out at me. You don't hurt yourself when you hurt me. That would be love.

I only wish hate could make me bold, like you. I could bring home someone pretty, too. I could kiss him passionately in front of you. I could ask him to share little bedroom secrets about me that only you and I would know. I think I could. If I hated like you do. I wish I could...

I can look back on the body of your work and see your broken promises and my stepped-on dreams. I let it drift. Load a fucking bowl for fuck's sake...

What's Up—4 Non-Blondes

--Rainen's. Of course. His new bitch came in the bookstore

all the time and I tried each time to let someone else help her every time after the first time. But she would ask for me specifically and the college has a policy... I tried to school myself to act not only unaffected, but as though I didn't even know her. And it made it quite easy for me. I was getting over him while I was still living with him. Even though I grieved over the loss, I was grieving in part, so I COULD move on someday. I have learned to smile while I walk on knives, just like our beautiful mermaid in the Hans Christian Anderson faerie tale. I am no princess but I damn sure relate to forced silence and pain--all for a dream.

070513 1035p

It came with a jolt today. I began to quit (very quietly) living for you. I know who I am. I had to see with my own eyes that you don't love me anymore and today I saw. But finally, I can start grieving the loss of the relationship. It will be hard to do while living in the same house as you but I think I can do it. I mean, since there is no choice, really. I don't feel at peace with this. I keep on doing the things I always do with the girls and the house and the job and the school and the art, and even the physical therapy. But I don't know what it will take to ground me to myself again. I feel like I am drifting in some random way, here. The fires of hope didn't die within me, you know. I hope and have faith in a love just for me somewhere. My stained-glass soul is beautiful in its own way. But if you don't know how to care for the glass you probably shouldn't bring the piece home.

Little Lies—Fleetwood Mac

--Rainen's. Oh man, does this one wreck me so bad to read now. it is shorter but there is so much of myself in this... I remember seeing them together that afternoon and how my heart caught. I just smiled as the punch to my chest landed, and forced breath in... walked the other way. Hardest ten steps

I ever walked, so straight and slowly. It felt like slow motion but I was determined to walk it unhurried--I don't RUN from anything EVER-- and with my head up. Easier to smile that time though...the dream readied me. It felt like hell. PROUD TO BE A TOUGH BITCH.

071013 0835p

I hold my head up, proud of myself and that I am the "bitch" that got us by. I don't even care about my past. It sure doesn't care about me. I walked away. I dreamed too long. Where will he be when he realizes I am gone? It still feels like time stopped.

No Time Left For You—The Guess Who? I think
Rainen's.

071413

The whole damn stack of letters is going with me to Texas. Ha-ha. No really, could you imagine? Please keep saying all those things (lies most likely...) you say. I know you don't say them for the reasons I think, so it doesn't matter anyway. I am not OK. I am nervous. I went out of my way NOT to dress up. I can't be that girl trying to impress you. You didn't have to try to be impressive to me. I just needed you to try to be a friend. I am not perfect looking. But I am a decent person. Why anyone would notice now...

I Walk Alone—Papa Roach
Cain's.

072513 1120p

There is a damned soul somewhere and he is lost like me. The one who came to me in my fallen moment. I remember every detail. I adopted you into my heart and don't know who you are or what you look like. I am a weird lonesome girl and difficult to love. I made myself better for myself but I had the idea in my head that you were there just waiting for me and when you knew it was me, you would be with me. I am not that weird. It was a mechanism to remain hopeful. And it worked for a time. I am still myself. And I wasn't worried about finding love. It will happen or it won't. I am optimistic. I hope I get to meet the apparition that gave me so much comfort over the years. It would be nice to know more.

For the unknown ?? I know as the shadow.

Tourniquet--Evanescence

072513 1159p

I am dancing alone in the Oregon rain. I found myself by myself. I can feel and not fear. I let it out. Every sorrowful heartfelt tear. I listen quietly in the night. I should feel love even though I am learning it may kill me. We all find something like that this life. I have wandered far from home. (I guess I can't call anyone I really want to speak to with this stupid phone. Darius, you dick! I have NO number for you!)

I was pulled blue and half dead from my mother. I pulled myself hated from the arms of another and another. I don't think anyone is born to suffer. I want to feel less alone and something real. I feel like murder is wrong even if it isn't your blood but only your ruin the jackass seeks. I am stronger than you, though. Remember that. I think my wait will be worth it.

Here I Go Again—Whitesnake? Damn. I don't know if I am right about some of these. I will have to look it up. Sorry... :/

The shadows.

080513 1006p

Today has dawned with the sunny disregard that I knew in the desert. Hey! Isn't this Oregon? Land of the flying with her own wings? And rainy beauty and little moments of flowers dripping with silver? I don't know if I will fail at this flying thing. I am a desert girl who is trying her best to make wings and then teach herself to use them. It is way harder than it looks. I had no education to fall back on here. I am unemployable. No job history and no experience in thirteen years. That wasn't what I wanted for myself. I wanted to have no babies until I was a successful fashion designer and had some college under my belt. I was full of impossible dreams I am making come true late in life. I will do everything else first and then finish the wish list. You laugh but here I go. One dream for me must fuel another and they are all woven together in the fabric of my soul. I am too damn dramatic. I guess you can take the girl out of the desert but the poetry stays within. *hard eye roll.

I will do my thing. Ha-ha. Sort of a laugh in the dark. I am usually not laughing so this is an improvement.

You shouldn't just read neat lines from a script. It feels too forced. People, people. Realism is so hard to achieve while acting...

Lie To Me—Johnny Lang

--People named Cain. I do have deep moments. I usually try to offset them with something funny. So... I make a cross-eyed face and stick out my tongue.

080513 1040p

This summer rained on my soul—welled into the deep cracks. I felt full. I only know that love is finding myself wrapped in their dirty blonde, strawberry blonde, auburn, and orange hair in the night when I rock any one of them to sleep. (That shampoo is citrus and smells amazing!!) I wish I could express the peaceful feeling I get from them. These girls have taught me love can be one sided and even unreturned and I will still feel the fullness of it. I hope everyone feels this. It is amazing. I think that was the major lesson. Am I turning into my mom while I hunt for a love? I have four loves right here and they are worth so much more than any other love I could ever have! They make me real. I think I caught myself before I turned into a weirdo looking for something I can't have while I am leaving the best parts of life out. My girls are so amazing. I know I am the luckiest for getting to be their mom. I let them grow and change as they like and be themselves. I don't think a lot of mom's will even make that distinction. We can't make them have our personalities!! I wouldn't want them to. They are so much... MUCHIER than I ever was. I love them for being so different and intelligent. What do you know about me? Not a lot world. Just that I am me. Mine are themselves. My love will be himself. And I am not even impressed with anything fake.

Pocketful of Sunshine—Natasha Bedingfield

080513 1015p

I made my way here. I came through scary high canyons. I feared my choice for the first time when I saw how high those canyons were. I really almost threw up at the wonder. Laughs but it was a fearsome awe. They were deep and cold. I came past unbelievable mountains. They sat high in their sky. I drove through endless plains of plenty. I wondered at the forests where I began to feel peace with this choice. My eyes lit on the silver rain drifting lovingly over the anger of the ocean. I finally felt the coolness of the fog. The feelings wrapped around me like a comforting quilt. I feel this place. Through the pain of who I am, I feel it.

I don't care where I ever go, I love this place. I will go back and dance in the rain again. Bet on it.

River and the Wind—Tanya Tucker

This song became special to me when my mother (a music aficionado) introduced me to her albums for the first time. She had been toying with the idea of making some t-shirts and when she did, she took her inspiration for mine from this song. My little Cherokee name was Riverwind. How romantic. Both me and not at all me at the same time. I think the song had significance for her and my father when they were first married and so very much in love.

The t-shirt had a simple rendering of my face and some lovely scenery along with my "name", Riverwind. I loved that shirt and wore it until I could not wear it for the holes. It meant something and some piece of my mother was struggling to tell a truth here in this shirt she painted. I couldn't hear the whole song but I did hear her ring of truth. And I tried hard each time I wore the shirt and saw her face to understand her a little more. Her expression would soften and she was a different person when she saw me wear it.

080513 1027p

You found your reality. I haven't found all of mine yet. You think me funny for looking. I can never see one way to happiness. All roads lead there. I am ready. I see myself in all reality. I am not even strange for holding out for someone real. I do have a destiny you can't take. I am joyful at least I still have that. I don't forget where I come from. Ever.

Jenny From the Block—Jennifer Lopez
99 Problems—Jay-Z and Linkin Park
Cain's.

080713 0250p

If I let go of all my immaculate self-control, will I be able to hold onto the person screaming inside of me? Let me out! I want to be free for once. I want reality to mesh with what is beautiful for one moment. I want to dance with my face upturned to the rain. I have listened to too many stories of pain and trouble. I felt what I thought was love but it was fake. As though I were in a zoo and the main attraction, they watched. I believe in the broken souls, so beautiful, like stained glass. I see the light of hope shine. I don't want to wait. I just want to dance barefoot under the rain.

081013

Hi. Another letter. (Poor trees.) I was thinking of you to-day. I hope everything is good. It's raining. I had a dream about you, again. I usually get vibes when others are seeking me out. I just believe in magic. Not sorry for saying what I like.

I am so tired today.

I try not to complain, you know. Energy mustn't be wasted on that pointless shit. I wrote another eleven items and drew a creepy picture and a cool dreamscape. I also read anoth-er twelve books. I should calm down sometimes. The busier I stay the better I can avoid us fighting. So that's what I do. After so fucking many fights, I don't think I can do any more. I am so tired. If only I could keep my big mouth shut. That is hard.

No rain now? I am a desert girl. I need rain, people!! I had to hike like twenty minutes of rain forests to get to the very cold beach. It was awesome!!! I love the beach.

Be good. Or bad. Whatever.

Dear Agony—Breaking Benjamin

Cain's.

081113 1212a

I let the world go with newfound ease. I must care for my-self and my angels first. It feels like I am bleeding out in a huge square and all the people I know are there and biting flesh from my not-even-cold form. It seems dramatic, but it's funny if you imagine those people I know with blood coming out the corner of their mouths... Flesh hanging out. Oh, man, it is funny!! When I was most alone, I didn't turn to them. I laugh when they offer their conditional shoulders for my bur-den. I know they shouldn't have to bear the weight, anyway. Luckily, I learned early from other assholes that I can bear any burden thrown at me.

Oh, you all love me? I smile because I feel like you never knew me at all. Is that what the girl you used to know would want? Empty words? All your vanity is ridiculous. I know you, remember? I knew you wouldn't be there if I gave you a chance. Sighs.... I will forgive it. But I will never be that stupid again. No matter what you think of me at the end of the day, I have learned a lot more than I dare to say aloud. Sometimes karma doesn't have a tiny, sweet hand to smack you in the face with! I do!

Yeah. I write things off a lot. Especially things I never even wanted. Your life seems made for you not me... too normal. Your insecurities tell me more than anything I asked directly. You play and I watch. I wait. I will not ever forget you. You retaught me lessons my step-father started teaching me back when. How ironic--the people I loved most fondly while I grew up could be grouped into the same category as my step dad. I never saw that coming. Really. I wonder what kind of life anyone could have with someone who does the shit (like online bullying and ignoring me forever) they do? *shakes my head and laughs because it doesn't really matter to me. I have miles to go but not with any of them.

It's My Life—No Doubt

Same date, different writing.

--I pulled the dagger from my body and asked the goddess-es gentle forgiveness. I pushed it into myself to still the heart that betrayed me every day. Finally, the anguish over things I can't change, leaves. She whispers to me,

"Yes. THEY may not forgive you, but I do. I will give you the peace to get through this. They gave you away and that means you are free. Live little child of the woods and waters and know you won't be alone, forever."

My tears meant SOMETHING after all this.

081213

I walk quietly. I am thinking too deeply. I'm in a dream, again. WAIT. This is reality? Why are the people still looking at me? Like I don't belong. Do I not belong here, either? Like everywhere else? I put on my worn tennies and go outside with no purpose.

So hard to keep being me when I could just be someone else. If this is reality, it will kill me.

SO WHAT--Pink

081213

It's a dark day, brother. All the love is still dying. I felt it less back then. Do you remember my fifteenth birthday? We were already on our own for all the parenting we had. We thought we were already grown-ups. Life stretched endlessly. We lived each second fearlessly. You will always be my brother. There was never one who looked out for me in those last years like you did. We ran the town when we were young and partied and gave all the best we had to give—just to fucking live. You told me things I keep inside...Remember never let them tame you. Always hold a demon and an angel. Flip a coin if you don't know. So, it's always fair either way. Just give it all you have to give.

I'd give anything to just remember how to live.
Eighteen and Life—Skid Row
Thunderkiss '65—Rob Zombie
Darius Michael's.

081213 0351p

It seems weird to wish I was human. Laughs a little. My time here teaches me that I can't join the club with no references. It cracks me up to think I would want that, anyway. I wonder what other people wish for in the dark when they are most themselves? I used to think it was love. A man. But I don't know anyone who lays alone in the dark and wishes he was with me. I hear these words so "full of meaning" but really, they are only full of motives I can't comprehend. Words fail. Can you be an adult and let me go? Or are there more laughs to be had yet?

This Is Gospel—Panic At the Disco

Cain's.

081613

Her bright eyes long for a sweet word or kind touch. It makes her do the bidding of heartless others. While she struggles to right the wrong inside herself, she grows up. Elusive, of course. He doesn't appear because he doesn't think she is ever worth it. He seeks other arms. She grows and it shows him he doesn't own anything—least of all her. He laughs at her and tells each love to go away. They do and she is alone. If there is no love, why should she stay here?

Hair of the Dog--Nazareth

Rainen's.

081813

I am remembering that dumb little uncompromising twit, all romantic and idiotic. It is hard to relate her to this me, now. Never change but let the world affect you because otherwise you aren't human, right?

It never mattered that I shared the deepest parts of myself with him. He used all the secrets against me. A moment of reality along with beauty? Compassion... It seems so hard to get from him. I can love him all I want, it won't make me any closer to love. He doesn't love me and I get that so much more than people think. In suffering, there is truth. I didn't want any more pain but perhaps I learned the lesson well enough, now. I am sort of full up on truth. I would like to see true beauty in this life. Not cute looks. Not pretending to love. Not bullying in the guise of love. I don't need a dad. I never had one and it didn't do all that much really. I gave myself the pep talks and I did my own encouragement and support through tough times.

I just need a nice garden where my flowers will bloom. I need a nice quiet place to write and a very lovely place to watch my children fulfill their potential. I want rain. Every damn day. I would like that place to be obnoxious and big and have too much property. Ha-ha. I'd love to sit around in my chonies and smoke a bowl in the nice rain.

Not earth shattering wants and needs. I can make those happen, right? Do you know what it's like to have a dream fuck with you? Love is a later deal for me. Being the only freakin dream that seems hard, I might go after it last. It really does scare the shit outa me.

It is a little daunting to think no man will know he is in love with me until he fucks it up forever. What a joke. I am worth the risk when it comes to love. No big deal that the others around me have no idea of what love is. I mean I don't exactly either, but I know it's not middle of the night calls from a pissed off ex.

I didn't do a thing to you and I don't care anymore if I did. Fuck you, if you don't like me. I am a person and obviously, you will find your way eventually and without my shabby heart's help. I am not sure you deserved the first chance I gave you. I don't care to try to protect you from your karma. I hope it isn't too bad on you. These things tend to go badly for some. Shakes my head and hurts a little. I am here though. On a phone, only, but I can do that. I have been saying new blessings so it maybe doesn't happen that way. I also have been trying to spend less time in real life talking to you, since I am probably part of that.

Sadly, the best feeling I have had in all these years was when I was so tired and down in 2010. I was sitting in the living room all by myself and had given the littlest her midnight feeding some time back. I sat really worrying over my broken heart and wishing I had just walked away. I wept bitter tears and reassured myself that if I wanted to have that good life, then I was on my way.

The first step was to be discontent with second best anything. I was really grieving for the things I had never even known I wanted. A life of art and beauty for myself. A life that included not wanting for food or the small necessities that other girls never asked for but instead expected. Like clothes and pretty houses. I can get these things for myself. I knew even then. But I wanted a man who wanted to give me those things. So, I felt a little sorry for myself. I was as low as I got. I had my earbuds in listening to my iPod. Suddenly, the song I was listening to turned waaaayyyy up, and I felt a hand on my shoulder. I turned expecting to see Rainen and instead there was nothing. I was shaken by the experience and went to bed to process it. The next day was changed and so was the rest of my life. I know there was a desert shadow that wanted me but I was determined to make my way. So that next day I chose the way I wanted to go and we went.

That is why the other day when I said I felt a touch on my arm in the night, it was jarring for me. I am not a big believer in what I can't see. I don't usually put much stock in ghost stories. Nor do I think this was one. But I did write of it often. And then feel and hear more from the shadowy...what would I call him? Apparition? Maybe that's why it is so easy to discount the people who screw with me. I just keep thinking of this guy who is waiting for me and loving me and knows how low I have been. Not only knows but has helped to lift me when I was. I bet no one knew and so they thought naturally I did everything for them. Rainen thinks. Cain thinks. I have my faculties and I am going exactly where I said I would. To the top. It doesn't even matter, Cain, if I am in NM or Oregon or Texas or China or Portugal or Australia. I will make it to the top no matter what I do or where I go. And Rainen—can't snap sexy fingers and call me back now... that, my friends, is why I didn't worry about either of your asses. I know what love isn't. Do you think love sits idly by and waits for some reason to fall in love with someone it KNOWS is all wrong? Or do you think it is on the wind and looking every moment for that one girl who doesn't need to change...she possesses the qualities love is looking for.

So, a phantom, shadow, or mirage-whatever word YOU want to make fit—showed me in brief seconds what I have waited lifetimes to hear from a real person: my sadness is not something I should have to bear alone. Even if that is the only way I know. And it is so great a sadness. Intense and shaking. Still I should probably quit feeling sorry for myself and do something, right? The universe can be beautiful even if looks ugly in the daylight. Three forty-eight in the morning is the time I find beauty. I am on a mission to make a life for my daughters. I won't quit. I know love is a dream, but my daughters will be prepared to live it at least.

I am eternally grateful to a shadow who showed me something like love in my damnedest hours. I wonder if he is as lost as I am?

Living Dead Girl—Rob Zombie

Rainen's and Cain's. Laughs. And more so, the shadows.

082013 1122p

This feels like a vague fucked up dream. Reality doesn't even try to intrude. It was only a spirit, Tabitha. He can't be with you anymore, whoever he was. Why is it that he is the hardest one to get over?

I feel like retreating into myself and my new dream. It is a nice escape now, while I am so tired from all the work and the hateful people I must deal with and be nice to each day. I am exhausted from the things Rainen could do but spitefully won't. I am so... weary. What does it matter if I leave this beautiful state? I will tell you. Oregon is a fairy tale come true. A place I could go and hide away in the rain and the lovely.

I know I don't want to go back to NM. Not for the reasons everyone that knows me might think either. I just didn't like being somewhere that the people could say that I wasn't worth the time or effort to either know or get to know. Well, I WAS fat and broke.

See, I get so tired of the "what can Tabitha do to win herself a friend?" game show. I know they all USED to have souls. And they used to care about things beyond themselves. And they even, SOME OF THEM, used to care about me. I can't be the only person on earth who is like this. Even if it feels like I am EXACTLY the only person and I am being stupid when I reach out for humanity time and time again. They sort of smack my hand down each time I do. No big deal. I am a "tough bitch" as I have heard a thousand times from a thousand people who hurt me and thought I should "get over myself". I get over things in a strange way these days. I don't look back. I have tried and tried but I don't have the capacity to.

I think anyone would be tired of the attitudes that I encountered all my life. I don't want what I can't have, people. Your friendships are something I couldn't have had even if I did want them. Which mostly I didn't. I understand what makes you behave the way you all do. I just refuse to try to FORCE any more meaningful connections with people.

Why did he do it? He knows I am alone. I hurt him, but I have been paying my entire life and I am too tired to pay any more debt that isn't even mine. He got everything he ever wanted after I left, right? I can't pay for everything, anyway. I am not Jesus or anything.

Some people leave and it's a bright shot of light, right? I hope so. I meant for it to be. So, go head for your light and be whatever you need to be.

Headed for the Light—Tom Petty and the Heartbreakers Cain's.

082013 1229a

You were always mine and I was always yours. But faint heart never won fair lady.

I don't remember who I wrote this for. Maybe it was just a beautiful beginning to a story...

082213 1126p

Can I watch this train wreck? Can I distance myself from it? I don't think I should believe the words from those lips. I know I will hear a bad lie. I have been thinking of that shadow-weird thing. Do you think I will even know who he is if I see him tomorrow? Laughs unexpectedly. I am changing so much that I don't recognize myself. Will he know me? I hope I am not believing a lie when I think I am strong enough to get through this. I hope I don't always have to live lonely. I am ready to stop suffering. I am alive and doing the best I can. I had to watch Rainen run around and pick up girlfriends. The one girl was so bold as to come into the college bookstore and tell me about her relationship with Rainen. It was hurtful and I spent the entire time forcing myself not to cry. It was quite hard. She laughed on her way out and swirled her little skirt around her tiny hips and danced out of the place. A coworker watched me breathing in and out very hard and not returning to work and asked me what was going on. I managed to ask if she would cover me while I went to the break room and freaked out. Bless you, Tran. I cried for a minute and then I pretended like nothing happened. I didn't tell Rainen because I know what he was doing. Trying to make me jealous when I am going through hell trying to love and care for you, you heartless man?? Hilarious.

Fields of Gold--Sting

083113 0539a

Another letter. Your lie is breaking me to pieces. No glass heart here. But still you persist. It won't be hard to forget me. So why don't you get started on that right NOW?!
Living on the Edge--Aerosmith
Cain's.

083113 0526p

I am lonesome right now, Rainen. I feel like I wasted my most precious resource on this—time. You didn't have any for me. I knew this. I feel like I haven't seen a bright spot in life in a while.
NONSENSE. I see my girls. That's a relief in my bleak mood. I am OK.
--And Rainen, why go back to being your same charming self as always? You act like we should be besties now. No, you don't love me and you treated me like horrid shit for about five years but you think you and I are meant to be homies, now. You knew this would break me and then you set me up and knocked me down. You saw the shadow in my eyes. You feel like your life will be better without me right now but you are insane. I am the only reason you lived through this. You endured but I cared for every single need you ever had. I wonder what you will do if I am not there for anything anymore. I bet you will find life lonely too. I hope someone rescues you from the lonely feelings and saves your day. Too much to ask that you love me with truth.
Diary of Jane—Breaking Benjamin

083113 1025p

It's dark. I am by myself. I know this gets easier. I am worried it will overcome me. How hard will it be the next time someone wants me to say those stupid three words? I don't know if I can.

I am brave. I am honest. I fight for what's right. I defend those who need it. I want the world to have fire. All I needed was a chance. There was no hope for me in this. I have been alone. I watch the sun set from the tower and I am wilder. Harder to catch. Maybe impossible.

Her Ghost in the Fog—Cradle of Filth

Bullhorn: "Miss Ruslon, we know you think these people won't be missed when you throw your ginormous panties at them and break their little disturbed necks...that's not true. Leave them alone, Miss Ruslon! Put down the panties!" Crowd chants..."Throw them!"

090713

Wish in one hand, I create a new world with the other. What can I say to make you see I cared about you? I should leave anyway.

Good Girl Gone Bad-Rihanna

Rainen's.

090913 0356p

I am a girl. Not quite the same one I was. I know. You didn't ask. These are awful, bright, real streets in this indifferent city. I wish I knew how I made it this far. I didn't want to trade my quiet for violence. Truth threatens to flip me inside out. I am still myself. I am. I can't be anyone else.

Be Yourself--Audioslave

092413 1055p

When I was in the desert last, I was sure of one thing. I could not make it one more minute. You came in one low moment of doubt. It was the most alone I had ever felt. You came for me. I know I am not a princess. You turned up the music.

I held that ethereal two minutes to me all these years. I need something more than two minutes of no one. Tonight, I will go walk in the blue rain and wait until midnight to go back home.

Blue On Black—Kenny Wayne Sheppard

092413

Hey, Cain.

I was out in the crazy pouring rain today. It was so beautiful. I even thought about you for like a second. I wasn't worried when I ran out of minutes. I figure you don't talk to me when I have them and you can't talk to me when I don't, so what the hell does it matter. I haven't talked to you in a long fucking time. You should enjoy the break and I will not bother you for plenty of time so you can get some wonderful living done. I am officially in school. Second day. I was nervous. Now it seems dumb.

092613

All you have to do to be with me (someday when you really want to be-when you realize what you did was wrong.) is just close your eyes. I will be there like magic. I am sad for the lost time but I lived. It turned me into the woman I am and I am proud of that. The simple seconds did sparkle. I looked away when I saw what you were doing. The weeping world will wait.

Don't know who it was for...ambiguously worded...

Close My Eyes Forever—Lita and Ozzy

092813 1012p

I will meet a man both patient and understanding. I have waited for so long. I can't dream about you because I don't even know who I am dreaming about. I asked the universe for some sign but it doesn't tell me shit. Who are you and where are you now? Sorry to admit, the night of the loud music and the unseen hand freaked me out. It triggered a fight or flight response and I flew.

At least the man I thought I would be with forever has finally seen me for who I am rather than who he wanted me to be. That helps something but I am not sure what. Sort of a lose-lose thing.

It is beautiful in this place. I never want to leave. It doesn't seem like the people anywhere I go ever accept me. But I am sure not caring when it rains and I am in it. It is the most Zen thing I have ever experienced. I know-I know. You don't believe in that sort of thing. Well it gets me through the day here, so I DO.

What is real or right anyway? The clouds have gathered in a dark cluster to chit chat about how much rain to pour down on the little desert girl.

Bye, Cain.

Coming Clean—Hillary Duff (old version)

093013 0756a

Good morning, Mr. Texas.

It is WAY to fuckin early in the day for math. Also, battling hurricane force winds for a test seems excessive. I even wore my fuzziest socks!!

I hope you aren't under a blizzard warning in Texas. I didn't look but I am busy. Give me a minute for testing and I will be back when I am done k.

Wow. That was much easier than I thought. Whatya know, Benedict? Missed ya last night. My neighbor who is terribly weird but very sweet texted a ton and the whole evening was chock full of homework for me, anyway. I like talking to you, though. I am ready to go out tonight but me being drunk doesn't guarantee I won't have to fight tonight, too. *eye roll. Oh well. My bus stop was closed due to the blizzardy cold and the weather warnings. So where do I get out....oh. My driver was so cool. Really, he didn't have to stop at all, till the next stop about a mile down the road. But he instead stopped me in a huge puddle in the middle of the street. That seems mean but it was nicer than me walking in the dark cold for another mile through many many puddles. So, here's to the driver that made my life colder but gave me a much shorter walk. I was up till almost two so maybe the cold water was what I needed. Or coffee...ha-ha. I gotta go take some math notes.

Bye

So Cold—Breaking Benjamin (hahahaha!!!)

Bullhorn-Officer Awesome, again: 'Miss Ruslon-is there no way to talk you out of this horrifying murder spree? Can we get you anything? Maybe a coffee? Your oldest daughter is here to talk you down, OK? Shuffles and Alyc's voice pipes in and screams, "Do it mom!! Throw them!!"

Bet you didn't expect that...

101613 1004a

Hey.

Was going to text you but I am sure I shouldn't. Even so, I did. I am sure if you had time and thought of me for one second, you would have texted me too. Ha-ha. Nah. You wouldn't have. You are a real piece of work. *shakes head because I knew better than to let myself talk to you to start. Sighs.

College is very demanding alternating with very boring. What an extreme range. You know you will never read these. There are just too many. I feel like a tree murderer. At least the paper was recycled and everything already.

I had to stay up late to color Alyc's hair. Hot ass pink. What other color is there? Laughing. She loves it and she is happy. All I wanted and worth it, then.

Just getting all energy drink-ed up for my keyboarding. Would rather be doing something more relaxing but what's more relaxing than making a good grade in college? Nothing, that's what. Chuckles with no real reason. It's NOT FUNNY.

I know you are (coughs out the word "bullshit") busy as you can be and I guess it mainly means too busy for ME. That is fine because like I said, it is funny for you to think of me over here and working my ass off while you and yours are all whatever over there in Texas. I don't want what she has, Cain. No matter how much glitter and bullshit you put on you, it isn't going to make me leave here for your little sancha-life. I don't want what I can't have. I like my own life even if it is hard as hell. I will be much happier doing things for myself. I know you think I can't do anything for myself or by myself but I AM.

Energy bux is bad for my head. I am going to do my class here.

Rock and Roll—Avril Lavigne

102513 1246a

I finally give in to the simplicity of the madness. In that instant, I am pulled away from all I was. I don't want to let them see me cry. I am grieving. It is a weak moment. I am strong. I am not even worried about the stupidity. I while away the small hours writing about nothing. I just have to make it to sunrise. I will be OK.

Jay-Z (feat. Linkin Park) --Encore

For the girls. I didn't want them to know how bad I felt that day...

102513 0100a

I'm tired. I can still feel the rain. It's not far. I am sad. It doesn't feel impossible. The dawn is coming. Look one moment past the pink-hued clouds. Today is the day. That door has been locked but now it is standing there wide open. I don't know why I ever wanted to go in before. The ghosts will chase me—even find me. What can they do to me? I buried them a long time ago. My moon will always rise. And tonight, it did again.

No Rain-Blind Melon

No date

It's another letter I won't send. To interrupt. I know why you want a minute with me. It isn't to wake joy in yourself or me. I know why I give you a minute. I worry over your stupid soul. I won't chase you anymore though.

Runaway Train—Soul Asylum

Cain's.

102913 1141p

This place glitters in the moonlight when it rains. I feel an almost magnetic pull from the forests around here. Like I can't stay inside or I will die. I want to feel the cold wind and the bright rain on my face. He might look for me when I am gone. I know him pretty fucking well. He won't.

Trouble in mind, I'm blue. But I won't be blue always...

Rainen's.

120513 0103p

I remember laughing and fighting like it was yesterday. Ha-ha. It was. If you think I don't remember who you are—really are—then you must be crazy. You got what you needed. You are so happy, right? I am glad my leaving made your day so much brighter. As it was intended, so long ago. You don't need me and I don't need you. You keep telling yourself that you got me. I waited for you to show your humanity. A kind word, which cost you nothing. But I am not worth it. You treated me just as much like shit as he did. So, you remember this, asshole: I am not your girlfriend either. That sort of makes me dangerous. I know who I am, too.

Forget It—Breaking Benjamin
Cain's.

120513 0911p

I have never let that idea sit in my mind for even one half a second, Cain. You never have given me a reason to believe a word you say. You are still waiting for the finale. I am almost sure you hate me. Does your soul match your eyes? Yes, and they are both cold. I will find peace without you. Blaming others for your life when you value it so much, makes you seem ungrateful I passed from your life.

Behind Blue Eyes—The Who

120513

The formula sets itself inexplicably. (No one even NOTICED!) I reinvented myself. I was more me with Rainen than I ever was with anyone else. I know what we could have been. I know what we still are.

I did walk to the woods and wilds. I love this wild inside me. I love that I am still alive. It matters because I have great things to accomplish yet. I am nothing in your world, probably means we don't need to worry about the little...whatever this all is. My list shrinks each time I pull it out.

Toxic—Brittany Spears
Rainen first, then Cain.

120513 0957p

You two boys can walk away, and not worry about looking back. One never cared anyway and the other will be sure to know where I am. I am walking away from the both of you, cold as I can be...the endless hours walking in rain soaked streets too lovely to express... I can't feel warm anymore. Something that didn't concern me. I told you both the words, even though the dreams told me what you each would do. You both lost my respect. I feel like it's fine since time always finds us. Even you two.

S&M--Rihanna

Cain's and Rainen's.

120513 1201a

You should take the words I wrote for you and walk away. I gave them to you so you would hurry your little revenge faster. I would have given you the paintings too, but you acted like my art was nothing. Like it meant nothing. So, I took them and burned them. They were worth much more than your "loan". I am past it and you can call me back as many times as you like now. Once its burned, it's gone. You will remember these days with regret sometime soon, my pseudo-friend. I am counting on you to bring my face up in your mind a million times after. Easier to be too far for you to come see me at all. Then we know you won't and I won't have to hear you lie and say you want to see me. Goodbye and all my smiles for your abilities to forget me- just like before.

Insert blue-eyed revenge poem

Cain's.

--I discovered I didn't write it down. Or if I did, I sure as hell tore up the original. Laughs at my awesomeness...I knew my words meant something but he is the only person who knows what the words are or meant. I hope you are good with the fact you erased it.

012913 1100p

I am trying to take this pain and make it something more. I can't sleep and I spend a lot of time scared. I wish I didn't need his love. That I didn't need him. If I didn't need him so much I could just let something go. Why fight me? Because I didn't do what I was told? He just started to hate me and to live for punishing me. I didn't put him in pain. He did. Live with that and don't make me regret all the care and time and love I have wasted. I am so angry at myself for not seeing him how he was. Truly he is a fantastic liar. I want more than this. I am speaking silently and only the rain can hear me, anyway. I love you, fucking Rainen.

Promises--Clapton

Rainen's.

021213

He is only a man. Sometimes scary sometimes sacred. I let him hold me down. When he kisses me, it feels like he owns every bit of my soul. Those words whispered so no one hears... no, he isn't ashamed, I am. His hands are like marble and I start to feel his underlying meanness for me. My heartbeat speeds. I don't recognize this chaotic rhythm. My voice breaks and I know he isn't playing anymore.

--For Rainen. I started to feel like the crazy stuff we used to do in the bedroom was easy-freaky compared to how it turned out. I knew he wouldn't remember much of it due to the overwhelming number of meds he was on and so I did what I could to make sure he was satisfied in that department. It seemed the least I could do for him during the bullshit we both were going through. I loved him fiercely. I did handle some things I didn't have experience with when it came to the violence. I did realize his openness to my off the wall suggestions before had paved the way for this. I did NOT think I deserved it or brought it on myself. I examined the facts I knew and decided I could handle it. I was after all a survivor of much worse from way back. Sometimes I found I could control the rhythms enough to make them easier on me. I didn't know how to de-escalate that but I did learn quite a lot through this experience. He wasn't actually aware of some of it. I don't believe it was all due to the meds though. He knew sometimes. And he felt triumphant for getting away with it, too. I saw, Rainen.

Pain—3 Days Grace

I Like It Rough—Lady Gaga (ironically...)

060713

I don't know what determines if you have a soul or not. Just the act of living could mean you have a soul—spirit to animate the body. But what about the fire within you that moves your world. Where is it and does it die if you live in chains too long? I still search for answers I cannot ever hope to know.

There are no familiar faces in these dreams these day. I saw yours. But I am almost sure it doesn't count since you are far when I see you and you don't ever appear to be coming closer. Doing nothing is a choice, too. Your presence used to comfort me, you know.

I always questioned people having souls when they acted like a tool. And he did. Each time he communicated with me he chose to show me how he had lost all his humanity in his casual attitude. I did nothing but think of my child before his feelings. But since I thought of her before I thought of myself even, I figured everyone saw this and knew I was in mom mode. There would be no joy for me in this relationship. No, he took it personally and decided to come for me with both barrels blazing. It is a law that if you cause a divorce in the great state of NM you can be sued for it. I wonder if Cain knows... maybe he wouldn't have wanted me so close if he knew. I doubt he thought through a goddamn thing he was doing. Just take a drink and think of other ways to make Tabitha feel slighted or whatever. I am nothing if not a practical creature. I never thought for one minute he would dare to drop down and try to act like he loved me. I know he is on a mission of doom for me and mine. It seems like he would just sit down like a man and talk it through so he and I could both move on in some semblance of healthy normalcy. He does LOVE talking about how normal he is. My house calls normal "fro-yo Tuesday, minivan driving, spin-class wifey, and missionary." Very god-damned vanilla. Well I am no vanilla. Ha-ha. He thinks I can gain nothing from this because he is bullet-proof. I hope that he is sure. Because sometimes things creep up on us unawares and we find ourselves tied to our own stupidity. I mean, not me. Not on this one. But he should eyeball his situation once or twice and see what appears.

Remember the Name—Fort Minor

021113

Dreams fall dreadfully short of reality. Things change too much. There are so many times I know magic happened and then the morning dawns and the sun reminds you that you hate me. I need some reassuring touch but I guess that can wait. No undoing the words now. No unsaying them. I spend serious time searching for this shadow in my dreams. I am not even sure if he exists.

La Isla Bonita--Madonna
Rainen's and the shadows.

012913 0756a

. Good morning. Another letter to someone I won't give it to. Rainen.

I didn't mean to intrude on your awesome sleep. I wish I ever had dreams I wanted to stay in. My dreams took me back over sixteen hundred miles to Oak Street, of all the stupid plac-es. I don't know what peace I was looking to find there. Maybe it's sort of like revisiting a murder scene for clues. Maybe. I could still smell blood. I wish I could leave my bloody dreams and go into yours where I could lay down in some green grass under some rain and just let my nightmare fade away. You did bring me to Oregon which was a great adventure and I got to have some peace despite you. I wish this love was real.

--Maybe the love was and is real. It was on my part any-way. He tells me still of his love. And how he knows he threw it away. I am glad he understands why I am doing what I am. I also hope Cain knows that despite all that, when Rainen gets something in his head, he is single-minded and I wouldn't swear that Cain had seen the last of him.

And I will laugh if after I am gone, Rainen sees a way to make sure he learns something about himself. He did quite a lot of helping the relationship to disintegrate. And yes, I take my responsibility. I always have made sure I take my part of blame. But he knew good and well he was doing this to say that his marriage is stronger than we were. Yes, Cain. For if she knew, she would surely stay with you. She would say, "You tore apart a relationship for your own selfish desire to say you are better? That seems like you want to deny you still feel about that girl."

I bet I would divorce you quick-sticks. Chuckles. I can't imagine any woman wants to know the man she is with is a damn fool who would throw away his own family for revenge on a broken and damaged girl. I'm sure she might be stupid enough to forgive you—you married her and she probably thinks your love is forever. Laughs...call me again, Cain. Do it. I laugh because you think I am stupid and I have been onto you from the first fucking message.

Talk about your not knowing about someone by now!

111413 1210a

Before you got started, couldn't you have quit. Before you thought to break my heart one more time, couldn't you have remembered who I am? I don't want you to leave your life for me. Nor would you. I don't want you at all. You gave yourself to me in the smallest way possible. My life is my choice.

Hit Me Baby, One More Time—Brittany Spears (say what-cha want about her, that chicky knows what's up.)

--Remember Tabitha. If he was hateful before, he won't change. Maybe he will even get worse!! Cain. Who else.

010513 0838p

I sometimes think Rainen is a wondrous creature. He manages to spew hateful language without choosing his words or thinking at all. He's sure to keep me hanging on if possible. He wants the idea of me still. I am already half-dead these days. I used to laughingly refer to myself as the living dead girl. I feel a little lost with the weird way my day goes sometimes. I think of the people who could do something if they knew but I never said anything. What would I say that would gain me any peace? I am gentle but not because I must be. Because I used to be something I didn't like and I decided to change it. I hope you can manage to be that noble person for SOMEONE someday. It couldn't be me. You don't have to lie, anymore. I don't care if you are telling the truth, now. Just go and be the best you can be, Rainen. I wanted you to be happy. Even if it isn't with me.

Say My Name—Destiny's Child

012913 1240a

I usually do show too much of myself. I won't be likely to ever forget this. If I could kill these little parts of me, I would. I am on this mission to love this world and it really gives little reason for it. I know. As always, the good things are hidden and unexpected.

I don't want one more fake. I am ready for the alone. I have felt alone in groups and in places I should never feel alone.

I don't know what would be so bad about loving someone like me.

Nothing is bad about loving someone like me. I am a very nice adventure. Laughs and tells it like it is.

Freedom—George Michael

Purple Rain--Prince

012413

I have hope but I sometimes still feel like I might not be adjusting too well. I feel like I am losing the magic in me. I don't want to sit all alone and wish for the things I want anymore.

Life didn't have to live up to any expectations but I think I can say with some certainty that I am finished sitting suffering for some ideal of how it should be.

I am not sitting anymore. I will keep going no matter what and moving on to the next adventure I want to live. Not for a man, mind you, but with the intent of learning and growing and doing something real.

Sexyback—Justin Timberlake

012413

This cold walk is killing me. I keep being myself. Even if he thinks he can make me regret all I am. Clearly, he sees what he is doing. Pick my punishment, judge and liar.

My little flowers have bloomed here and that is after all, why I came. So, let's not play like you gave a damn, okay.

Shambala—Three Dog Night

Rainen's.

010513

The new year's sunrise brings me some hope for myself and those I love. I wish you gave your love to some other girl. You instead chose to betray every day. All because you had no will to say, "My feelings have changed." A man could have easily recognized how this could benefit everyone.

Not Afraid--Eminem

Rainen's.

040413 0146p

I am taking some pointless walk through the nice slow rain. I came here and looked for myself. I found her. Today matters. My hopes and dreams matter. Arguing today matters. Makes me uncomfortable.

I take one more walk through the cherry blossoms sweet smell and little pink petals. I know for sure this day matters. I kept my promises. My words stay and my promises are real.

I fight for my truths.

Love Me or Hate Me—Lady Sovereign

041613

Cain-

You mean more to me than I am willing to admit to you freely. What a fun joke the whole entire thing turns out to be. The next time I switch phones I will decide when I talk to you again. And it won't be soon. Chuckles...

I am funny, so why can't you come by and smoke a bowl and be sociable. Not invade my privacy and just try to make me feel like shit. Funny. If you kick the girl you used to love when you see her already down—you might be a passive-aggressive-bully-dick. I bet she is wise enough to see you coming and decide her own plan and fate before you get there. Luckily, I was working on my life for quite a little while before you came to tell me how beautiful I was. Thoughtful but unnecessarily simple. Did it work on the last girl? Or did we still think I was 16 and sweet? I sometimes wish I were.

And yes. I genuinely thought I was in love with Rainen. Too bad he is so far from finding himself. I guess we all have a path. I want a person next to me for the ride. I can find someone who will find life better and more interesting with me in it. I am not a weird enough person that I need to be locked away unloved and alone.

One friend is not too much to ask. I shouldn't have to pay

with anything. My body, my sanity, OR anything else.

Down With the Sickness--Disturbed

041513 0400p

You will never know the hope you took with you the day I fell apart. You stormed angrily away and peeled out of the driveway of the little blue trailer. He knew I loved you and he was keeping you and I apart. It was funny to him until he had to deal with me every day. I was still joyful and always loved my child.

You and I dreamed of life beyond this. I never saw your vision, because you didn't like to talk about it. Just vague promises I could see were fast fading for you. I wanted all of you but not your hate. I knew he already resented me. I didn't know if I could handle raising a baby or not. I didn't want a man that would lie and make me feel alone. But I have been on a repeating loop since then. I don't want it back. I can't have it if I did want it. But I gave you up that night, fully. I told myself I was done feeling sorry for myself and I would make the best of every day so I could make a life for my baby. Whatever life that turned out to be.

I missed your sure arms around me. I knew I could do anything with you. But I knew how I saw the child change the relationship with him—and it made me scared for what you would do to hurt me if I said yes. Some proposals might feel fake or forced if they do not get made for the right reasons. Many men have asked me to marry them. I didn't do much for there always seemed an underlying reason. Shouldn't it be JUST for love? I mean, if it's real. And going to last.

I won't forget because to forget is to repeat the past. But I also won't forget how your gentle treatment of me wasn't very goddamned gentle. I am not your woman, but I am a human being. I deserve to be treated like one.

Have your life. Leave me out of it if you can't be civil. Really civil.

Civil War—Guns n Roses
Cain's.

041613 1200a

I am thinking about my whatever you want to call her. I used to call her my best friend. I would never do that again. She is sitting somewhere drunk and with twenty-five people just laughing her night away. I don't begrudge her anything. Even now-I will admit she works hard. I don't care if she does, it still isn't right the way she treated me as a girl. I am grateful to her mother and father most of all. I know she doesn't want to think they cared about me. I did hear them call me a stray dog many times. I never called them on the crap because I had already been called so much worse in my house. I loved her like a sister I got to hand pick. I don't feel like I deserved any of the rough treatment her and HER friends gave me over the years.

And I feel now they missed a great thing by pushing me away. I guess they can figure out their own shit. Someday maybe they will evolve. I sure did miss having someone around me that cared. But it was only a lie after all. I shouldn't be so hurt. *shakes my head at the mean and hateful.

073013

I dreamed I was looking down at the power lines, flying over the tops of the tall pines. I feel the holiness of the snowfall from up on the heights. My heart is beating loud enough to consume us all. I know without a doubt that I am on my way.

These times without strengthened me and made the grateful me you see now. You can see inside the walls but that doesn't mean you learned anything about me. I left it all behind for the reasons I have stated. There was no love nor life for me or mine in this place. I told you I wouldn't be here long and you didn't listen. I am not running, but rather walking a very simple path to where I want my girls to be. I doubt my hard decisions but I know they are right in the light.

Your cool glances from the porch were something to behold. I didn't try to read them for that way lay madness. The rain felt almost too unreal. Did you plan for me to be there during the rain? Maybe. I tried to take nothing from the time we spent, since you and your time weren't ever mine to begin with. A sense of the shadow in your eyes. A strange thing for me to see. You were a powerful force. I know you hold more than I saw. Or see. You hid well.

More Human Than Human—White Zombie

Cain. One of the very best liars in the world.

073013

Your eyes seemed afraid. My eyes weren't the blue you remembered. You had both remembered me and forgotten me at the same time. I tried to remind you of other things.

The lightning was a nice touch. The rain made me quiet for a minute. I would have gone outside alone. You didn't have to come. It was MY rain, not yours.

Art is a tool of war. --Picasso

Cain.

090113 0916a

I had to unlearn certain things I held to be truth from my childhood. The entire childhood was a study in futility. I had a hard time keeping myself to a code. Truth became important and not just truth but truth told with an honest and kind soul. One should be kind-not a hateful douche. Sorry—raised by wolves my Aunt says. Ha-ha. I hope I am well understood when I use my language. I am a creative speaker, so when I use the term, it must mean the term applies...Auntie.

There is greatness in me. I know no one saw and identified it within me, but I did know my potential from early. I guess I took a cue from my mother after all. She spent so much time looking for love she forgot to live. I have broken the cycle already. I believe in my girls. They share a desire to make life new and amazing. We all do things each day to make it happen.

A figment of a memory inspired me to put my positive words on this so his words can't tarnish my effort. I am keeping to what I always have. I am capable and overqualified.

Men. Sheesh. Act like boys and then get mad when you call them on it.

100613 0107a

Come walk with me into a rain soaked field--into the deep grasses...it is dark in the moonless night. A dreaming god's silver rain pours onto the earth... bathe in the beauty of the dream...
The Briar and the Rose—old Celtic ballad
Just for me.

111413 1215a

I want to make the old me go away, sometimes. I would like to be able to see my soul as good, one day. I just stay on the path I had planned. Nothing sets me back. I can be seen, if someone cared to look. I mean from your own eyes, and not a screen that seems to lie of its own accord. You don't know me and what I have to live every day to get by. You don't know who I am and what makes me strong either. So how about you don't talk to me and lose my name. I don't need such bullshit in my life. I can do it on my own. Without love or tough love or hate or whatever you bully-dicks want to call it. But please remember to fuck off.
Cyberbullies suck ass.
Stand By Me—California Raisins
Same date 1220a

I love the dark. Moonlight seems like a vague way to call attention to everything I look at. I walk slowly on the wet grass. I open my eyes and look right up into the rain. I feel joy from this simple interaction. My icy body doesn't register the cold. Nor does my cooling soul. You hurt me with your broken promises.

Alibis--Clapton

Rainen's.

081913 1122p

I love the moon from afar. I can leave her. I wish for love and at the same time release the dream so I don't hurt myself too soon with this. I let it go and the chains fall away. I made my way out. I struggled for a while. You helped a little, though I walked the miles. I made a promise. To him first and then to you. I don't have to honor promises to people who take advantage. Nonetheless, I kept them both.

I can arise and take what's mine. I climbed and as I climbed I became charged with electricity and fire. I walk alone and crackling like crazy. Now it's all about what I want.

--First time I have had a dream like this in a very long time. It makes me catch fire when I wake I am not the same person. I understand I will be doing some very great things soon.

Lose Yourself--Eminem

Cain's and Rainen's.

120513 0920p

I am balanced but you should learn when to leave well enough alone. I know you never planned to love me. I know you don't have the patience to be with me. I know you aren't free to be with me. Now we can agree this is all wrong. I don't care what you want anymore. Your love is only the same as his. Designed to hurt. Keep it. I will be peaceful and quiet somewhere.

Shut Up and Drive--Rihanna
--Went back and forth here between Rainen and Cain. Laughs because I can only tell a little I wasn't talking about the same man. Shit. Hope neither is too mad about that. Behavior is so key. Feels like I expected it of Cain, with no surprise and didn't expect it at all from Rainen.

120513 1013p

I don't feel alone when I am by myself ,anymore. It is strange for me. I don't want to care about your heart. You have it all, right? I stand by all my choices. Even the wrong ones. At least you finally went towards your life instead of trying to hurt me. I imagine you will show up when I start getting serious about someone. I won't be so easy to reach next time. And you only have the power I give you, right.

Silly Cain. Remember I can only be me. It's not quite like it seems.

120613 0303p

One more letter you don't need. See? These fuckers were firewood the whole time. And you don't know I write you so I feel like who cares. Ha-ha. Rainen loves to fight over whatever he can. You and your texts, that mean literally NOTHING to you, mean the world of war to him. I appreciate you being hateful and acting like that is love. I get your little stupid lesson. I do. I mean, I am not ever going to do anything because you think I should. Whether or not you are right, you have no idea what goes on here with he and I. We were in love and you now say that you love me when it is so obvious you don't. Remember that no matter where I am, I am never at STUPID. At least Rainen deserved to have my undying loyalty. I would know the dif by now. Just because I am alone doesn't mean I am desperate to believe YOU.

Am I left behind? Gods- I fucking hope so.

Far Behind—Candlebox

Chalk Outline—3 Days Grace (man that singer is yum yum yummy! He is my other-other husband, you know!) too bad about the neck snapping on stage incident with that one crazy big girl. Hahahaha!!!

021714 0924a

I am walking through an icy storm. I just can't see what will light the way. I create something you can see and learn from. And I give it to the broken billions. See if they can feel it, since I am so cold these days. Let it be what stirs my blood or maybe the mud in my veins.

I will let them call me whatever they need to. I will let them be certain in their stupid assumption. There is my garden full of trees. My peace. Thundering thoughts asking me who I am looking for.

Killer of Giants--Ozzy

--I don't think I am looking anymore. That's ironic and funny to me. I just keep seeing myself while rereading these entries. I wonder why it took me so long to be done.

021714 1000p

I have both created and destroyed myself a million times in a million different lives and with a million different methods. Ultimately no one can decide my fate but me. I am one of the six that saw. I am the only one it happened to. I know what happened. No one else.

I am alive still and for once, I am walking ahead of the dreams. It's incredible to just not know for a few minutes.

Lighters—Bad vs Evil feat. Bruno Mars

Just for little old me.

041014

My chin is tilted up and I am alone. My strength doesn't mean much at three a.m. I can only run so far. If I let it all out and set myself free-I won't be the same. These responsibilities are what keep me from being that woman I grew up with. They keep me working towards my goals and moving in the right direction. I wonder what I will think when I look back in two more years and see this.

Riot—3daysgrace

Just for myself. I was reminding myself to remember who I am and why I came so far. I can do it again. In fact, I am.

041014

The days I wasted I have to make up for. They are hounding my quick steps. I am fully running now, and no one sees it. I was asked to teach and now I am. I have to go get the lost minutes back. I am running to always stay in my own good graces. I will pluck the best of my dreams from the top shelf and I will have them, I will live them. I will work and be fulfilled. I can appreciate myself now.

Bloodsugarsexmagick—Red Hot Chili Peppers

I knew I would teach only for a time and then go on to the next thing on my list. I just know I have a limited time to make these dreams happen. I am on it.

041014

I ran like so many other artists and poets before me. To the woods and waters wild. I walked reverently barely daring to step on the green and springy moss. I listened to the wild winter creek making loud murmurs. She drowned out my own thoughts and pulled me to her. She felt as abandoned as I did. The trees petted her sky gently and whispered simple platitudes to her sad soul. Her patient forests wait for me.

Naturally—Selena Gomez

--I never could get over the beauty and joy I felt at the forests in Oregon. I love the enchanting desert's sparse and delicate beauty. I can appreciate something more because I grew, here in the enchantment of this desert.

041114

I have so little time and now I can't complain. I have grabbed time by his slow ass hand and dragged him with me to ensure I get the list complete. I let him heal the wounds inflicted by this one's truth and that one's beauty. They will listen with breath held while I move from her shadow and closer to my light. I can live now. I am grateful to be back to myself.

I'm Me—Willow Smith

--All for me. I am not even worrying about anything anymore. Things come and go. I am one of them. Ah. I relax.

041114

Hello sunshine, my old companion. I needed to be a child of the rain. I ran to where the woods and waters met and felt peace for a moment. I used to feel left out and solitary. I don't feel so lonely with myself as company, now.

I search for truth by looking for love. I look out at the world you love and finally feel ready to conquer the place. Thanks for waiting.

I knew I could keep my joy through this. It was hard as hell, but I am a champion! Laughs and hears "Rocky" theme music.... funny picture of Tabitha all decked out in boxing gloves swiping the air before the match... Who said I couldn't kick ass? Laughs...

041114

How does a heart break? Shattering in the stillness into

vague shards of beauty. Burning with a fire we can't kill... when I thought to put it out, the dark ashes blow away with a puff of breath. Pierced with barbed arrows that stay and fester...ripped into unrecognizable shreds fluttering wildly in every breeze...broken and cracked like an unfortunate egg at a hurried breakfast...sliced open and dug out until only a husk remains...stabbed, until spent, you walk away...smashed by many bricks from an old torn down wall I once knew....

I would wake each day and sneak a look at Rainen's sexy sleeping face and just breathe in slowly and let it out... sometimes words were needed.

041214

He can break every rule, even my resolve. He laughs because he thinks I can't break things. I can of course. Not him. He didn't deserve it. All he wants is to feel excited and alive. No more tears for me. Time to go home.
Road To Nowhere--Ozzy
Rainen's.

041214

You knew you shouldn't -you know you will hurt me in the long run. But that's been the point, I suppose. To see how much it takes before I lose myself.
These Dreams—Heart?
Cain's. But I must say, knowing it was coming didn't make it easier. Thank my gods for sending the dreams. If I were unprepared, it would have been so much worse. I wonder sometimes if he ever sits in the dark and just wonders if I am OK. A normal thing. I do that for all the people I know. I wonder if he is so cold under all the reserved.

041514

I can't see beyond this one repeated moment. Let it go. Let him go. He's a good man. He's a joy -he's just not mine. I can be strong.

Rainen's.

041514

".... like water under a bridge...dirty, nasty water under a horrible bridge..." -Chuck Charles (Pushing Daisies-2007)
I heard this on Netflix one day and it made me think of you, Cain. Laughs. You were a bad example for me, there, sweetie. You forced my honesty. With myself and you. Thank you.

043014

Another come to save my little angels. I might not have love for my own heart but my girlies ARE life. I will never be far from joy and sunshine. You thought this would be a little laugh... Don't you love and treasure your children more than yourself? Don't you live to see them smile?

043014

You knew I was fragile. Why would it be fun to watch me hurt? Your laughter won't go on forever. You bleed too, I think. I didn't come back for you but you could have shown me I wasn't forgotten, as I did for you. I won't wait for you anymore. I know where I am going. No time for anymore play-ing around.
I love a lot about this world. I also know that I don't want exactly what you think I do. No one is paying attention and they have really been in possession of all the info from minute one. Utilize learning tools people.... Shakes my head because

too many will say they just didn't understand. I was plain.
Bad Company-Bad Company
Cain's mostly.

043014

Short note of thanks to myself for all the hard work I put in
on this killer revamp. I was lost and had to find my own way.
I never believe lies when I see them for what they are. Even if
they are told with silver lips.
You avoided a nightmare of your own. So, we are all happier, right. Go enjoy your life, would you? I am pleased you are
happy. It is inspiring to me to think I could be happy. Thank
you so much for the things I DID see you do to help every day.
Your Star--Evanescence
Rainen's.... Man, oh man.

050114

This flannel is something I won't wear again. I do believe
still but not because of you, anymore. I can't reconcile this,
Rainen. I wanna do more than just burn your sweater! Do
you ever decide to make me smile anymore? Or do we just
fight because neither of us is where we wish. I just wish I were
somewhere with no yelling.
How You Remind Me—Nickelback
Sweater--Weezer

050114

I only wanted friendship from you. I really did enjoy your
conversation. Whatever you may think, I was willing to be your
friend so we could have some small contact. And it doesn't
matter what you thought of me in my low times. I tried to still
be there for you and you hurt me by ignoring me like I meant
nothing while you knew Rainen was, too. That is forgivable

but I can't stay. You can have your bright future and I will have mine. I wish you ever looked back and saw me for who I really am. Not the bad press I get for the name I have. I tried to see you for who you were. Sorry it wasn't really worth anything to you. But I do think of you sometimes. As you are. Not were.

Killing Me Softly—Destiny's Child

Cain's.

050214

Never trust ME. One life to live. One chance at life. One time to prove it. Not to anyone else. To me.

Starstruck—3oh!3 feat. Katy Perry

050414

Dandelion puffs from the past. I wished over them. As they flew away, I never thought of them again. I never got to walk with faeries but I sure walked to the woods. I have been wild too long.

Where the Wild Things Are—Maurice Sendak

050514

For all the endless watching me, you failed to see what was going on. It was obvious. You wanted me to wait. Why? I don't know what you are about, anymore. I just wished you were the real Cain from long ago. The boy did grow up. I am just happy you did. And happy you did find light. It is worth having no matter what dream you go after in life.

No. I don't think you sold out. I heard those words from someone I knew, but I thought you went after love, which is what you always did. Have your dream and do your thing. I hope you do great things and your family gets to see what some of us already knew. That you are diverse and full of surprises.

The Only One—Melissa Ethridge (I fought for you and over you so many nights. He finally knows who you are to me—much different than anyone imagined...)

Goodbye, as usual.

050514

You feared me enough to shout at me about your weapons. To threaten me. In my hurt and sad state, you worried I needed to be yelled at about guns? Yeah. I guess I see where you think I am some beast. Whatever.

--When Cain could contain himself no longer and had to call drunk threatening to hurt me and Rainen, though we were split up. Rainen had indeed once said he would tell Cains wife if he didn't fuck off and leave us be. But Cain lied this time. Again.

Come As You Are—Nirvana

Irresistible—Falloutboy

050514

I don't need a visual of you standing between me and another one of your females. I am fierce and I have fought. I never threatened you or your peace. Please do me the fine courtesy of not threatening me or mine. I am a pretty understanding person. But I think you crossed the line. Could you please just leave me alone?

050514

I grasp the dandelion puff in both hands. I close my pale green eyes tightly over the wealth of tears held in too long. With a deep shaky breath, I blow the tiny helicopters away, like pieces of my soul being life-flighted out of here.

Time used to own me. Lately, I find I am time's biggest fan.

I never minded the quiet darkness. I survived on moonlight.

I watch these tiny wish-makers float into the rain and for one space in time it all makes sense.

Life is simple. This is what I found in my wishing. A happy little reminder lesson.

When Doves Cry—Ginuwine (cover)

050814

Desert flowers in full bloom subtly perfume the super heated air after flooding monsoon rains. The downpour brings all of life out of hiding and creates a brand-new melody in the eerie silence. Leftover storm clouds gently retreat to the edges of the horizon. The clean of the freshly washed sky stretches from me to oblivion. My ancestors pull me home with a small thrill: each bolt of lightning and deafening peal of drum-like thunder. I walk through the dusty mesquite patches in a state of enchantment.

(I wrote this while I was missing the desert in my poetry class. I wanted to let it out and I think I painted the picture for the class. A great group of poets, and a writer-professor. They were enchanted!)

050914

You brought me here. I challenged myself. I didn't complain, except to my paper in the night. I did what had to be done. I was burdened with sadness that made me dark. I won't need another monster or demon. Or love since that's what most of them turn out to be as well. The armor I need to survive your leaving isn't available. I see her on your face and smell her perfume all over you. Here I sit, worried about your feelings. You can manage.

--You could have stayed with her, Rainen. I would really have let you be. I bet you would have made her so happy for the time you let her keep you.

050914

I am watching the time slip quickly from ten to midnight. A muse by herself. Unasked but ready. My pen and brushes will not hold me back. They reveal deeper things. It won't hurt anyone to see some art, read some art. Am I so dangerous?

We all have the answer to that. Laughs at my very inspired art.

Counting Crows, "Mr. Jones"

Gray is one of my favorite colors, too.

050914

THIS is crazy. I keep listening to them go on about their life. They try to kill my importance. Why would anyone want to strip my life of its purpose? I can't believe they don't see me trying to make this ugliness into something beautiful. Something I can bear to see. These four beauties are all I have. You can watch the change. I have been asked to wait. I can't do it. I am kind not weak. I have already given you all the space you need. Just leave me alone. Let's pretend that Tabitha is still too fat to bother with. Please.

Faith—George Michael

Men don't want revenge on a scarred and damaged girl. What does it make you if you know someone is down and pull back to punch her?

050914

I have been carrying around a burden on my own shoulders. I am creating some beauty for myself and the world. They are all turned to stone while I sit and count raindrops.... Add all of this to my collection of things I will not grasp this lifetime.

--I don't mind the world. I don't know if its relevant now. I like the line about them all turning to stone. I sometimes feel like I would rather people would try to be real to my face and then it wouldn't MATTER what you said when you were kicking back laughing at me.

051114

Your icy eyes once inspired me. Now you just look at me and don't get it. Its fine. I am nothing like Cinderella. I don't need a damn prince. I did need a friend. I quit wishing and started doing what I needed to do. I don't need to see the ice in your eyes to know what your feelings are. I understand you.

Unfortunately, Cain.

051114

You weren't interested in my life and what was happening before. Why now. Did you think I would just call you and chat like we were besties forever and ever? I am moving to accommodate my daughters schooling. As I might have mentioned thirty or forty times since I got here. I found a few good ones and I think I will move somewhere pretty and green. There are so many good places where it rains all the time.

Alone isn't half bad. I didn't think I would love it. I do get lonely. But I don't socialize a lot. It's bound to happen. I don't get too down about it.

--I WILL come across someone sometime who won't be afraid of Rainen and his tactics. And Rainen you damn well know you are terrorizing guys into not even trying with your stalkish ways. I will know who is serious when I see him. Though I have no idea when that will be. Not to say I don't understand Rainen and his being upset but why try to ruin anything. If there is one thing I have learned it is that men are specially equipped to fuck things up all by themselves.

Everyone seems to be getting old and dying right in front of me. I always thought of my good friend Dowayne as indestructible. He was always my other big brother. That's what he called himself. I guess when I got back here I found he had started looking at me in a new light, I didn't know how to respond to him and his new overtures of romance. He was the one man we can all agree wouldn't be scared of Rainen. He knew Rainen and had respect for him and the proper irreverence for him as well. He always said he wasn't attracted to those girls he called sisters. I found myself OK with that. I was never a classic beauty or even cute in the days he knew me before. He was such a great guy. He went overseas with the Marine Corps and took pictures for me because I had to stay home and care for my little Alyc. I knew I would not travel the world yet. So, he always let me join him on his adventures. It was a sweet thing to do. He was so brave and real. I will miss him always and I will always wonder about him. Such a great person and real and funny and bigger than life. I feel very sad for all of us who knew and loved him. He meant something grand to this world. I will miss him forever and I will always tell him of my own adventures and how I am staying true to who I am. He knew of those people who faked through life. He knew how hard it was to have a soul in this age. We always lamented together over that. All the people my age are dying and it worries me I won't get all my shit done. I am still working on the list. Eight items left...

Cain, I don't know how to keep going with you sometimes. I wish you cared and tried to be the person you were once. I guess I always think of who you showed me you were and it feels like you don't try to be him, anymore. Maybe you changed too much, already. Or maybe you never were what I thought and I just projected onto you what I wished. That seems likely. I have been known to do that. Laughs. I do still make sure to see what is there, but I always see what people say they want for themselves and attach that to their profile as well.

You aren't here, so you won't know. But I am getting my stuff finished up. I know some people can't help it but to hate me. I don't care. It used to matter but I lost the capacity. Must go now.

You have things to do. As do I.

051214

I can almost feel the tiny wish makers fly as I gather breath- or courage-and finally wish my future into being. He drove off in a flash. I didn't even look back at him. I understand him so well. I haven't had a meaningful moment with him. None of this is really meaningful. Unless he can get what he wants.

I did try to offer him the chance. Meaning won't matter until I am done with the entire mess.

051214

I remember how I thought I must stop looking at the scenery fly past from the window. I have to choose something to engage my tearful eyes so I don't cry in front of anyone I don't know. there. A ravine soothing in the darkness of the three-days solid rain. The cool shadows of the leaves and the algae colored water are inviting. Breezes blow and waters trickle. They tempt me away from the enchantment I had been under.

An enchanting love or hate story? I can't say the words to him ever, knowing how I will feel when he gets around to telling me he doesn't love me. I won't lose myself. He wants me to chase him. I won't do that either.

--All my writing for Cain is goodbye. I notice that because it's sort of a waiting game for when he gets bored so he can try to hurt me some more. And he shows himself in unexpected moments. Always saying something someone else said first. Why? You have nothing of your own to say? Surely something about how Tabitha is bad at being a "NORMAL" people? Gives a wry grin.

051214

Your still heart can't feel mine wildly beating. You will have to keep your hate. My single moment of pleasure at seeing your eyes was cut short when you turned that look on me. I tried to see nothing but the light. But there was no light in your gaze when you looked at me.
Strangers—Hillary Duff
Cain's.

051514

I wake up again at four a.m. and cannot remember why I am not held close to his heart like a treasure. Slowly it works itself out in my mind as I remember. I can't heal from knowing. I can never be that for him again.
Hello Again—the Cars
Rainen's.

051914

Thanks for the painful lies you both told me in the dark. I didn't need your love. I wanted your compassion. No one tells the truth anymore. There is love for me and I will find it.
Rainen's and Cain's. Always Rainen's first because DAMN!

052214

I fight on. I keep telling the girl in the mirror...that I am doing well. That weight loss like this takes time. I am beautiful even if the stupid people judge me by how I look. I am not a bad person. I deserve to be happy.
--I don't care about what others thought. I haven't seen anyone I know lose two hundred in five years. That was lot of extra weight and I did it right. Think whatever you want of me. I don't mind. I know who I am. I know I am a good person

with the will to make it no matter what. Gotta love the haters. They are the ones who make it all possible!

052214

I am watching the many hues of beauty whiz by me on the Trimet. The little pink houses behind gates slip by. I never want to belong there. I can let it all be. No one who knows me understands the cost each day to keep the emotion out of what I do all day. Even this simple ride on a bus. I fear this is where you and your memory belong. Buried. You love her. Yes, you might have mentioned that. I respect myself enough to NOT compete. (CLASS BY ONESELF...me.)

Cain's.

052214

I am a simple creature really. I have been looking for meaning and love for who I have become. I look for invitation to bliss just like everyone else. I look around me for honest gazes. Honesty makes the eyes of the righteous bold, I hear. We all hide so much. If I sat and spun my words for eternity on the wheel of my mind, I would still hear only echoes of truth.

Say You Will—Foreigner

For myself and I wax philosophical at the least provocation....

052714

Stupid Tabitha.

Writes one more letter. Why on earth did I listen to Rainen when I knew for a fact that you were no good for me? He was so nice to say life puts us on the path of another for a reason. I knew it was going to come to this, though. You two are fuck-ing funny. I try to see it from your pov but it is hard for me, I confess. I think you are crazy and I don't know what I did besides try to do the right thing for my child so long ago. I didn't fuck you over. I didn't want to do any damage. I knew we would hold you back from your dreams and I knew you would treat my daughter as less because of it. I know I was a child and you were too, but can we agree neither made good choices there? I don't mind if you think you are better off without me. Go be better!

You loathe yourself for sleeping with me. I can see it on your face and I am tired of seeing that look on anyone's face. I say go home to Lovely and the house and kids. I was still glad to see you being happy. It's not a thing for me. The world has enough of everyone being hateful. I will miss you but I can do that from anywhere, right.

This has been quite an adjustment for me and the kids. Not to mention Rainen. I hope we all make I through this with all our shit together. It has been hard and we made it, anyway. I can't forget some things. I can praise him for the tenacity it took to get through this time. He is superman.

I would just like to chill out and do what I am meant to. It's fine. I like this me and I can do anything. It doesn't matter right.

I don't really care too much anymore. I just think I am me and if that pisses anyone off, well too bad.

I am going to head to class. It's sociology time. Eye roll...
Freebird—Lynnard Skynnard
Cain's.

061114

Our relationship once full of magic died. His scoliosis and subsequent surgeries caused him pain that was too much for my love to get through. I didn't know the horrible things he would scream at me in the latest nights. But I knew he blamed me for everything. I began to believe it was all my fault as well. I sat up till three or four in the morning just trying to be awake when his medicine wore off. I cried every night that year while he recovered. It seemed unreal and in my lack of sleep I became faded and dreamlike as well. I went over and over harsh words I spoke wondering if I could've said (or left unsaid) ONE word that would have made him hate me less. I remain failed in my thirteen-year attempt at love, wearing all black and wishing myself invisible so nothing else hurts me.

3a.m.—Matchbox20

For Rainen. And Elizabeth. My poetry professor who helped me to distill my thoughts and cried as she walked with me through this awfulness. It was the first time I told anyone about most of this stuff.

061114

The distinct buzzing comes from that blue-eyed Texan. We both thrill at our separate boldness. My old nickname spoken in my favorite medium, his quiet voice at two a.m. Cherished texts transport me back to the desert. I smell rain and after-shave and the cigarette he just smoked. He murmurs midnight promises I know better than to believe. I order him with crossed fingers— "Go to bed, Benedict." We will both be tired tomorrow and neither of us cares.

----I did the cutting process that my poetry professor asked for and I don't know why but the whole poem lost some of its integrity. Laughs. I cut the few lines out and it changed the entire meaning... but I liked it nonetheless. It sounded like the sixteen-year-old me that Cain so wanted me to be. I laughed because I knew it was what he was hoping for. I do care about him and probably always will but he sure does assume some erroneous things about me. Someday maybe he will come across my book somewhere and read it and recognize himself. I hope he does. He is so worried about what I will write of him now.

061414

He watches me ever vigilant. in case I turn into what he seeks...what he wants me to be. Last minute. "Oh, don't go now, Tabitha. I love you." I am not her, not Lovely. Just me. Since he is failed in trying to break me, he will taunt me. I had enough. I am sure to let it all go.

Cain's. Do you read this and know yourself Cain?

061714

I lack the qualities you two require. I am still perfect for someone. Some man sits alone at three a.m. and remembers a glance or an innocent touch and wishes for me to let loose, to be his forever. He would love to obsess over me, send a knock to me in the small hours of the morning. I don't want to be lonely. But I will make it.

Written with Rainen and Cain in mind, but only for myself. I push the positive always because I know how negative the world is. I use the horrible past I had to further the future. It's the only way.

062114

I grab at my happiness. One hand pulls me up to the next knot on my rope. I am nearing the top. My hands are blistered from the effort. This is different than when I was young. It was easier. Now my happiness sits on a high shelf. There is no way up but the rope. Sharp things that cut are dropped carelessly on the floor. I am only a few knots away now...My face is turned to the goal.

Bette Davis' eyes—Kim Carnes

Meaning, I look away from all the bullshit and ignore it.

062114

Simple smiles remind me of an old love. I could have some shade of it still if I could forget the words. We could be sort of us again, if I say I am sorry when I am not. Everyone I know lies. I don't want to. Words of invitation beckon me. I imagine I am already sitting at that table from the dream I had in 2004.

The table is representative of something archetypal in this dream. I have hit all the books for meanings and found little there that applied. I painted the table and I saw the man. I am sure of who he is. I don't know why he would be in the dream at all, let alone as the sympathetic creature I saw him to be. He seemed to be a picture of an almighty figure and his green colors must have represented something more. The symbols on his skin were ancient and I couldn't figure that out either, since I knew he was not of my oldest religions. But maybe there was something there I was needing and the dream had to let me know that jealousy is THE OLDEST religion by far. I wasn't doing anything to rile him in the dream. He wasn't there in the beginning of the dream but this smart ass kid was. He sat right down and kicked back at the table with his feet all propping his chair up on two legs. He was eating from the table which in the dream I was seeing as extremely rude. No one should eat till the host arrives, right? I saw two girls and they were both in idiotic poses of submissiveness. I knew all these people were going to get asses kicked when the host got there. I was worried in the dream about what they would do when he got there. I saw him turn the corner and he was the biggest thing I had ever seen. The people scattered and ran to wherever they go when they piss off the boss. I was feeling scared and I didn't even DO anything. I shrugged and decided to wait it out.

I knew he was at least nine feet tall and I could only look at him from the corner of my eye and so I saw little to identify him to me later. But he came in and gestured to the seat next to him. I knew he wanted me to sit on his right side. I sat and he passed me a bong. I was extremely confused because I thought maybe he was some all-powerful leader and that weed seemed contrary to his assumed nature. I smoked.

I smelled the smoke though and the smell lingered long after I woke. I also remembered thinking, "Oh damn. He invited all these people and they weren't being reverent or polite and he looked pissed."

There was a girl on the table trussed up like a pig at a BBQ. She was dead and cooked, apparently quite well. It smelled wonderful and I knew I didn't care how fucking good that smelled, I wasn't eating a goddamned thing while I was there. I sensed danger all around. I did what came natural to me. I sat, relaxed, and smoked and looked at his arms laying on the table. I was thinking how I could immortalize his patterns in art. I had this art work in me for eleven years. Since my daughter Iome was three. It was a wild dream and when I woke I committed it to paper in many ways. Drawings and writings. And the smell of that smoke haunted me until I finally smelled it again. I was in Denver and the strain was called, ironically enough, "Blue Dream".

I know who the dream was about and I am not worried about this book damaging anyone. But perhaps showing the errors in thinking. I am not quite like other people. I don't care to be. Even if I like or admire someone I don't believe I should try to be them. I am me. And I am spectacular.

062314

He never stops looking in at me. In case I do something new or unusual. Something with which he doesn't mind aligning himself. If I am not careful he will go. I am no princess. I am not your women either. Only this girl. Determined and fierce. He can't build my hope. He haunts me with his declarations. I am sure to let it all go.

Rainen's.

062114

Helluva day.

I need to paint but I am blocked. When I left NM I really didn't want to go back. This effort I am making here is enormous. My goals didn't change just because you want them to. I am working and filling my days. I am going to do exactly what I said I would.

Cain's.

062414

Ha-ha. I am in class and instead of taking notes I am writing notes. Funny shit right. I don't want it to be my birthday so I am not bringing it up to anyone and no one seems to mind. Least of all me. Sheepish grin. You know I miss you even though I know that I am wishfully thinking you are my friend. It's a psych question for sure.

You are a huge ass. I mean you must know this. You know how I am mentally set up, right now. Not a cool friend. Not a cool friend, Cain.

I shouldn't even be writing you a theoretical letter because Rainen doesn't realize these letters ARE theoretical. He thinks I am romanticizing you. Which is just not true. I think by now you know that I am on to you. It matters to him. I try to keep you from affecting us. He doesn't realize that I spent a great deal of time putting you and your little plans in their appropriate places. He would rather see me eaten alive by something large and carnivorous than write a letter to you. Even if you will never read it, ever, in the history of me or civilization. Tilts head sort of philosophically... I guess I don't deal in absolutes anymore, so I can't say never. Though for these purposes I think maybe I will just leave it. Not a little boy anymore, huh. Well I don't know about the validity of that statement. I sure hope so.

Bye Cain.

071714

You will dream about me, careless man. My touch. My "alright" looks. You will think about me... boring as I am. I can create a very beautiful place to be.

I heard all the words you said. I know what you think you are doing. My dreams are far bigger than that now.

080814

I stab the pieces of raw chicken with a big fork, throwing them carelessly onto a broiler pan. (This won't help," I say to myself.) I pick up the salt and pepper looking for my preheated light on the oven. I put my spices on the pink chicken-garlic, onion... (The first "I love you" was a lie that scarred me.) It needs basil, sage; some lovely to kill the gross. (The second one I saw coming-it didn't hurt less as he peeled out of the driveway and left forever.) More salt. (Eyes blurred.) More pepper, turn the nasty pink flesh. (Tears falling freely now.) Beep, beep goes the oven-prehet at last! (The 3rd time should have showed me but I was young and believed I could overcome anything.) I grab the broiler pan full of tonight's food with shaky hands. I pull out corn tortillas, green sauce, cheese, lettuce, tomato... prepare for enchilada night. (I know this one wanted a party girl full of drugs and dick and nothing else. I dared to believe him when he said I was his dream-that he wanted something more than these girls.) Blurry eyes make reading digital temperature difficult. But dinner will be ready, come hell or high water.

And the last liar I will ever believe will walk through the front door any minute,

And ask why I am crying on the chicken.

082014

No one's secret. I burned in the sun's hate. I left it to burn alone. The charred remains of the soul I used to cherish finally begins to cool in the darkness of the rainy forests. Hunted while I was wounded, the blood washes off my form in the rain. I was sought to be kicked repeatedly. He didn't know I was already dead. The cold was bitter. I won't lay here any longer. While he pulls back to laugh at me from afar, he loses sight of me. I pull myself up quietly though every step is fire and glass. I won't let myself cry anymore. I drag myself into the trees and wait for the rain. Can't be colder than HIM.

Oh, I hear he wants to see me, again. He searches the fog, rain, and woods so wild. I am not where he left me. The cold puddle of mud and blood is empty. I told him I would be gone. My voice whispers to the dark: I AM NO ONE'S SECRET.

082614

Night is when I need arms tight around me so I can find my way back after the long wearying nightmare paths take me far from my soul. This is all I wanted from any love. Shelter my soul from the lonely walks I take in my dreams.

I didn't have anyone in mind when I wrote this. I was just lonesome. I always seek shelter from the dreams.

082614

"If I can't have her..." all the jokers talk..." then no one can."

I am faintly amused by this archaic expression of machismo. In my mind, I chortle and rewrite the saying more accurately..." I don't want her and you still can't have her."

I am about to set myself free and wander much lovelier streets full of fog and rainy moments. I can enjoy my life. Seven worlds will collide and I don't fear the prophetic dreams. Always someone saying SOMETHING. I listen to beating drums and hold my head high while I wipe the last of my tears away.

No one will need to love me as wild as I am.

Wild creatures—chuckles. We are a rare breed.

082814

I walk through the lovely places you are. A stroll down a worn path with a boy I thought I had seen the last of. Doesn't matter how long it's been, it feels like forever. I fell asleep with thoughts of you swirling dangerously close. I slept with great dreams and awoke with good feelings in my heart. I think that's sort of more me than you relating to me. I just take the positive feelings you have inspired.

I wanted that joy walking hand in hand. The elation of looking in your eyes and seeing that you once were mine. Hold you close right now. maybe you are forced to dream of me too. And think how much you hate it. I do feel bad for you. I wish I could sleep minus the damn dreams. Just for one fucking night, if it's not too much to ask.

2014 (only date that appears on this writing. Placement in notebook is only indicator.)

In the interim of my loss, I asked once for your help. You told all the same old jokes. You aren't alone or worried. I am pleased. So, let's quit playing and move on already. I have to go get what suits ME. Lean on the ones you have with you. Learn to love someone with all of you. Be yourself because he isn't a bad man. Stay blessed and far away from me.

Please, for real, Cain.

083114

A little diversion while I go away. A tiny thing for himself. So, he can go on his way pleased. His happiness is only achieved in using me for his anger outlet. I feel like I walk into the room through broken glass. I sometimes can't find my own way. I am a sad child next to the other one's blue-eyed revenge. Make the cuts fast already. I will go somewhere quiet and remember why I left.

Get Out Alive—3 Days Grace

Rainen's then Cain's.

092314

Dear whom-the-fuck ever,

I love this rain. I don't want to ever be away from the rain again. It is beautiful. I hated the desert hot for so long. It is a darker day than I thought. I feel out of place there in the desert and here is no different. I am embarrassed by being seen in an overwhelmingly honest moment.

Whatever.

Unwell—Matchbox20

Mine.

092314

I either have too much time or not enough depending on how you look at it. Today's dawn is just like yesterday's sunset. His hands were made for love and he uses them for a way different purpose. He needs to go love while he can, before I ruin him. Or that's what he said. I'm surrounded by energetic noises and voices. The noise of life. I wonder if while I was silent, I died. Must have the noise to believe I am alive. Simple silent hermit me. I just write my stupid page of crap and listen to all the inane chatter to keep from going crazy.

Those words he spoke were immortal. I have to look at them every day spray painted seven feet tall on the bricks in my mind. I shake out in the cold world unprepared for the rains. I wrench myself upright at four a.m. It's quiet at last and I am once again wondering if I have too much time on my hands. He invites me back to his room and his bed... I just

consider his eyes with no words and go.
Time On My Hands—Styx
Rainen's.

092314

Wednesday in the same ugly green chair. I was sitting in this chair when I found out I lived ten of twelve years in a lie. I open my notebook, my hands wiping hatefully at the last traces of my weakness under my eyes...such an ugly shade of green. No one remembers they are green. Just call them blue, like always. I sit in this chair rocking now and then unhurried. I wither inside while I wonder to myself and the chair, "What the fuck am I doing?!" For the millionth time. I sit and listen to the creaking springs. Appreciating the worn comfort. I understand this chair. Passed around because no one wanted it. To owners sure to mistreat it. Ultimately doomed to being torn again and again until it is tossed aside with the trash. I sit in this same chair when I find my daughter is part of the mess. No daughter should want to hurt an already hurting mother. Despite us both being thrown out-me and the chair- we won't forget the lessons we learned together. Fucking ugly green chair.

INSERT The friend from Texas chose to help me out financially so me and my girls could come back from Oregon. I wanted to stay but I couldn't handle the every day pain with Rainen anymore. I was about to lose my mind. I choose to not be remorseful for the decision. I needed to go. A kindness I should have never accepted. Rainen was telling me he was staying behind in Oregon with the new girlf. I shrugged and said whatever you like.

He suddenly became worried over his girls. I mean the three days before I left were really some flurry. He didn't seem to care until the last minute, as me and my girls got ready to leave. I guess he thought he had done something to keep me there with him while he kept miss thing at beck and call. I didn't care anymore. I fulfilled my promise and I was done. I really was too. So, I said I will lower my pride and do what needs to be done before I end up in a worse situation and Rainen lets it happen. Just by doing nothing at all.

Rainen went out of his way to make sure he took care of a lot while we were newly back in NM. I did go immediately and get a job waitressing. I also started applying for a substitute license and began to think of a house. We stayed with Rainen's mom and she was kind to us. I believe she began to know and understand me more over the years. I tried to do as much as possible to get out in a hurry. I felt uncomfortable because every second with Rainen was killing me. He would lay down next to me and flirt outrageously each night. and I had quite a hard time keeping myself away. I was still very raw and angry, though.

I was most angry at Rainen for not trying to pay back the money. You know Cain has a family to care for too. And he could have spent his last money doing this for us. I don't know. but I didn't agree with the flippant way Rainen thought I would use Cain and then be done with him. That is not me! It fired me all up and got me so mad I thought I would not be able to make it back without saying something. I might know I can't be with Cain, but that gives me no right to discount that act of kindness. I never and I mean NEVER will forget it. He thinks I have already, but I know what it takes to do what needs to be done. Just because I get mad sometimes at your casual attitude to me, doesn't mean I ever would say it meant nothing, Cain. I sure did give him a birthday gift. He deserves someone to look and see how his nature is, and reward him for his generous spirit.

When I went to move out to a house, Rainen just moved with me. We would just –what!? forget what happened? No. However, it did become apparent I would not be able to make it if I didn't rely on someone. He tried his best to help what ways he could. He worked a little and I worked a lot. I tried to keep my understanding. He was as lost as I was in those days. I could feel it. I would not sleep in the same bed with him. I refused because I could see where he was going. He should not get away with the things he did to me. And I still believe that. I am tired of making excuses for people's bad behavior. Everyone's.

For Those About to Rock—AC/DC

--I began to start an account for Cain. Sort of secret and unofficial. When I got my taxes in, I had enough to give him a smallish amount of the money back. I just did it for his birthday since I knew he would say I couldn't pay him back for the help he gave and gave. And even now gives. His soul isn't as hidden as he would like it to be. I do see you, Cain. And I respect you as well. Please don't change.

Bitch Better Have My Money—a nineties rapper once said...AMG?

Last minute fight was Rainen yelling I was going back to be with Cain. I most certainly was not and he was insulting to imply it! I went back to NM because I figured why not be where I could succeed if I had to do things all alone. After all, I was. And I knew my promise would end someday soon. He wanted to stay in Oregon with her. I told him he should. Instead he made it his mission to follow and make sure I wasn't getting with anyone he didn't like.

When we got back to NM, I waitressed for several months and later got my substitute teaching license. It was decent work and the kids were no easy creatures. They sure made me work on myself to be better equipped to deal with them. I had little nervous breakdowns when I subbed in the developmental room with all the babies that had learning challenges. The emotional issues from these kids were things I didn't know how to deal with. Children of dopers who gave them away to other relatives. There were some few who had parents up there all the time. And some children needed us to be that too. We did fight every day and work hard to keep these students learning and growing and doing more than they were projected to be able. We tested and continuously argued, cajoled, asked, and retaught anything forgotten. It was so hard I thought I would lose my mind. I had to leave those sweet kids and start doing something a little more my speed. I wept the entire day when I left.

I taught middle school at one of the very innovative but still lower rated schools here. I enjoyed it. I was scared I would mess up the entire time. I fought my own instincts every day and went forward. I listened and learned, I fought and taught. I helped the students in any way I could. Some of their stories broke my heart. I thought about how no one listened to me at that age. I would listen all day to some of the problems. I heard more serious issues with body image and bullying due to looks or money or popularity. I heard about crazy parties with all sorts of bad things going on. Since I could never prove any of the information- I gave the councilor all the dangerous stuff and tried to dispense valuable advice and much food to the masses of always hungry babies. I feed mine at home, and so I fed mine there too. I loved each one and even bonded with about twenty or thirty students I never had in any of my classes.

I kept letting the lunch time kids come in to stay out of trouble with bullies or just to keep from having to hang around mean people or even not wanting to be around certain teachers or staff. I did what I could to create understanding and solidarity for all of us as teachers. Sometimes I got backstory and sometimes I didn't.

I still think of the kids and I am not even gone from the job for one month to finish my story. Don't quit. This message is for not only the adults but the babies. Please never quit. Even if you are a boy who is having a hard time coming to terms with his sexuality in a tiny town of older values. We are growing here in this place. Don't give up right before it gets good k. I need to see you succeed so I know anyone of us can. We are all people and need the same love and acceptance.

Please little girl who lost her mamma too soon and then started a steady life of hard things. Don't you quit. Don't get down when you are hungry or you feel like you have been ignored. Just keep yourself positive. I lived through some very hard months where I ate a record breaking five times in one month—honey-I will try to let you know about the resources we have in this town to help too. I love that you are fierce for your people. I know how that feels. You must go on and do your art so the world knows your extraordinary powerful story! You must make it. So I can. We all must, honey.

Also, little boy who got into so much trouble. Who has a hard time in his house where the food is not abundant and the kids are everywhere asking for attention that he feels no right to. I remember how I told him to call out that sister on her bullshit when she lied to the school authorities about her brother. It not only got him out of trouble but made her respect her brother and the staff all said how grown up it was! I was SO proud of him!

He made the kids in my class be respectful even when he had a hard day and I could tell. He got kicked out of school and I didn't see him anymore. You make it, you tall green-eyed boy, and don't be discouraged that you are older than your peers when you DO go back to school. (I know you will. I know it!) Keep that ambition and remember: a clean white shirt, pressed, and a new pair of shoes will make a difference when you go to that interview. And yes. You must take out the earring to make them look at you seriously, hon. You just fight on and do what you have to. Make it. So, we all can, little man.

I will remember you all, forever. I will never be anything but humble for my time I spent teaching and yes! Learning from you. I learned so much. I am so much more now that I have experienced your lives for a few years.

You are all amazing creatures and I am proud to have been there for you when I could be. Please stay strong, children. You are our new hope for tomorrow. What will we do without you?! Even though being back in NM was the hardest thing I had to do by far, I loved every second, because of you kids. It made Rainen and Cain not matter so much when I could see where I was needed and do the good work before me.

And my colleagues—though so many of you were so much more educated and so damn cool about it—you taught me the most. You let me make my way and do my own thing and backed me up only if I floundered. I did that a lot. But you never judged me. Only gave me encouragement and trust. I tried to remember that in my mirror first thing in the mornings. I understood the awesome responsibility and the irreverence we had to treat it with so we didn't lose our ever-loving minds.

Please parents and anyone else, understand that no amount of money can make up for the huge job these wonderful people do out of love for YOU and YOUR KIDS and YOUR TOWN. Remember to vote on each proposal for teachers. And dammit—vote YES!!! These men and women do the angels' work and get no fucking credit for it and most of the parents treat us as lepers and nosy pariahs. We spend our money on your kids too. We feed them and talk to them and work with them. And we love them, each one. We are the last line of defense for these kids in some of the cases. Please remember to show your appreciation. These people are so important! To us all. I never knew what this would do to open and change my mind.

Thank you to my little town for giving me a shot at something I needed to do to prove I could. For myself.

Coming back to NM possessed its own set of challenges. I chose to look at it with some optimism and lightness. After all I could always leave again. No one keeps me here now. I can take my little girls and we can go anywhere. Really. Anywhere we want to for the rest of our lives. No one has watched my struggle like they would need to if they looked for understanding. I grew and changed some more. And now I think I learned what this place had to teach. I think I can peacefully leave without worrying over anything.

I am going to have to expound upon the desert again. I can't say enough I have found beauty and small days of peace that were so rare my whole life. I love this desert and I love many people who live here. The universe has been showing me better and better people and places I can be myself and make a difference. It is amazing and I have come to see beauty everywhere I look lately. I smile more and I feel like I have come to a new understanding of this place. Just because you grow up in a place that shows you hate and hurt doesn't mean the hate or hurt have to impact you forever. Or at all if you can manage to keep yourself above it. I had some trouble getting to where I could but I think I am cruising now.

Where It's At--Beck

010315

I stand outside myself, looking at my desires. I am ready to have it all, now. I walk right to the iron gate. Grab it with both hands and my strong intent. It was open and waiting and easy. I want the great career and the great house and the great life I have dreamed through this hard time. I saw it and know it. The magic is there for me.

Dreamweaver—Gary Wright

061015

Dear my Ionthe-

Oh, darlin little girl who made me sing again! I was surprised by your appearance and I am still so surprised that I had such a bright, lovely and bold female within me. They say moms split pieces of our souls off to give to our daughters. I had four so I know you girls will make me proud. I have a lot of love to give. I know you do, too. You made me think I wanted love again, even if just to prove to myself this world was good enough for YOU. I want your birthday to always be the day that reminds each of you that you are special and dear to me for so many different and perfect reasons. Your father doesn't know how proud he should be of you, and he may never know. I don't even think you needed either of us to be the fierce you I see before me. I just want to give you the wings to achieve your dreams. I will never leave as long as you need me. Even if that means I have to be here forever. I love you more than my own life. Easily. Please stay the bright and lovely creature you are and never change for this world. You be the change you want, baby. I know you will do great things. Never fear anything at all and you will make this world your own.

The specialness of this day will always make me smile. I remember just after the doctor placed you in my arms, your little tiny face looking up at me examining my face to see what you could see there in my eyes. Love, baby girl. Only love. I just sat in love and stared at you. Waiting for you to say OK mom. You will be a good mom. Nonnie and Poppy and Grammy all enamored of little Ionthe...Your oldest sister fell in love and later we all found our love with your younger sisters, too. Even your auntie fell hard. How could we not love you?!

Happy-oh darlin-- happy birthday!!!! Have a fantastic day and remember why we celebrate!

Mamma loves you so much!!!!

--I didn't write many things as full of me, the woman and mother, as these birthday letters to my little girls. I found them sweet and so rich with memories. I always love these girls and love the little light they carry with them. So beautiful and truthful. They really made my entire life worth it. I could never have wished for more than them.

072215

Sweet oldest girl who holds a special place in my life and heart. No matter how old you get or how long you stay away from me, I am your mamma and I will never stop being that for you honey. I love that you have grown to healthy independence and you are making me proud each day you take the time to plan the day and work to make it happen. I know how hard these things can seem when you are young and you don't know everything you need to, yet.

Happy birthday and never let anyone tell you birthdays aren't special when you get older. You are always special, peanut. I remember you all nestled into the crook of my arm and though I felt like I had been attacked and beat up from the entire ordeal, I felt triumphant. I had a busted lip and cuts and bruises and needle marks and bumps from the allergic reactions to everything in the room... but I made this little, tiny PERSON! She is beautiful and dainty and so sweet and I created this beauty inside myself from a man who didn't think so much of me. I didn't care what anyone said. I might have died that day twice as they said, but I also came back. For you. Even when I gave up my young dreams and moved on to the newest and most beautiful dream of all—YOU! I felt proud to be your mom and I always fought for you even when others told me I wasn't going to make it. I damn sure did and more importantly: YOU DID. Yes, you may have had more candy than I liked and you may have listened little and bounced off walls much but you grew and learned and changed into the amazing and fierce woman I know and love so much. Who else could inspire such love and tears and madness? Just my little girl I stole from the rain. My own sweet girl... you have a very happy birthday and remember what's important. LOVE and HOPE and FAITH in yourself and in this world. No matter what, I want you to go out there into this world and stamp it with your name. It's yours. I brought you here to give you something real. The world is yours if you want it—take it, baby. Don't let anyone tell you that you can't! EVER! Do you hear this?

Mamma loves you more than you will know.

080915

I sang a simple song, not even written for you. You tried to make it yours. Whatever. You thought my heartfelt voice needed to be silenced? I don't need you, which to you is a huge crime. While I gain my independence, you watch each of my valiant stands. And they ARE valiant. I don't guess I needed anyone after all. Love is simple and so is the lie. It was easy to figure out how to gain the trust of a girl like me, right? You thought. Why not leave me alone and save yourself? No one gets off scott-free this time.

Numb —Linkin Park

080915

Last night's restless sleep took me away. I went to a new place. There were people to whom I was apparently familiar. The discomfort of the evening's dreams never receded as it usually does. I knew little about this dream city. I felt it was mine. The magic was there for me even if I could find no reliable lover or friend. I own my moment. I stride confident to my future. I learned how to be free. You should try it. It is wild and comforting and full of huge light.

I am so glad I didn't quit.

--I am a fighter from way back. I learned several lessons from my brother that I needed every day and one of them was: Don't quit no matter how many knots you put in (he taught me to tie my shoes while I was four-- in three and a half hours and five thousand knots, which he patiently untied each time!). Another was: don't ever stop fighting, for it will surely kill you. I learned this while he fought the cancer in the last two months. I saw his hair fall out and his eyes go dark with pain too many times. He ran off to the dealer for some more chemicals. Whatever he could get his hands on. The pain never left but sometimes ebbed with the self-medication. I asked him if he wanted to be a bad example to others who would need to know they had to fight the right way --no matter what. He began to understand why I was arguing with him after that.

No dying with a needle in the arm for my big brother. He walked away. I didn't get to say goodbye properly but I will remember the day etched forever in my heart. He fought till the very fucking last second, like the warrior he always was. He makes me strong today when I want to quit. I have to fight. Always. My girls never see me slip. They have to know it matters.

In Stereo—Fort Minor

080915

You take yourself back and revisit, asking for another chance. He did the same thing but wanted it all. I have been abandoned a few times. You laugh. He asks to be mine. You do nothing. Nothing else I can say or do for either of you now.

Eh, Eh, Nothing Else I Can Say—Lady Gaga

080915

Another letter to the ever-unreachable Cain.

I don't have minutes and I am not sure I could to talk to you if I had them. Thunder is rumbling heavily outside my window. Rainen's gone. I'm not sure I know how to feel. I understood the words he left me with so long ago. It still seems like he left me even though I asked him to leave. I guess your part is done. That is OK too. I am sorry you were involved at all. You can go back to your life—I am sure you will be fine. As it should be.

I feel lost. I wished for things I knew better than to wish for. I am alive. So that's going to have to do for now. Thanks for being there. Though you couldn't bring yourself to be.

T.

Home Sweet Home—Motley Crue

Remember, self-assurance is good. Cockiness is very, very bad. One gets rewarded and one gets you nothing.

081015

ON RELIABILTY—

Did you ever have an off day? One where you needed me more than you needed anything else in life? Promises broken matter. You never wanted a part of me. Why play like it matters now? You can find your own way out, right. I need love to be wild and free.

What would you know about being reliable to me? Goodbye is a nice reliable word.

T.

Cain's. Yeah. Goodbye IS a nice reliable word. I always try to say it. For some reason, I wanted him to know I didn't leave him behind. He matters to me.

081015

Late last night alone on that awful green sofa, it felt like Oregon in so many ways. A lonely place to be, but good to remind myself of who I am. I have grieved for these long years. After the love is done, he can't seem to let me go. He must be SURE I won't recover from his love. If the love isn't mine, I can't keep walking with him. No glances back. He is simply not mine.

My Lovin' (Never Gonna Get It)—En Vogue

--Rainen's. Sighs because I spent the better part of my life loving him. I can't decide why I am upset so often. Maybe because he tried his damnedest to break my spirit and then treated me poorly. The man always said he wanted me. I always tried to believe him. It is unlikely, though. Now I find he is attracted again and I could have him back. But what does he learn from my giving in? To treat me bad and get what he wants out of it? I think not, Rainen. I won't forget any of it.

Even though most of your relatives and friends were sweet to my face and often out of their way sweet when it came to the kids, I felt so isolated and alone. You let me. It seemed you and your friends and family were there, but only for the superficial shit. Never for the deep stuff. I try each time I make friends to let them know I am a soulful creature. That way if they are ever in need of some real talk or heartfelt words of hope or joy, they know to come to me. I loved each one of them. Mick, and Wyatt-too-naughty, little Misty, and Reston. All the neighbors we had—Sanette, and Don and their cute and sweet kids, Chico and his family, who were with us most often, Rainen's sisters and mother and brother-in-laws. I care for them all. When they hurt, I do too. Even when I think they brought it on—I am there if they ever wanted me to be. No one called on me because it was funnier to leave me alone and be rude. The isolation made the weight worse. I had little love and so I ate for comfort.

Sometimes my house was cluttered. I didn't think of any housework as half as important as the happiness of the kids. I don't care. I never will. My house wasn't dreadful. But comfortable. My kids live in my house. You only live once and the time is precious. All my wonderful friends and family who passed away will say amen. Spend time, because there isn't a lot of it no matter how you look at it!! It seemed dumb to judge me when NO ONE is perfect. I wept for myself many nights in those times. Please remember, I am there. I know I had to work through it on my own, but you don't have to. I will help anyone if they ask me to.

As for my own "friends", I sit and think of you so much. I worry over you and your kids. I wonder if you are doing well or if you are back to old bad habits. We all have those slip-ups. I think of and love all the old times we had. I knew some of you so well and I knew very little about you at the same time. I worked hard to keep in touch.

I am that fucking pleased you all got married and moved on to adult lives. Most satisfying for some of you. I will keep your names on my lips and bless you and yours but you can stay away from me. You seem to enjoy not hearing from me, so let's stick with what works. I don't mind.

081215

I wake slowly and remember the dream in its entirety. Did you dream of love again last night? I did. I walked through the dream alone. Isn't that love? People I don't know, places I don't want to be.

Who Says? —Selena Gomez

--I have a creepy look at the bright side thing that is weird but works for me. I wish others didn't perceive it as strange but I guess walk a mile before you smile.

081415

My paintings hang in the local museum today. It seems like...

My sorrow hangs sad on the white wall, painted in evil colors I have never used before to portray pain. The people glance and walk easily past it. Either not recognizing the message or more likely just not caring what is spoken there. The second painting-- My greatest joy hangs in simple pieces split from its bright meaning. The words are lost forever. The people's simple ignorance appalls me. Not an ounce of love in one eye for the little girl within the painted dark sky.

--I didn't like the way the paintings were lost in the generalness of the show. I had to leave one piece by itself and it was part of a three-piece work. It looked like a half-finished sentence. And the other painting they loved because of the New Mexico color scheme but I hated for the same reason. I was practical about the museum show. I do need a gallery showing to properly show my art off advantageously. And I will. Like I said. It is on the list...laughs and waits patiently for the next item to go crossed off the ever-dwindling list... ah. How sweet it is.

081415

I feel a little alone. Life doesn't stop even for you. Sticking around thinking to apologize to me is silly. Just go do what I had to and calmly head that way. My choices led me here and my choices will lead me away. I guess. That's the plan. Doesn't lying about love hurt your soul? It always did mine. I am simple too. I don't have to have any of this.
Simple Man--Skynnard

081515

Letter from the edge of the earth...
To anyone from someday in the future who might give a rat's ass...
I am finishing with this list. The promise is finally crossed out. I feel lighter every time I look at the list. I only have eight items left now. it's getting easier to do these things. And these things I saved till last thinking they would be the hardest... I wonder if I just chickened out over nothing. I believe these may be easier now than when I gave up on them. :/ as a young girl they seemed daunting, now as an adult woman, they seem sort of easy and I don't think they will be that hard.
I really just wanted to share an adult moment with a real adult. Not to be lonely for five minutes and feel like we could be whomever we needed to be right then. I tried to be real to everyone to whom I spoke. Understanding would have been nice.
Chuckles. Sometimes they tried too. Mostly, though... they didn't. Lots of reasons but no excuses. Right.
No Excuses—Alice In chains

081515

I can hear the thunder quietly shake the earth under my feet. I see the threads of lightning piercing the darkness. Those threads stitch together the holes torn in my soul. I can smell that scrubbed fresh ozone cleaning the world of the bad stuff. I breathe in the smell of clean while I dance under the blue and silver drops. I can taste the desert rain's dark flavor. I have faith that the rain can heal me. I reach for the warm drops as they cascade down the sides of the sky. The drops hold me together while the world falls apart. I loved him.

What Is Love--Haddaway

Rainen's. I thought this was some of the most beautiful imagery I could paint for anyone inclined to read this. Almost as beautiful as him.

081515

The revolving door brings around an old friend. What does he want? I watch his face while he processes. Live it up like high school. Wait, what?! I didn't want to live high school while I WAS living high school. I barely lived through the violence of one high school adventure. No more. I am an adult. You have access to adult faculties. Why can't you BE one? Leave me alone. Stay with your wife and family. I know it seems like nothing to you but I am not really the type that wants to be in the middle of this sort of situation.

When I was at my lowest and needed him the most, I pushed him away because I knew it wouldn't end well. I just pushed him away and ran a little so I could gain perspective.

Guess who. Laughs.

081515

Breathe in and breathe out slowly... it seems like my heart was never necessary for real life. Why is it difficult to do without? The girl me fades but doesn't ever go away forever. My deepest beliefs are questioned every day. I only know I have to go on and make it. I want a new love and a kind touch. Hands that seek me for pleasure and don't even WANT to hurt me. A heart that always reaches for the pieces of my own heart. 3A.M. wake-up calls to wrap himself in me and my changing mystery. I need love. Wherever you are, I can't hold onto shadows forever.

Shadow thing. Presence. What the hell ever.

081615

I have waltzed with bloody feet in an indifferent ballroom. I watched and learned with every step, what life was about. I trusted wholeheartedly each person and saw the advantage I gave them. When extended chances to prove themselves honest and honorable, they wounded me body and soul. They are remorseless. I still look for love.

Much later, I found new partners with which to share a few steps. The half dead girl wasn't asked to dance often. It became clear. I danced alone. I hunted love. It seemed easy for others to find. I could not learn love. I remembered back to the days before, when the words hurt and the promises went unkept. I don't need to remember each of the lies anymore. Don't worry about me... I can dance alone.

And I notice people are looking... they want the joy of my solitary dance. Not everyone can make this dance joyful. But I found my peace within that dance.

Cheers--Rihanna

082015

The music sustained me before. I don't get the same calm from it now. Like each of the other unnecessary things, I give it up. I danced in the dark before. It changed nothing. It was still dark. I sang for the moon before. I dreamed of the hope for which I looked. I still search for familiar music. And dance and dream. I hope in the dark.

--I have spent this time learning and changing and growing. I used to think people who said those kinds of things were full of shit. So, I get it if you don't think I am telling the truth. But I am a real girl with a real heart. It is one I give with my all but just now it is broken. That's OK. I am healing every day. I don't care if no one saw what made me and Rainen a special and wonderful couple. We were. We loved all the way the first few years and those wonderful years made me real. I hope anyone who is in pain will pull from this a lesson and remember that pain is temporary. You will overcome it. No matter who holds you down or lifts you up. You will be OK because we are people and we are made for this. Living and loving and growing and learning. We will all be OK. A kind smile or a nice word is sometimes enough to bring hope back. It is getting to be, we forget that we are all people and worthy of love.

Revolution--Beatles

082115

I mourned for this man. I didn't leave him for another as many believe. The man I loved was my world. I gave him everything. That man's love changed me. Made me better.

--I would never have even thought of looking at another man while I was with Rainen. I thought he was the world and I just a moon put here to orbit him. In the beginning, he never let me turn away and he smiled his radiance on me. Sounds so bad and corny, right. I did fall for him fast and love him insanely.

Cover Me—John Cougar Mellencamp

082715 0910p

It doesn't matter. I don't think of him as often these days. You never know when love will sneak up on you... I had a dream the other night...

--I had a dream about the new love I will meet. But he was turned partially so I couldn't see his full face.

082815

I miss his warm hands all over me and his lips whispering between kisses to my wild body. I can't wait for this anymore. I have shit to do.

There You Go—Pink

--I kept sleeping with Rainen over and over trying to keep ahold of some of the magic we had. I understood it was not a thing I could continue to do. So, I stopped. But as I read, I notice untruths or biased truth and I change it.

I must say I broke my own heart by doing it again. I love him and he says he wants me back. I can't keep it from myself that a habit is made by behaving a certain way for three consecutive times. He did the violent and hurtful things for years... How would I be able to live with myself if I let my girls see that one more time? I would be no better than my mom. And I choose to be someone else completely. Me. I find her refreshing in this day when no one will make eye contact or talk to you.

I like being a weirdo. I love being a nerd. I love Star Trek and art and singing and dancing in the rain. I love stars and my moon. I love to stay up late and get up early. I love the complexity of the forests and I love the simplicity of the desert. I love to be nice to people and to hear stories of adventures they have had or wait to have. I like to see the many different and unusual eye colors around me in a room. I don't even mind if someone catches me staring. I might just be stealing one of their features to draw later. Probably. Chuckles. I like throwing my phone when people act dumb. Hear that!

I like to wake up and chase my youngest daughter through the house while she screams and laughs. I smile a huge smile when I see her orange hair streaming out behind her. I love to listen to my third daughter speak because she reminds me of myself at that age. I love to watch Ionthe smile. It takes a minute to get all there because she really has to want to... and after a full minute her smile is big and beautiful and beaming! Her happiness is nice to see. I like to see my oldest fighting for her relationship with her sisters after her running off. She is a fighter too and she really has to work hard with Iome. She should have to. Easy to mess up, hard to fix. But keep going. It is working!

You are all my pride and joy and love forever. I will always have your back and I will always want to have you in my life. You are not only my children but extraordinary people all by yourselves. Each of you have your own things and your own beliefs and you all coexist. The world could learn from the four of you a new way to be. You fight and work it out. You get sad and work through it. You get feisty and put it out there to the world. You should never stop. DAMN—I love my girls.

21st Century Girl—Willow Smith - ALWAYS for my girls. It makes me understand their souls.

082815

Black and blue clouds pull together. They sing a rumbling solidarity to me. I listen joyfully. I see the flash of a beacon that lights my way. Back to peace. I need hands on me and arms around me. I need whispers in the dark. The clouds murmur, "Until then, we are here."

Thunder Underground--Ozzy

--I was thinking of Rainen. I just had to keep reminding myself not to give in. He is persuasive as fuck when he wants something... I fear he wants me again.

083015

I can't accommodate your schedule. We will change it? I

almost couldn't believe you. I can't accommodate your busy life and not be left behind. If you cared about me so much, you would see me weeping and extend a hand like a real friend. It is silly and tragic. You are offended by my flippancy but that's what holds me together until you get finished here. I can at least care for myself, can't I?

Under the Bridge—Red Hot Chili Peppers

Yes, Cain. I can. And I am.

083015

Well-wishers want he and I together. Fourteen years is a long time. On this I agree. But there is no reason to force something he doesn't feel. It's sort of amusing. If I didn't have to be in the situation, I would probably find it funnier.

Janie's Got a Gun--Aerosmith

Rainen's.

083115

Caught in a most compromising position. How offensive that you think I am here for material gain. I can get that my-self, in case you haven't noticed. I will deal with my mess and you just leave me alone k. I can feel that you will. How simple I really am.

But don't forget who I am. I damn sure can't.

I Remember You—Skid Row

Cain's.

083115

It was an ever-odd sort of night. It promises to be an even odder sort of day. He thinks I should have to chase love. I am a noble prince? Not a princess, and so not a prince...laughs. Maybe I'm not what he's looking for. Maybe my odd day will best be served by doing exactly what I need to be.

I am walking slowly through the rubble of my walls. I notice how dark it is here. I do want to feel other things besides pain. I want to be held like it matters. I want one just for me. I haven't found it yet. Doesn't mean I quit looking.

Would—Alice In Chains

--Cain's. How do you chase a married guy? Clue from a smart lady—I think we all know it isn't wise. Especially if you have ever had the joy of being left behind. Which I have. By the same married guy, if I recall correctly... I like to think I have grown mindful over the years. Maybe learned SOMEthing. *hard eye roll

083115

I wake up today like the days before...tired. I do what needs to be done...pushing always forward. I continue to have faith in myself. How do I know what I am doing is right? My daughters smiling faces and screaming laughter down the hall is all I needed all along. I don't cope well with knowing I am alone. I slowly pull out my pens and brushes to create a little more beauty.

Art washes the dust of everyday living from our souls. --Picasso

My own. I did it too.

090115

I will unplug this tangle of wires that bound us before. Even if they aren't easy to sever. It will never be the same. I can burn the paintings and shred the shitty poetry. Maybe it will let you get on with it. You didn't act like it mattered when I was far. Now that I am close, not being worried about me seems normal. He does still care what happens to me, in his weird way.

I knew exactly what I was doing when I got here. I have followed my plan and I am not doing it for you. When I see you,

I do it, sadly, out of a sense of selfishness: to see your eyes. I wonder why you see me? Do you feel? Do you scheme? Do you care?

091815

A small gift from the universe came today. Unexpectedly, it reminded me that I am alive. I do forget. Surrounded by purpose and all those things I must do. All my all everywhere but here. Within the crumbled walls I notice dust growing all over everything. This place hasn't had me back in so long... the vault stands open and I go live for once.

What About Love--Heart

--I got myself a sign from the natural world. A simple little flower came on the wind to me after I let myself give a little tiny prayer of hope for myself. It was meant to lift me. And it did. Sort of like the shadowy thing I feel.

091815

I dreamed of a cloudy rainy night and looked up into the shadows face. It was so deep a night I didn't see his features. I ran back to the dream to see his face but I couldn't. it's OK. I will know him when we meet.

I saw enough in this dream to identify him when I come across him. Smiles. My own spoilers. Chuckles...

091815

You want me to say those fucking words out loud? You want me to say the tragic line written in my notebook which I buried away long ago? Haven't you all moved on from me yet? The time for this stanza has passed... even the words pass. But I will say it. I won't take it back. I meant it. I love you.

Don't know who I wrote this one for. It is beautiful still.

091815

I am no west side story. Fuck you. I am from this neighbor-
hood. So. Get over it. Let me be whoever or whatever I can be
now and leave me alone. Go sing Maria, Maria by your fucking
self. While I dance, smiling, to another song.
    You Gotta Fight For Your Right to PARTY—Beastie Boys
    Bohemian Rhapsody--Queen
    Guess who.

092115

I am waiting for time to be right. I don't sit idly and do
nothing. I work on all the things I need to put my energy towards. I have so much to do still. I would love to see if he does
what he says. He doesn't seem to have real interest in me.
Someone's always angry. For once I will not try to please everyone. Or anyone. Except myself. I miss the flippant way he
casually thinks he owns me. He realizes what matters most?
No. Let's back up and let the universe do her thing.
    Even though the darkness guards me jealously, I am well
loved by the light. Love will find me. In this senseless competition, there are no winners. He only has the tiny privilege of
being held close and loved well by me.
    Hell is Living Without You—Alice Cooper
    --Couldn't tell since they started to bleed together in the
way they both had to be out of my life. I can only do so much
to keep a friendship going. I really don't think I should have to
have sex if I am just a friend. Do you?

092215

Happiest of birthdays, my little sparkly, orange-haired
daughter. It took so long to finally hold you in my arms. That
wonderful day made me see the world and not care if I saw
the world all at the same time. I knew that you would brighten

my life and holding your little hand in mine is a joy I can't put in words. Your mommy is not perfect but I will always love you and that makes your birthday super special for me. The simplest things...my four little women and our divine struggle for something more. We are okay and I will always fight for you all, my little beauties. We don't need anyone else. We have made it so far and been OK! Let's celebrate our sparkly, orange-haired, six-year-old! You will remind me always what can happen when you fight for it. Because you fought to be here and then I fought to get you here. And then we fight all the time—to comb your hair or to eat a dinner or to brush your teeth. You remind me to keep looking up and questioning everything. If we don't stay curious, how will we conquer the world? Make no mistake—I expect to find you crowned emperor, one day, my little Blysse. You have what it takes to conquer worlds, my darling. You better go do just that. We will be waiting to cheer and sing for you!

I remember how big you were and how I thought they had to have switched my baby because you looked like a six-month-old!! I did dream about you when I was six myself. You were in a little cabbage but when I opened it I saw a huge baby that seemed switched at birth. She was so BIG! And the red hair...I would have laughed just like your uncle did when he came to see me in a dream before I had you. That red hair is wild, honey. Keep it in check...the temper that comes with it must be disciplined well, so you can fight for the real things and ignore the rest. You are an angel, whether you know it or not and you are here to remind sisters of the real and important things, too. Don't let them forget, my princess. My wild warrior princess.

Mommy loves you sweetheart.

092215

In the beginning, it is always dark. So, it was with the quiet girl that was once me. The beginning was dark so I would firmly embrace the light. The beginning was dark so that I could learn to stand alone in the blackest nights and have no fear of the dark or the creatures that live there.

--And I did. Cain. I must care.

No honest conversations with me. 3 a.m. or otherwise.

092315

I don't wonder who I am anymore. I have been shattered and rebuilt. I don't need to be alone anymore. I am finished with promises from liars. I am breathing still. I could be any-one. I don't care what you think of me. I am busy. Hate me if you like. It's easier when I am not yours to command. I have taught and learned. I have created most of the beauty I see. I wrote about my love and then burned it. The world rang with my song. My voice is rich and powerful. I felt. I dreamt. And even now-I will not fear tomorrow.

For my lovely soul. I am a real and wonderful person. I can make it through anything. I have. It has been tough. I will fin-ish the game.

092715

I don't sleep well with you on my mind. My phone died while you pouted. I didn't break the damned thing. I think I should have, though. I did miss you. You can't expect me to lay down and die. I already had taken a nice step back and had a look at the big picture. It's what us arty types do...big pictures. I am aware of many things I don't talk of, yet.

Sighs. Even though I am not your enemy, you seem to want to be mine. Why?

--I hope I find someone brave enough to love me, too.

092915

Hiding the shining crystal pieces of me isn't easy but each day I push them down and wait for five more minutes. Breathe Tabitha. It's over soon.

Don't Trust Me—3oh!3

--Cain's. I hope he knows I learned like five new words for revenge because of him but that none of them ever worked as well as the favored line from the poem I didn't even keep a copy of.

I left it with you Cain. Blue-eyed revenge. I still gave you time after time, until the cards said I didn't have to anymore. It seems strange to think of you not there anymore, but that's sort of how I need to look at it, right?

092915

Happy early birthday, Darius.

I love you. Thank you for making me feel good on my own birthday when no one else could be bothered with the quiet, little me in the corner. Thank you for making me feel special. I miss you, big brother. I wish I could say how much I feel, but I am sure you know. Mwah. You big old asshole. I miss you. Remember the sixth birthday with the tinker toy cake? Me and Charisma were both in awe. It was shocking and we were forever in love with birthdays after that. Smiles and re-members the day and the joy on your face.

092915

The shadow was here one more time. I felt his hand on the small of my back guiding me to a place more private so Rainen didn't see me fall apart AGAIN. He will show up. I will see him, soon. I saw the time in the dream.

The End of the Road—Boys II Men

I have a lot of hope when I have a good dream like that one.

It made me feel light.

092915

You belittled my heart. Doesn't make freedom any less wondrous. I packed away my heart with the other breakables. Somewhere safe from marauding pirates. If love isn't there, it can't conquer shit.
Rock Me--Scorpions
Rainen's.

092915

Can you let fourteen years go? Of course, if I have to. He wasn't mine. I still loved him.
Freedom--George Michael
Rainen's.

092915

In love, on guard. What's the difference? Wake in darkness and walk through the ruins alone. I put the walls back one beautiful brick at a time. I am careful to cage no one. No wild boy would know what to do with me now, anyway.
Control—Puddle of Mudd
It felt like a great deal of being on guard against stupid people and their lack of understanding and knowledge. I was sooooo bored.

093015

I am only myself. I let go the illusion of control. After all, I am in control of nothing. You should try it once. When you feel the freedom of imperfection and the joy of being away from my supposed ownership, you will feel yourself soar.
I walk slowly through the equally enchanting desert. My

mind is set on something I haven't encountered yet. He is somewhere. A shadow waiting for me to set him free and let him be real. I'm not waiting anymore.

Keep the dream for yourself.

Drops of Jupiter--Train

Where the shadow gets his ass booted for being too mysterious. Ha-ha. Gotta let it ALL go, right.

100315

Happy birthday to my one and only big brother, Darius. Thirty-eight...low whistle. You old motherfucker. Smiles because I think you would be a striking man now in your old age. Chortles and gasps.... I am funny. The ladies always did love you and your weird Irish... WEIRD.

I wonder if you will ever know the little things you did while you were here that made such an impact. I miss you each day. I pray for your continued peace wherever you are. Your fire and wildness often inspired me my entire life. Your balance and faith keep me going when I lose my own. Your generous spirit makes me relent when the world pisses me off. I love you always and miss you forever. Happy birthday. Darius Michael.

Fearless leader, crazy asshole, troublemaker, and this little sister's hero.

I love you.

Tabi

Thunderkiss '65---White Zombie (His song to me...the first two lines in the song...)

100315

Hi Cain.

I hope you are doing well. Everything is peaceful. I wish I had my phone but I don't think it matters anyway. You manage to be there at the same time you manage to ignore what the real issues are. I don't think it would help. I miss you while understanding you don't miss me. I knew right when I got here. Shakes head and wonders. It is fine. I am going away though. You keep acting like it didn't matter and it won't, I guess. It's a stupid letter and writing them doesn't help anymore. I guess I'll stop. Worthless ink.

--Na. the ink was OK and the message was OK. The dear whomever might be better served by just saying dear whomever rather than making it to Cain. Right. Even when I know I would like to talk to him. Scoffs and rolls eyes at self.

101415

Darius,

It doesn't seem like thirteen years ago, you know. I always feel like it was some more recent day you sailed off to your peace and fucking quiet. I'm not mad, just miss you. We always seemed to be alone when we were young so I wonder why it bothers me so much now. You found friends and I decided when I went out into the world, that if I needed friends then I would have had them when I wanted them. I survived well by myself. Your mother...shakes head. I wasn't much to her all along and now I try to give her the things she could never give me-- you know, a home, a loving place to be oneself, a house full of love and children's wonderful laughing. I can remember who I am and where I come from easily enough. She could have just not given me to him that night and you know all could have been forgiven. She won't even acknowledge she did something wrong that night. Save yourself so your daughter can take your place? I would kill before I let my daughter go to a soul stealer like him. Any one of mine. But that's why I am the mom. Laughs at my good sense. And people's selfish ways.

Oh, Darius. You would be so proud of these girls. They are so amazing. Alyc is working hard and struggling through finding out that mamma was right about most shit. Such a hardship to learn that her dumb mom was always fighting for her and protecting her from the struggle. I hope you look in on her now and then. Sometimes I worry. She is doing well, though. It's hard to reserve my opinions and keep my damn advice to myself. I don't want to be like mom. In any way.

Ionthe is a constant source of reliability and smart-assery. She's very creative. Ionthe is always here for all of us and she is giving and stubborn and ferocious for her sisters. She takes no shit, brother. And she will drag us all on her adventures. I love that about her. She is always looking to see where she could make her dreams happen. I am ready to take her there. Little Ionthe so serious about most everything.

Iome is smart and I mean brilliant. She complains about not having friends and then complains she doesn't like how dumb most people are. Remind you of anyone, asshole? I try to keep on it and remind her we all are human and fallible but she thinks since I try so hard, everyone should. It is frustrating to try to get across to her. She is so strong and she has a lot of that wild in her. I worry for the world when she goes to claim her part of it. They better stay out of her way! I am glad she loves Ionthe so much because that's how she stays balanced. They are like twins and it is weird but true. Always together and talk weird and act like sweet little girls... except for the smart-assery. Can't forget that. Laughs.

Lily is always herself and makes no damn apology for it. You would be her brand-new pinky ring, Darius. She is adorable and honest and rotten and she loves so much. Her red hair and sky-blue eyes remind me to be gentle but tough. Like with you. She must argue and about everything. Not just one item. Every single thing from bath, not shower to pb and j over eggs. I mean she will argue till you just have to get up and get her booty. She is just like you, Darius.

I know you would love them. I tell them our stories. The good ones and the bad ones. They listen and they are in awe of how much we didn't have, and where we went from where we were. I am so proud of them and their grateful little spirits. They make me better than I ever was and I love them so much. They love books and each one is so smart about her own thing. They have causes and hold firm to them. Alyc is all about babies and kids. Ionthe is into saving animals and people's souls. You know we come back as animals. And she sure doesn't want to save any shithooks! Iome loves authenticity. Research. Knowledge being power, she is powerful. Also, very beautiful when she lets you see her in a rare movement or dance-step. Little Lily is just wanting some snuggles and to be chased around the house like all of us are idiots, poking her and laughing. They are all RUSLONS. I don't know if that's good or bad though. Ha-ha. I miss you, big brother. Your advice was always so open minded and double edged. I love you. I hope peace is as good as it sounds. I won't see you soon but I will be thinking of you always. Love you big bro.

Tabi -your least fave sis. Ha-ha. P.S. You go check on your mom, please. Sheesh.

102015

Sacred silver drops of beauty greet me quietly. They fall to remind me where I came from and where I'm going. Today simply pulls me from a dream and deposits me on the steps of my Tuesday. What a gentle waking. The thunder's very deep voice is like a lover's sleepy whisper. I jump. I can hear my name on each peal. I don't think anything moves me like this.

--The NM rain is something you must experience to know exactly how amazing the wild weather is... it always seems like someone is trying to get my attention during the rainy season. I always jump when the thunder peals.

102015

The best of the rainy morning is mine. I wake just after

three. My dreams still disturb me. These are ancient dreams I haven't had in some years. Strange they creep back up.

I dream of Rainen; my once universe. His dark green gaze so magnetizing and mesmerizing to me. I dream of Carl, his soul I once thought of as kin. His guilty blue-green eyes never fully meeting mine, like it always was. I dream even of Cain. His cool reserve and his ice blue stare pinning me like the spotlight it turns out to fucking be.

I wake and I look around, not expecting anyone. I know this is the time and that soon I won't be waiting anymore. The puzzle falls quickly in place and I see it moving with momentum now. for once, I am not in any hurry. My patience seems limitless now. After all the time I sat in such torment wishing things would move faster...

--Chuckles because that's just the way it bes. I am finally happy and wonderful and the bullshit is let loose. I don't care what happens because I tried to engage honestly and be a good friend. I was a damn good girlfriend. I also did my dead-level-best to be a good person. I am seeking ways to see the good in people refracting through their eyes. I want that to be the way it is. But I know what life is. I live in no fantasy.

102015 1050p

I sit quietly with the TV as background noise. The clicks of a protesting furnace war with my first love. The rain. The slow dark words from the thunder drown out all thoughts of TV or furnaces. I am embraced by the clouds. The lightning jewels my neck with soft cloud-bristled brushes and the steady cold rain washes the ugly world from my skin.

Ah. Rain as art. M. Yummy.

102115

My pen and I fell asleep together last night. And we woke together this morning. The pen holds all my rain soaked dreams and me.

--My new boyf...the rain. Can't help but laugh. Truly while I was in Oregon, I spent more time in the rain than anywhere else. And yes. I will be in the rain forever. Not just something I say. I'll take NM rain or Oregon rain or Ireland rain. I just gotta have the rain.

102115

Lonely soul-like me.
Wandering dreamer-never finding one path.
Lost heart-if I had one.
Senseless tears-crying doesn't help.
Generous spirit-finally quits looking.
Cautious steps-toward healing.
Stormy night-the night I meet him.
Rain soaked morning-at least now I know.
Disbelieved love-his words fall like fired stones.
Stubborn fighter-I fought for him every step and he lets me go easily.
Remembered friend-I will always want.
A ten-year lie-or was it? I will never know.
Uncondoned untruths-how can I believe a liar?
Bared psyche-I tell others who I am.
Gentle runaway-I never tell them where I am going. They should know.
Painful memory-I don't let it rule me.
No more tears-I won't be alone and I won't wait for you.
Patient runaway-I can hold myself up.
No more lies-actually plenty more, I just don't believe them anymore.
Careful fantasy-I am careful to leave out love, in case I am looking too hard.
Simple life-I can do whatever I want now.

102415

I can take off the black now. I feel like I have mourned for years. I want to pull out the nice grey and wear that for a while. It isn't like I would stay in sadness forever. I did give it the time I needed to move beyond it. Now I can. I can even leave a shadow.

--Rainen's and the shadows. Sighs. Hard words to say. I am done grieving and ready for life again. I can't wait forever for a reluctant love. While you all sit and figure it out, I will go ahead and get on with this.

You know it isn't like Star Trek. You can't fuck everything on board while you "love" the one girl and wait till you are both fifty before you do anything about it. I am the greatest adventure and I don't want to wait to start living.

102515

Happy, happy birthday little miss hallows-eve moon! You are growing up so fast I have no time to catch you at one stage before you are off to the next! You better slow down a sec and smooch your mamma before the next adventure begins. Endless potential and wonder are yours, my third daughter. You are special in your place and special for your awesome sweet huge heart. You are never fooling anyone with that Gothic thing you do. It just makes you even sweeter when you find out that light shines from within you as surely as you are loving the night. I found myself as a young girl embracing the same mystery.

Remember the moments that matter. The moment you came out and stirred your father's entire world up. He didn't know he could love like that. Your older sisters made him sure he could be a father and you made him sure to do it. And well. He stepped his act up a notch for each girl. Every time he thought about it, he was doing one more thing. I can't imagine he would be the same without you, my little toe eating monster. I remember you smiling and I smooched you and sent you to go with dad so I could make his world a little more special with your big giant eyes and little beautiful artist hands. I knew you would draw. Even then... your eyes were so dark and green. I wondered after a minute what color they would be. Haven't they changed like three or four times? You change and grow. We never stop so enjoy it. Revel in it, baby. It doesn't make you crazy.

Be yourself. Be only yourself for it is special and precious and anyone who tries to dim you will get a fat face full of my foot. You are going places, darling girl. I will see you succeed with every goal if you NEVER GIVE UP.

So, go shine my brilliant and beautiful daughter. Have the happiest birthday ever.

Your mamma loves you so much. P.S. I made dirt cake. It has gummy worms and Oreos. I love you, baby.

111815

I won't say it to you. You told me you feared me. Why the hell would you say that to me? I remember you thinking I would steal your fucking wallet. Has to crack up because I never stole a thing from you the entire time I knew you. I would never hurt you. Or be an idiot. I was only pushing on the barbed wire to feel something. I told you that I wouldn't hurt you. I knew I could feel again. I could move on in a way that would leave me feeling something rather than numb. I know you wait for him to be done with me. So, you can say ha-ha-I got you kind of. And I will laugh because I was waiting for it too, but for a much better reason than fake love. For a real chance at living for me.

Here comes the champion of it, to lie again and tell me he is honest. He lies as he says it. He pushes his pack of cigarettes down in his pants pocket. I smell them all over the place.

Another man could smoke, after all, people deserve choice. He can't. If he wants to stay out of the wheelchair, the good doc told me to keep him away from them. I couldn't. My one failure with him. I tried to keep him active and working on himself... eating right and being worthy of the faith we all put in him for his well-being and health. I fought and helped him through the entire thing. My promise mattered.

He doesn't want me unless someone else does. Which is funny... a most chuckle worthy group, you guys are...

First part Cain's, then Rainen's.

111815

I can't ask myself to feel love again. I know I can't lie and say it isn't there. But I am sure I don't know how to be that girl. I do want this feeling. I want to feel. I need to dance. I want to twirl in the rain. To feel the cool... to feel the joy... to feel anything again! I do want to see beauty before I leave this place. I look for the sparkly prism moments.

I know well what my feelings are and I laugh hardest because they both think I have no intuition whatsoever. I am not running my chubby little ass over to Cain. Nor am I holding my awesome hands tied to my chubby ass waiting for Rainen to decide I am what's good. If I hadn't slept with Cain, Rainen would have just known I was the one, right. If he couldn't figure that out in twelve years, I don't see how he ever would. And why would I want that, now?

112115

I did recreate myself. I hadn't expected to change so many things about myself... I made it through learning he didn't love me. Whatever I have gone through, whatever comes next, I am ready.

I feel the hunted heartbeat in my chest.

Pay attention.

--The words here mean so much to me. Rainen's love did force rebirth and I am better because of it. I do love him still but I don't need to worry about love finding me. Of course. I am a good catch. I have noticed lately that I am a lot of good things. I can make it. I wasn't sure for a very long fucking time but I am now.

112915

Did you want me last night? Maybe you got bored Friday. I didn't have time to notice. I was extremely bored. I made other plans. I remembered you saying you didn't care who I slept with. Excellent. As it should always be, dear. I am no woman who will stupidly wait for you.

I did find a lost moment with someone who knows I have a problem being patient.

112915

I was locked away twelve years before I found out. It had suited me well. I cherished my chains. They bound me to an eternal love and to a home I never had before. I worshiped the man who had thought enough of me to hold onto me. The sunrise who bound me couldn't hurt me. My soul felt calm and peace. A wanderer like the sun always leaves though. The light that bound me never had the key. I sat alone and bewildered by the open locks and what it implied. I saw myself as I was instead of how I wished he saw me. I changed my mind and my form. I changed my heart and my soul. I changed who I choose to be. That wanderer came back, chains in hand, to beg the butterfly for another chance. But now I can't BE chained.

Rainen's. So exactly how I feel.

113015

I am still amazed by the way you SAID you felt. The beer had to speak for you--exaggerated by far, I am sure. I know you don't love me. You haven't stood for the right thing since I have known you. I can only thank you for the lessons I learned. It was only for yourself, though. I knew. Be blessed in your life that you built for you and lovely. I plan to have a nice slice of peace and I did find a quiet, little happiness for myself.

Cain's.

113015

My walls have been rubble on the meadow grass for a while now. The wet charred bits of paper dance around with my hair. Pieces of hollow melodies drift through the bricks. No one is here. The night has brought icy drops to chill whatever heated passions I still had inside. Nothing reaches me here. I used to run here to hide before the destruction hit. I need a place where the violence can't find me. It's a peaceful, vacant apocalypse. I dreamed of a rare wild boy who loves only me. The dreams were true.

--This comes from the recurring dream I spoke of before. I have had it since the age of three and it has kept me through many bad times when I didn't know if I had the strength to go on. I shared these things for the first time here in these pages and it is a very personal thing for me to talk about. I am also giving the world a little bit of myself since I have had so many experiences that enriched me while I was here. I wanted to give back. The bad things and feelings we experience really don't define us. It's what we do with the time we have. Take it and make it the thing that moves you. Truly. If you don't do something about it, you will always be unhappy. It empowers us to change things. The world brings a lot of change and humanity IS a state of change. So, implementing your own change says you know what you want and you can attain it by simply creating it for yourself. Magic, we humans, after all, huh? DAMN, I hate it when I am right. laughs.

120415

Rainen, it isn't that you don't love me. But it is! You told me so many times that you didn't. I slept hardly at all and cared for you each minute I was awake. I lay alone each night and wondered who the hell I was, if not Tabitha Ruslon-for Rainen Kelsey.

You certainly didn't stay for the kids. But you did! The attraction was long gone and therefore your shallow love went, too. You don't want to punish me. But you DO! You burn my soul with your ability to take what you want and leave me nothing. You can't get over the tiny betrayal from a woman you swore you didn't want until that moment? You cut me and the babies off our supply of your light. Which betrayal was worse?

Don't worry—he never showed me anything new there. It was the same for you both. No amount of me wanting it to be different would help.

I saluted like a toy soldier and now you don't need me... I really was a boring old toy.

--The curse of the men who love me, is that for some reason, revenge or hate or love, they always want to come see me again. I wish that was ever different. I don't know why I let them see me. I guess that's a new policy for the Tabitha campaign. Must bring myself some law and order. Laughs... this one was Rainen's and I briefly spoke of Cain at the end.

121415

At nine fifteen his low, sexy voice melts through the phone line and over me. Sincerity wraps my jangled nerves in the calm that is usually his special thing. I relax for one moment, engulfed inside his easy whisper.

My simple smile fades slowly. An older tear-filled night shoves itself forward, telling me gently not to forget how deceptive that silky voice has been before. It sighs and tells me about the lengths he will go to find a way to break my peace.

His pain might have made him lash out, but he knew how to stop it. I was fighting these pains with him-by his side each day. I am not weak or some princess that hasn't handled pain. At what point would my love be able to break through? Never it seemed. He moved on in his city and I sat there, half-finished, super-gluing myself back together, frantically. I sat in black not able to grieve or be angry or move on. I counted a billion tears in that one sorrow.

His voice is asking me not to hesitate to call him if I need him. At nine twenty a tear slips down my face as I breathe out a quiet okay and then goodbye. The only forceful thing I feel is when I throw the phone and it hits the wall and falls apart.

No more of THAT tonight.

121415

It went unnoticed since long ago. It meant nothing. I am better equipped to deal with it than most. I wished in the dark lonely night that I could pretend to forget so well. I let the hurt go right back where it belongs. I didn't feel it then, and I don't need to worry about it now. I am simply waiting for it to be done.

121515

You believe anything. Especially in your infallibility. You are special because you are there when it falls apart. But do you make it fall apart? I am skeptical of perfection. I know about failure. I have tried to be everything but myself.

I don't hate you though. Like you seem to hate me. I wonder how you get satisfaction from hurting someone who has suffered.

You have what you love and I have what I love. We will all just have to love where we are.

--Which I did no matter how I felt or how anyone else

wanted me to act. I chose my path with my decisions. I bet you hate how I was assured even when I was on the floor crying. I knew what to do. I had to endure for Rainen and the honor he showed me in the newness of our love. I did. My promise stuck like no one would dare to believe. Yours? Mmm. I can't say what YOU call it. I call it unreliable, Cain.

121515

He reminds me now each morning that he wants me. He thinks he can save me from what he did to me. Which seems strange already. He reminds me every night that he will be here in the morning. Doesn't matter if I share an intimate moment or hours... I still insist I sleep alone.

For once though, today's desert darkness wakes me before he can. I was strong for so long, I thought I had no other option. But I can rest. I can walk away and even if it is dark, I will find my way. Like I always have.

Boys are so sweet when they are lying to you. I fight back the only way I know how-by revoking the trust. They can't see my sparkle-even right up close. I whisper my secret to the moon.

Boys. Sheesh. Ha-ha.

121515

I rest in the ruins-lying to myself, like every good addict-"It will be the last time." The door inside still locks behind me as it always has. The walls are crumbled behind the vault doors. No one looks for me, here. The cool grasses soothe my wearied feet. I don't care if I am forgotten; wish I would be again. The soft rains fall like they always have. The physical pain is finally bearable in the peace. The wind brushes my face to wipe rain and tears dry. The clouds pull me and hold me tightly, as no one here chooses to. The rain is murmuring quiet nonsense just for me. The peace will have to hold my soul until I manage to disappear into it.

122615

Some men don't think you are worth it. I don't think I am some great beauty over which wars are fought. I am no perfect flower. I don't listen to most advice. What I am, I can't even say. People always swear they have it all. They think much of themselves. Turns out I am one of the stronger and more equipped. I didn't know because I hadn't tried. People tend to tell me I am not good at something before I do it...I fulfill my promises and even the ones that others make and break. I STILL believe in magic. I smile the same easy smile and let them all be. I'm already dancing in the rain and I feel fuckin free!

--Just for me. And I am free. Free of promises and ties and little things I never even worry over anymore. I feel like I am warded well and ready for anything.

122915

This fog is new in my transformed desert. The white blankets the whole street and it soothes my soul in a quiet and simple way. I have long loved winter. It's a cold silent presence waiting for change. My inner fires are lit and my home is toasty with children and all others warm in bed. The world is brand new and I am the only one here to see it. I wait just outside the door with the fog, under the hanging dripping knives of all sizes. The clear sharpness hangs from every edge. They seem ready to enforce the peace.

--I love the imagery. I don't try to force poetry, but it leaks out my pen every time I set it to paper. I tried to pull myself back in so I could make sure I was going to be understood. People understand words they see and feel.

122915

The fog is emanating from each warm home. Our lives and jobs and movement cease. These several days of unexpected blizzard stop us. The large cones of clear ice cling to the edges of my roof. We all wait for the desert to unveil itself again with the melt. To see what changed. No one knew this little desert town was so beautiful—not even me. I must see beauty in truth no matter what.

The truth is that love should bring me peace. I can't fight for nothing or everything anymore. This is beautiful though no one can see it. I will wait for love under my December blanket, three feet buried within it's pure white chill. THAT is beautiful. I wait on the edge of the future like my icicles. This is the truth and finally it's beautiful to me.

122915

I wish I could be there for you during this. I know you don't need me to be. I know also that letting the crazy doctors chop anything on your body is stressful. You are probably calm and practical about it.

I wanted to answer the phone badly. I am sorry I couldn't. Rainen and I had a decent night and it went all to hell when the phone announced loudly and repeatedly, "call from: Texas". I know you could care less. But I have to. He is helping me out constantly and joyfully with rides to and from work and many other things. He shares himself with me. I don't have many in my life willing to do THAT. I don't want to fucking fight about a fucking man that isn't even interested in me. Sighs. You are married. Go be married.

I don't think the constant trying to get back together is working either. I don't think you or he understand why I won't be with either of you. More boring Tabitha stuff. Laughs and shakes head.

I get bored of people and they haven't managed to surprise

me when it comes to being honest or good people. Some just CAN'T.

I was still going to give you this one painting I found after I burned some of the first ones. I doubt you will miss it, though.

The stuff from Oregon has a few more. I think I should burn the rest of them. Maybe I will do just that.

Cain's.

122915

I wonder if pain is like a stray dog. If you feed it will it follow you around forever? If I kick the shit out of it, will it hurry up and go the hell away? If I call the pound will they give the original owner a ticket for letting the rotten biting bastard dog out? When the original owner calls and i.d.'s it at last, will they show up for it, so I am not stuck caring for a biting, jumping, and not well-trained pain-puppy?? Not as cute as we all imagined. Laughs...

123015

Just admit you are wrong. Give up on killing my soul. I never had much of one to begin with. Go on and let me go. You look for something from me that I can't give. I would never do that. I go on and check things off my dwindling list. I didn't rally too much belief in me. I didn't expect any. Three truths all said the same things. Not immaculate muses but inspiring nonetheless.

I am worth it. To myself at the very least. Thank you for the inspiration!

--Three truths...Cain, Carl, and Rainen. Who knew I could think of people as truth embodied in physical form? What an adult thing for me to to think.

123015

You can't break me. You try hard. You can't shake me, even when I let you. I step back one more time. You push and I am sure it means I should go. I give you back again. I wish you would just go. Me versus you versus stupidity on my screen. No one wins here. It doesn't hurt to be bullied when we both know you weren't even slightly interested in a living dead girl. You must work on your believability.

--Cain. Shakes my head. Because at the end of this I can recall your words and I am thrilled I kept those out and running across the ticker in my head. Chuckles low.

123015

You thought you remembered who I am, but you might have never known me at all. Really that's only who I WAS. You torture me each way you think will break me down to do what you want. I have already suffered through this a few times. I am sorry I can't cry for you. I told the devil I am fresh out of sympathy. This man did your work too well.

Cain and Rainen.

011516

I want to breathe the beautiful free air. I want to celebrate life, though I don't know much about it. I want to see my path clearly. I want to feel slowly and carefully. I learned some good lessons. I want something real. I understand myself. I dance anyway and remember who I always am...

011516

I dream of the little gardens I have planted everywhere I go. And I dream of the green already sprouted taller than I expected. I dream about the strength of those people who were there and didn't want anything more than to be my friend.

--I dream about the new life I have been seeing and creating all along. It's freedom. Keep the dream alive, the faith inside, and your love everlasting. Everything will be fine.

011516

I am looking for my life. I wake up and I am grateful. I found a little peace for myself. I would like to share my hope. I learned to accomplish. I can do whatever I want.

011716

I remember flipping the tarot card. And two more beyond that. It was a rainy Oregon day in October. It predicted some things I am watching coming true. These life experiences I had let hold me down have finally taught me what I needed to know. I will hold close the memory of being in the hated trailer house floor at my nana's and being grateful that I wasn't at the house on Oak St. I remember thinking I was learning about faith hope and love from a mother that didn't know about it herself. I knew then I would have to keep raising myself if I wanted to come out the other side. The people I could look up to were not interested in taking me under their wing. I didn't care after a while. But I did know I had to sustain myself because no one in this place would. I agreed with myself that I would not let the place I came from model my future unless it took me away from it.

And each thing I read in those cards came to pass. With different people than I thought but it sure did happen. Laughs.

011816

I am awake on this Martin Luther King, Jr. Day. I have been retraining myself to wake differently for the past month. I lay down stretching and listening to my youngest daughter pitter-patter through my hallway towards my room. I have been practicing my visualization for the last six months or so. It seems to work. I have noticed that the stress is going away.

My little girl climbs in my bed and snuggles under the warm blankets for the entire two minutes she can manage to sit still. She is such a bundle of energy and light. I kicked her out of bed. Too much bouncing. Off she scoots with her little nighttime ponytail swinging crazy behind her. She is off to wake the rest of my girls. I had a little time of loss when my oldest daughter moved away. I told her if she and her Grammy wanted her to move away from me so bad, then she should hurry and go. I worked hard to get my family through the hardship we had just finished with. I didn't want to give her up but sometimes the child needs to learn her own lessons. I love her and support her when she needs me.

I texted a short text to Cain, and then thought better of it. He didn't want to talk back then and he damn sure doesn't want to now. Game playing is for cards. Shakes head and laughs.

As I erase the message, and start to shut the phone off, Rainen texts and has to be at my house for his flat tire. I guess he is going to be here all day strutting around with no shirt on and all sweaty and awesome. I do care about him but maybe that's just it. I spent fifteen years taking care of him to the detriment of my own life and now I need to not look at him for a little while. He thinks having a pseudo-relationship will keep us close but really at this point, I don't see how. Sometime, I will have to make myself ready to do this thing and now is as good as any time. I want to be where I can say no easier.

I got my early on positive prize from the taxes. I won! A thousand dollars only but it was a nice reaffirmation for me to stay up and keep going. I can do this. Everything works out when I stop stressing and do what I know I need to do.

The simple predictive reading I gave myself said things I finally understood.

032216

This will of mine has to be enough. I am at my crossroads and nothing really sways me. It's too long and I am done now. I have changed. I was changing all along. Every day changed me. My will must be enough. The empty intersection gives me no clue which way to go. I picked a direction and walked. I couldn't say why. I am grateful for this difference. I was suffocating. I am glad I had the will.

032216 1258a

I will know the right words. I know what's true and what isn't. I don't even mind my own company. I can hear the right words. I watch your eyes for truth. Sometimes I see it.

032316

I like myself when I show kindness to assholes. It keeps them off balance. Laughs. I like to be soft and myself. I can be a decent person when I put my mind to it. I was broken hearted but I have been grieving for such a long time. I knew I could pull myself out of it, it's not too hard to be who I am. I don't enjoy pain like most think. I studied myself to make myself better. I know how to cope. I am a huge fan of life. Always have been. It's crazy but I like learning and growing and becoming more. I do want to be me.

032316

His eyes haven't looked in mine in so long. The differences are obvious. My eyes haven't looked at him in so long. I guess he isn't too concerned. I am not either.

Cain's.

042016

The weight keeps lightening up. I know my love wasn't

something to bear or be endured. I will be fine and I will keep knowing love is real. Somewhere it is.

Rainen's.

042016

Another place calls to me across distance I can't understand. A green rain soaked place...I see it when I dream.

042016

I hadn't felt alive in a very long time. I walked around mindlessly helpful to others, and kind, helping life run smoothly for others. I waited patiently for a sign to begin and I found the sign. I can't be everything all the time. I don't try to do all that. I am almost ready though. My smile might NOT reach my eyes, but I mean it nonetheless...

042116

Another question for me. Why am I sure that the shadow is someone I know?

042316

I keep looking ahead and being the real me. I can't share this grief with anyone yet. I need a hand to hold through the deep nights. Are there still stars out there? There are still other wishes, other worlds to see. I keep walking although it is a sharp pain. My distractions fall away.

As I keep to myself and do what I need to do I have decided that I can't be distracted by friends who fake their way through my time with them. I guess I knew I would keep going. It isn't so bad for me. It shouldn't be so bad for them if I treat them the way they treated me...

042616

Spring has arrived. I feel the rush of newness and light. I haven't felt the simple joy of spring in too many years. I feel the overwhelming pull inside to something more. It is very difficult to not run into the bright day and go look....

042816

I look around and down the usually busy street... There is no one for miles. I just water my garden with a surge of joy. I keep teaching my daughters with all my energy. I don't mind living a smaller version of life. It makes me happy. Since you were so blind, I will step back to the garden.

I find so much joy gardening and just living. It's amazing to be so free.

062316

So. Did you forget what the actual day of my birth was and so it's just more broad-ranging and insulting to make random appointments and break them? Laughs at you. You seem to have a problem keeping appointments you set. Did you just have too many pressing things?

Well, my little old feelings didn't even get hurt. You haven't kept any of the appointments you set for chats or texts or whatever. You are a superior friend there, Cain. I mean, thanks for lying your ass off. Enjoy your week, month or year. However long it will take you to get ahold of me this time. Chuckles. It's sort of sweet. Laughing. Dumb but sweet.

102116 1049p

I take a deep cleansing breath. I always find understanding in that place. Confusion bleeds away. I imagine all the blue clouds. It will wash me away from that stupid word. Love. Like that matters. Imagine a perfect world where they both have the love of someone better for them. I also imagine a world in which I emerge a butterfly, beautiful and brilliant. I know I will be noticed for the lovely creature I have been all along. Seems wrong to have to leave behind all the people I ever love.

010417

Good morning, I tiredly greet the early cold. I take time this morning to feel grateful for what I have. I grew my little family and I love it with all the fierceness I have in me. These girls are beautiful and wild. Before them my words carry more weight. I arm myself in preparation for keeping my big promises and the ones he STILL makes randomly. My daughters have learned to proudly carry themselves and their hearts are grateful and full of love.

It's all we needed after all.

We will keep moving forward with all the joy and we will dance under the moons and rains. We are free. My own collective of pixies. Wry grin.

010417

I watch him learn to keep his word. He still makes me proud every day. I smile because he wants me near him still. It might hurt sometimes but I am grateful to know what love might feel like. Should I happen across it, I will know it feels good. He made me feel again no matter what he thinks of me now. it feels like brightness sometimes. If he can pull away from the controlling long enough to see the me I am now...

I walk back across the street (-my choice-) to my toasty little home. My daughters are strong and healthy and living here in a new harmony. I do not wish for him. I dream of the loss with profound sadness. His friendship means something still. Even if Cain can't see or understand why I am still loving him and caring for him. I can't and what's more WON'T treat him like he doesn't matter to me. And Rainen, you can't expect me to want Cain to vanish like you want him to. He made me see the little smart-ass go-getter I was and that is valuable to me. I can't sit around and be bullied by people who think I can't do anything. And the both of you are sort of behind on all things Tabitha-related. Catch up, please.

010617

I feel like I am already back. I hear the steady thrumming of the rain on a simple roof. I feel like I am walking cloaked and warm through the fields. I smell clean earth ready to parent blooming life. I see greens slipping into shadowed tones as night falls. I walk in the empty roads and decide I am both in danger and safe everywhere I go. I walk fully hidden in the advancing fog and taste the sharp rain.

031117

I greet the strange foggy morning in this desert. The earliest birds sing outside. My earliest daughter readies herself for a day of creation and painting. I pull myself back inside my own head long enough to promise myself solemnly that this is almost over. I can't be checked against their stupid list of what I am not doing their way. If I change, it is only for me. Never anyone else.

031117

I am sure as I look in the mirror that I have lost four more inches around! I am so excited. This weight has made me strange and I return to myself the more I lose. I feel alive and powerful. I can sizzle in the electricity. I expect things of myself. Makes your expectations look silly. I know I COULD be who you want me to, but that thought makes me violently rise inside and say, "FUCK WHAT YOU WANT!"

No matter what I look like, I don't think either of you can love me as I am.

031217

I realize all that I am. The suffering has ended and I am so pleased I made it. You watch me struggle and look for ways to prolong it. I have no taste for the suffering. I watch myself love all wrong and forgive myself. Even if you will not. It didn't bother me before. I find it bothers me quite a lot now. I can carry on just like you can and I won't brag about what I am doing this weekend, you ass. I will just go do the things I want to and keep it to myself. You want, need, and love huh. It's very late for that series of emotions. Couldn't seem to find the capacity for those while I was heavy... hm. I don't think it matters much now, does it?

Rainen's.

031217

Maybe one day you will outgrow this. I hope for both our sakes that it is soon. You need to get on with it. Live, love. Create beauty. The world can always use more beauty.

Rainen's.

032817

Getting to know me is hard since I am still learning myself. I know I am loyal. Like crazy. It isn't as desirable a trait in this new day. I have many extreme tasks I am busy with. I can't stay here and wait for you to decide I am worth it. I know I am.

032817

Spring is here. The cooler is running with all its lovely white noise. The princesses are all tucked into silken sheets and dreaming of magic I am sure. Prince Jim the first is fed and happy in his tank of blue goodness.

My peace sits in front of me. Spring.

My friend from Oregon is texting, and my friend from Texas isn't. Same shit, new day. You must love seeing people be exactly themselves. Some have such a hard time admitting they are lying...

I have been adjusting to my mornings without his arms around me demanding my love and his kisses insistent and ever-present. I will make it through this spring. I don't know how, but I will have to, wont I, Rainen?

032817

The rain came back and washed the winter off the face of this town!

Hi again. How are you? Why I continue with this after all I found out is beyond me. My blank paper stares at me like I'm talking to myself. Which I guess I could. The fun fantasy you give a fuck doesn't stand any more.

Let's start over... How about this?

Dear fabulous, fabulous Tabitha. Finish this stupid book so we can move and be peaceful. I miss when I didn't exist for them. When I was fat and therefore not worth it. Chuckles. I don't care about too much of this shit anymore. Even when I was the right AGE, I didn't love high school bullshit. I was isolated for a long time. What makes you think I can't stand to be alone? Alone. Not afraid. Only eight more things to go. Laughs and feels free. My cards said I could call it when I felt like it. At long last, I am done.

I feel like no one knows how much I rely on my smart intuition to see where I need to go. What I need to do. When I need to do it. Who I will do it with and why I will do it at all. Call me superstitious if you like but I am a helluva girl—intuitive, you know. The cards haven't left me high and dry yet.

When I read the cards about this entire -I don't know what to call it besides an affair- I was told the requirements had been met. I was after all, anticlimactically finished trying to be everything for everyone. I could (chuckles...) diminish into the west, as it were. Those real nerds will know what I am talking about. Laughs. I did try with you Cain. I tried my best to be understanding while you played around like I didn't matter. I understood and kept flipping a card so I would know when I could let you go. I had no real wish for revenge. I am sad you did. I felt like I knew a piece of your soul in the old days but I guess life changed you too much to be my friend. I was all in to be your real friend. I did many things in a day you might not have believed me capable of to maintain that—whatever you want to call it. I can't be the second girl. I never could be. I am a good person, Cain. I didn't deserve what you and the other assholes did to me. I think I deserve at the very least an apology. I am quite sad you turned out to be such a different person than I thought. I didn't want to change you, but some force made you reach and punch wildly at me. So, something obviously thought I was important to your human growth and development. Well. I didn't want your left overs. I only think I deserve the best no matter what. I don't think that turns out to be you. I wish you had shown me any bit of your real self instead of playing like you were some awesome well-adjusted adult. We both know it's not true or you would have been able to do what I did. I looked at profile pictures for each Cain Benedict on Facebook. I didn't recognize any of them as you and so I left it be. I didn't want to disrupt or intrude on you. But you. Now you had a much better plan in mind. Let's go ruin Tabitha because she looks like she might be happy. And as I said, you didn't have to do anything. Rainen was well on his way to running me off. There was no reason for you to hate me. I didn't do anything to you that you didn't recover from right away. So, you see? You had the power all along. You don't love me now and you damn sure didn't love me then.

No one ever even asked me what I would do when I appeared pregnant and alone. Did you know I didn't tell Carl the baby was his for way too long to be acceptable? Did you know that I broke up with him for several weeks before I ever told him? Did you know that I knew what he said about me behind my back? Did you know that I knew what YOU said (and did) behind my back? Did you also know that I told him and watched him fuck it up that same day? Just because I chose to let him be in Alyc's life didn't mean I wasn't aware of who the hell Carl was. I was unsure if the rumors were true but I saw quickly how you were. Wishing me and an unborn little angel dead? Yes. We were both children. But for some reason you deserved forgiveness for it and I did not. In your eyes.

Well. I am sad that you turned out to be so. I am sorry your beautiful soul was hurt by anything, but most of all by me in my misguided attempt to let my daughter know her father. I never thought I mattered to you. While I was in Roswell with my mom and sister and mom's creepy boyfriend, I found when I called, you weren't in. I started making alternate plans. Mostly I cried to my brother and he took me to hang out so I didn't do anything rash and crazy. I was so all by myself. I know you love to hear about me hurting, so there it is for you. I am sorry for any damage I did to you. I never wanted your ice blue eyes to be so cold. And I do hope you and your wife are together forever. I hope it is always fabulous and that your kids grow into good human beings. Please go on and forget all about me like before. I know it was easy. You think it was easy for me. I knew who Carl was. In the back kitchen at his work hitting on another girl in front of me the night I told him I was having his baby. He had only just asked if I would marry him. I guessed he wouldn't be a good dad and I wasn't wrong. That hurt me to admit then and now. I just wanted my daughter to know him. So, she could have one thing I didn't. A meaningful relationship not based on what mom thought about dad.

Thank gods for Rainen coming into our lives when he did

and making us all a family that meant something to someone. I loved him so fiercely. It will never matter what anyone says about him. I know him better than they ever have or will. And he is a deserving soul and a good father. I don't need anyone who has to get revenge on a little broke down and sad girl who has already been through hell this life. Whether it's Rainen or Cain or even good old Carl. I don't need the added pain of more bullshit. I am a good woman and if none of you can see or honor that, I can't be bothered to do the same for you.

Someday when you happen across this little book, which may very well be never, I hope the words make you all know yourselves better by how you treated me. I did nothing but love. Rainen, I wish I hadn't hurt you but I don't want to lie and say it meant nothing. To me anyway. Our time was a miracle to me! I had never had a family! It made me real in ways I can't even say. You deserve a woman that makes you thump.

And Cain, I didn't want an affair with you. I wanted to be there and try to make up for what you imagine was a deliberate slight. I didn't ever expect to see you again. Honestly, I doubt I would have if you didn't decide I looked so happy you had to destroy me. I own my mistakes and have never tried to say I don't make any. Just go on to whatever wonderful stuff you have planned OK. I don't want to be even a speed bump on your path. And I am sure I wasn't.

For the rest of the idiots who hacked into my accounts: email, phone and otherwise, I want to let you know that whoever you are, I couldn't care less about your stupid insignificance. I didn't listen to much that was subliminally thrown at me. Lucky me, so much time in my very young childhood was spent with bullies, wishing I could kill myself. I spent so many nights under a table by an open window praying for rain, so that monster would leave me alone. And after a while, I spent those nights holding a razor to my four-year-old wrist hoping I was strong enough to make it to one more great day of the abuse and hatred. I could only just barely hang on. The knowledge I could stop the abuse and fix my own problem was always in the back of my mind. If I held the power, no one else would be able to make me regret living. And lucky for you, the asshole cyber bully, that I didn't choose to take my own life. My daughters are beautiful creatures and it says something about you and your lousy soul that you would take me from them. What a huge jerk. I hope you learned your lesson and if not, I am very sure what goes around comes around. I have never tried to make another being hurt unless they hurt me so bad I couldn't recover. So, if your sorry ass ever comes across me in real life- you better pray I haven't already learned your identity. I would pray to my gods to keep me safe and out of Tabitha's way. Then I would disconnect myself from the computer and start looking around for safety. Just a heads up, dick wad. I hope your own family never must be without you, but I can't promise what my gods will do for retribution. I don't have the say so to call THAT karma off.

I wept too many nights and prayed for sunrise to come so I would not have to be alone in my head and with the bad thoughts swirling around. And I never wanted anyone to be alone like I was. I realize the rest of you have your own coping stuff you do. I really didn't have the same story-telling, smooching parents to teach me how. I had to get dropped into the deep end with no floaties and try to be a girlfriend to my stepfather and a mom to my own mother and sister. So, who cared for me in the nights in Oregon?

We all know the answer. ME. The little black hen had to be all and do all. She can enjoy it all, right. Remember I forgive easily, but I never forget. Anything. Chuckles because some people just never fucking learn.

041817

Last minute rabbits out of hats. Unemotional creatures who want to leave me alone but can't. My life is arriving.

I don't care how anyone justifies bullying. It is wrong. If you knew, you are accountable. Revenge is different for everyone. Laughs very softly. I know what waits and today is so much easier. I kept a hard promise. I can be kind to him even after he broke me. As surely as taking a bat to a crystal vase.

--I managed to keep my other promise to Rainen and not take his girls away forever. I know that it was hard. He started dating. And he always wants to show his new females pictures off to anyone who can make me feel bad about it. But I don't feel bad anymore. I am glad he is moving on. He should. I think I have moved on enough to say I won't spend anymore nights crying over him. I am tired of being alone while I am with people. I would like to feel like I have solid relationships and real creatures around me. So, I am going to work on the things I have been already. Keep being strong so my girls will see me be what they need to be to make it on this planet. They already tell me to stop being so alone all the time and just go on and have fun. I laugh because I am sure I don't know what that is anymore. But I am getting where I am going. I know I am strong and I know I have what it takes to achieve my goals.

I hope Rainen knows that no matter how much time he spends saying he's sorry, it won't be enough for what I endured. I spent all that time loving him and caring for him and he still managed to discount every effort while I did it. I care for him but I won't be led by him anymore. I will lead myself and he will either go his own way or at least get the hell out of MY way. I have shit to do.

042417

I never cared much for money. Except as a means to an end... you know-feed my babies and buy paint! Laughs...

I will have plenty of my own money. I never liked the filthy, nasty shit anyway. I will use it to further what I am doing. That is what it is useful for. And feeding those babies of mine.

060217

I had a hard time thinking about the losses I suffered through the writing of this work. I went through quite a hard time with losing Rainen. I knew he was my once in a lifetime guy. I didn't think much of marriage and I still don't. But I will always know he is a wonderful guy and someday he will grow a little and figure it out. But I can't say I will ever be back at the point where I would put on my faerie dress and carry my flowers and walk with my little tiniest girls all dolled up like fairies. Walk down a long path and see him there waiting for me. He is amazing and I hope he knows how much he soothed me in those first years when I had no doubt he loved me even though he didn't know who I was.

I am glad he finally knows who I am. I am also glad I know who I am. Little people like to think it only matters that they think they got what they wanted. I had this dream see... laughs. I pay close attention to those dreams. And I have thousands I don't talk about with anyone. I am a mystery for sure. I can see what happens to people to make them assholes but I don't have to hang out with assholes do I? I forgive myself for not wanting to be around that sort. I hope I find some peace and quiet. The dreams have been oddly silent for a while. It is nice at the same time it is disturbing. I guess I will flip another card tonight—silly superstition seems to keep me in the know. (Please Tabitha, remember to keep being just myself. It is beautiful even if I have to hide it away from assholes who don't understand me.)

I still think this could use a swift match and a little barrel for burning.

060817

I lay down last night. I didn't know why I felt so light. Maybe the two Bahama breakfasts, as I have taken to calling them. I don't drink so much anymore, so when I am in the mood, I try to indulge. I felt light, though. I got repeated texts from Rainen trying to get me all riled up. I already was, but I suppose it doesn't mean much these days. I have been working on saying what I need to say about each of the people that have made my life hell in their own way. I wanted to let it all go and I feel saying it "aloud" as it is, will help. How can I have sex after that?

I don't care if the world disagrees with me. I don't care if they never come around to my way of thinking. I don't even care if I ever see most of them again. I am moving into the life I should have already been living. I am proud of myself for making the mistakes I did, and having the balls to admit it. I am proud of the way I have carried on and met and surpassed my own expectations with the weight-loss and the job and the tireless effort to be a great mom. I am proud of my stick to it and my solid reliability. I am proud of myself for forgiving the dicks that worked on killing my soul every day. I wonder if it will still be as satisfying to watch me rise to my rewards. I may not be perfect but I never asked anyone to think I was. Just to accept me the way I am and to come as you are. I love myself again. That took a very long time and a great deal of soul searching and work to get to the spot where I am. I feel for all the people I know. From the girls' dads, to the once upon a time friends I had, to the exes I left for their betterment. I feel for the town I left behind without ever getting to see its beauty. I feel for the people I never got to meet who showed me this time they were great and fearless people bent on making their world better. I feel for the lost time with family who never wanted to know me. I feel for my children who will never be allowed to know that family because they are so horrible to me. But if they would teach my children their wrong values and their hatred of me, why do I want them to be a part of that sick ass bunch anyway? I don't. I feel mostly for myself having to grow up in the harshness of the desert with the harshness of the people who tried to hurt me each day.

I feel the lost time waiting for them all to see who I was. Who I am. I am a good person. I know I am. I wanted all those I knew—not just loved-KNEW—to be well and have a great life. I wonder what I did to make them so hateful, but mostly I wonder why I feel sorrow for them at all. They did nothing to earn my feelings of compassion. They showed me none.

Of course, I have no stomach for revenge. When I said I would have mine, I never meant I would shoot at or blow up anyone. Whether they need it or not, laughs hard.... I wouldn't hurt their kids like these jackasses have tried to do to mine. I wouldn't even send monsters to ruin them as they did me. I would have been the best friend, daughter, sister, cousin, co-worker, artist, writer, singer and their biggest fan. But I had no place in their lives. I was cast off by the place I tried to make mine so long.

I have moved on from wanting this place to be mine anymore. I learned to love it well this last three years. I will never forget it. For the evil it brought me when I was a baby, and the new good it showed me and my daughters these new days we have spent here.

I am not staying here. I choose to leave this place again because I know I can't sit here and look at some of these same lying faces and forgive them every day for the struggles they made sure I had and have each day. I won't try to be friends with them again. I am sure they will not miss me, but my daughters. I raised them to be real and tell truth and to be as wild as they will. Even if the world doesn't think them princesses, mamma will damn sure deliver them each a crown of their own. I will not allow any more senseless violence to me or my girls. I will not allow anyone to tell them they aren't lovely and precious to this world. When they come to take their bit of the world, I hope they will remember the hard times we had and try to make it easier for some other struggling soul. They are such good girls. Always being so tender to those who need it and always being fierce when they feel it is required. I feel I have raised them without the help of the bad people. My heart won't be the same. But you people can't change the love I hold inside. You just don't have the power anymore.

061217

Can you chuckle through this day? I am laughing as I wake up and think of Rainen getting invited over last night and his simple act that said he is finally finished. He is surely moved on now. I have made my number available to certain ones and they show me with their simple acts that they are moved well and truly on as well.

Sighs in a satisfied way.

Sometimes it is hard to be amused but today is not one of those days. I can hear the silence and see the empty spots that are just there. It IS hard to be a friend to me. I know Rainen wants to be with me. You can't terrorize me into it, though. Instead of letting go and doing the dating thing he wants to, he will only go far enough to hurt me and then come back. Every time he does it once more, I find I don't want that. He can move on. I can make it without him. I can make it without anyone. I think I proved it.

I want to feel a love just for me. I know I will have it and I don't think he will be someone easily intimidated by Rainen or anyone else who might stand as a warning to stay away from me.

I am readying myself for new things and new people and places. I really want to make my life mine.

SO—a priest, a lizard, a wolf, and a smart-ass dude walk into a bar and ask the waiter for a whiskey for each of them...

061517

I have really been looking at my life through a jaded lens. I am very tired but I don't need to think about it so much. The more I focus on the relaxed feeling I have been feeling and how I am enjoying this time of my life, the more enjoyable it becomes.

I am developing a good relationship with Rainen. It is getting better every day. I am trying to be there for my friends and they are doing well. I am working more with my kids and they are focusing and buckling down on their goals.

I have those few items left on the list and I plan to systematically check these items off until I am quite happy with my life and my good effort to make it happen. I think seventy-six items marked down to eight is a miracle. Especially for a girl who does nothing but "sit on her ass and let life happen to her". I didn't find the bullshit true then and I damn sure don't now. How dare anyone look at me and make such stupid judgments based on one day's activities. I like it that Rainen loves to cook and does so for me and our girls. But he never spent every day cooking no matter who said otherwise. Also, my house spent plenty of time in disarray but never to the point I watched my "friends" houses get. I sure didn't ever think more or less of anyone due to their skills or LACK of skills to clean. Even my own damn sister who turned down each offer to help her get it in order. I tried so hard to be there for her but she chose to wallow in her misery and liquor, just like dear old mom. I watched it happen to many. My mom lost Charisma to the system and then Darius to cancer and she completely forgot the child she still had. Booze it up, mom. That's the best thing right. Don't try to be a family for those left.

I can see my way to forgiving so much from others and the idiotic lies they tell, but I don't need to any more. I have put up with a great deal of bullshit and I won't any more.

My life has been full and I am not ever making any more decisions based on others and their faulty eyeball into whatever I am doing. If I stay with Rainen, great. If I don't, great. None of any of your concern. I have no reason to hold onto such flighty friendships when I am sure they mean nothing to you. Now they mean nothing to me either. I hope that moves you and makes you sure of yourself. Maybe you will go on and use the example of how you and your dumbasses tried to shoot me down to find your own wings. Until then I plan to go back to how I always was. In forward movement mode.

I am not all too sure about anyone else but I am getting ready to get out of here and go do my thing. I have a few things left on the list and I am done! Whew. I am ready to go sit in a lovely rainstorm and not hear anything but the quiet.

It feels like I have been non-stop working and running ragged for a very long time. It is nice for things to finally slow down. And to get to feel the good feelings again. Sigh...

I am ready for my vacation now. Smiles and feels good. I hope everyone can manage without me now. I don't really care so much about the little shit. Just be yourselves and if you should need me, look around. If you learned anything at all, you should have no problem finding and chatting me up.

I am grateful for my life. Please remember to be grateful for yours. No matter how bad it gets, only you can change it. Do it now. Don't wait. It will never be a better time than right NOW.

I must go pack and plan the next adventure. I hope your next adventure finds you learning and living, on your own path, never forgetting for even one moment who you are.

As a final little word, I would like to say a few last things to Rainen and Cain.

Rainen-

You have been the source of the greatest love I have ever known. You have healed me when I was wounded and never thought twice about helping me. Even when I chose to move away from you. You showed me a brand-new way to look at myself. You made me mad and made me unsure. I encountered your violence and your gentleness and your heart. You made me know I wanted this family with you and all our unconventional ways. Our religions both different from the closed minds we encountered all our lives. We knew the right way and went for it. We are the real pioneers. Sorry fucks who thought we didn't need each other because they wanted us to be unhappy. Who cares about them now, Rainen? Not us. We always manage without them and I finally see how I placed too much importance on their opinions. Who cares what tweakers and liars think anyway? NOT US. We just locked the door—remember, when they all pounded on the door and were miserable because we found love and each other? Remember we didn't answer the door for ANYONE? Just wrapped ourselves in each other and loved?

Remember when we lit our fires and made our bright love right there not caring? That's where that painting came from this birthday. Remember when you showed those fuckers who you were by getting your job and keeping it longer than they ever knew you could? Do they know if it wasn't for me, they would have never seen that side of you? Remember when I dove off the deep end and got myself a job and went to school? Remember how the jackasses were jealous they weren't a part of our lives and we didn't miss them at all? Remember how they all scrambled to tell you that education isn't important so you will fail and they can get you back into drugs? You are a miracle and they are mad to see people happy.

Do you remember me telling you that you can do anything, Rainen? Because I still believe that! I want you to remember who you are. You are a creature of unimaginable strength and power. You are a fabulous father. You are a kick ass lover and don't forget my best friend in this world. If anyone ever tries to harm you, I will have their heads. As I am... I am tired of fuckups telling us that we aren't all we should be, when we are all that and fucking WAY MORE!!! It doesn't matter if we find our way back to each other or not. We will always arrive on top and with our top shelf shit, just like I promised. So, let's get ready for the next big adventure, Rainen. Even if it isn't with each other. Don't you ever think I quit on you. I won't and I don't think I could if I wanted to.

A word for Cain—

I know you want to believe that you can step in and make some sancha life seem fun and exciting, but see, I said to you before, and now, again—I don't think I have EVER belonged in second place, anywhere. I wouldn't let your woman ever have the need to wonder. Nor would you. So, let's call this thing a bust and remind you that you are full of absolute shit if you think I would ever settle for half-ass love. And you couldn't even give me that. I am on my way and I will find love. Whether it is with Rainen or not, I know it isn't going to be with you.

You saw an opportunity to be rude and slight me at each contact. I didn't say many things to you, Cain. You are a jerk for how you used me the night I went to Texas. Rainen had no right to use me roughly the night before, either. But you. All you had to do was attempt to be a human to me. You could have endeared yourself to me far easier by not sleeping with me and being my friend. I just needed a friend, Cain. I was alone and sad. No reason for you to feel compassion for a fellow human, I know. but you still think yourself superior to me and mine. I don't believe that bullshit and I never will. My daughters are my pride.

You didn't get to have the one that got away. How else could I keep my title if not by saying goodbye once more to you and your outdated ideals and hatefulness? Your traditional family may give you peace. My nontraditional one gives me mine. I don't care about it really. I had said my goodbyes in my head a very fucking long time ago. I knew you and your motives the moment I saw you pop up. I know that Ann and her lackeys are dickheads for playing around and acting like they cared when they were so jealous they couldn't see straight. I find it funny that you and she had something going under your "friend's' nose. After all, she bragged about it and wanted to take a picture of FAT TABI so she could let you see how superior she was to me. And maybe you even fucked my sister...

laughs...I am finally washed clean of this place and I am tired of trying to have relationships with people just like my mother. Emotionally unavailable...

I hope you write a book. Respond about how I misrepresented you. Ha-ha. Or try being a human and worthy of having a BADASS friend like me. I could have certainly helped you and I have been working on a cool formula (several years of work.) for a skin treatment for you. Since I know you are too good to use a pagan herbalist remedy and only the super expensive and worthless doctors could help, I haven't given it to you. I still have the information if someday you manage to suck it up and work at having a real friendship with me. I would give it to you for nothing.

Good thing I am an adult and ready for the next stage—you know—the "forget this bullshit and move on to my great new life I promised I would have soon" stage? I didn't lie.

I cared about you and worried you were losing something vital to yourself. I dreamed a great many dreams about you. But forcing something so you can get yourself something you don't deserve, well that is bullshit, too, Cain.

I won't forget what all you did for me, but I won't forget what all you did TO me, either. I will make sure you get your money—the most important thing, is to make sure the bitch has your money, right.

So, go do your thing and make sure you are being who your kids need. And your woman. She obviously had NO IDEA whom she was dealing with. I could destroy a lot in a few seconds. I don't think I want the responsibility. I wanted you to be happy. Remember.

I get it.

I don't care anymore. You should have been here for me like you said, instead of making sure you bailed in the moments I needed you most. I can easily let go now because I got to say what I needed to about cheaters and the people they manipulate to get what they want.

I learned about the type a very long time ago... you know-George. The asshole step-dad who made sure I was alone for my entire life. Well, fuck George and Ann and the tweakers of this city, and the relatives who left me behind so long ago because I was unfortunate enough to be born to my own mom. Yeah.

So long and make sure you smile. I sure did miss that cute smile.

T.

This book has been a culmination of time from 2011-2017. Six years is a very long time to hold such things within and I believe I have reclaimed my personal power within these pages.

I hate to feel like a bitchy person, which is why I always try to spin people in the best possible light. I loved all the people I wrote of who interacted in my life in any small way. I also felt betrayed and alone from those same small-minded actions and I don't regret one single word I wrote.

Please do hold true to yourself.

If you suffered at the hands of bullies or random violence, take heart. And if you suffered at the hands of those you lived with or loved, please don't ever stop believing you can do more and be more.

You can.

This life is short and tiresome enough without the assholes who try to take your magic. I am in love with magic and life. I can see great things coming from just smiling and sitting and letting the dumb bullies do themselves in.

I do care about this world. But the lesson isn't to just be kind, people. Stand up if you need to and kick ass for what you know to be true and right and real. If it is yourself and your beliefs, so much the better. Your friends and family, too.

I miss being confident so I decided some time ago to be just that. I love to laugh and be joyful. So, I am. I love to hear my daughters laugh and play and be real girls. So, I do watch them and smile.

I don't really care who decided I am not a worthy person. Fuck off.

And you should adopt that attitude as well. It will save you so much time and effort when anyone stands in the way of you and your happiness. I earned my rewards so long ago sitting on the kitchen floor on Oak St. all alone wishing for the rain and weeping openly for my ruined innocence and all the things babies should hold sacred...love of mom, joy in the simple things, food, clothing, house to live in, and friends. I prayed to gods who never listened and discovered what I want, I must go get. No god will hold my hand while I am alone. I waited patiently for the rain. I had to wait a very long time. I feel I am under this new rain and no one can stop the little dark-haired, giant-eyed girl now. HUGE difference in where I came from and where I am going NOW.

I don't need to earn Rainen's love or Cain's love or anyone else's. If they don't see my worth, see how I made myself wake each day with a clean slate to make this life joyful and free—they don't either one deserve ME.

Time to get out of this enchanted desert, my dearest new friends and all others.

With love and joy and peace spreading to you all. Hopefully to the whole world.

Tabi Ruslon

THE END???
I think NOT!

www.ingramcontent.com/pod-product-compliance
Lightning Source LLC
Chambersburg PA
CBHW030646020726
47493CB00006B/1895